Golden

CHOICES

Noelle —

Thanks for the support
of my dream.
If you enjoy the book —
tell everyone... if you hate
it, don't say a word! La

Dic B

Published by Mindstir Media

1931 Woodbury Ave. #182 | Portsmouth, New Hampshire 03801 | USA

1.800.767.0531 | www.mindstirmedia.com

Printed in the United States of America

ISBN-13:978-0-9863057-5-7

Library of Congress Control Number: 2014921300

Golden
CHOICES

written by

DIONNE BELL

MINDSTIR MEDIA

To my mother, Stephanie Bell.
My earliest memories of kindness, love, forgiveness, and all good things were exemplified and embodied by you.

ACKNOWLEDGEMENTS

It has been said that teamwork makes the dream work. There are many wonderful people who have contributed to transforming the dream of this body of work into a reality.

Encouragement: Tammie J., Robin P., David F., Crystal B., Katika F., LaShawna G., Shaneen H.

Hands-on: Crystal B., Katika F., LaShawna G., Laura W., Mindstir Team

Cheer Squad: Tammie J., Leslie B., Phillip B., James B., Laynell B., Ebony S., Sherry S., Lisa P., Laura K., Laura W., Thomas C., Denise Q., Brian C., Terri M., Vanessa N., Stephanie B., Glennie J., Val B., Edna M., Juanita M., Denise F., Lindsay F-B., Krissi T., Tori H-G., Richard M., Tamara D., Natasha N., Lula M., Logan F. Lindsay F., David F. – my P. L. F.

Special Teams/MVPs: Christopher W., Kayla F., Kristin K., Crystal B., Katika F., LaShawna G. - - I'm just sayin'!!! There are no words to express my feelings for the love, support, encouragement and old fashioned elbow grease given by Chris, Teek, Tammie, and Shawnie. Soaring is so much easier with strong propellers. Thank you for helping me to fly high. I love you so much.

In Memoriam: Virginia B., Vivian Q., Eunice M.

I thank the Holy Spirit for His inspiration, comfort, and peace that surpasses all understanding.

I thank God the Father from Whom all blessings flow.

Finally, I thank my Lord and Savior Jesus Christ whose sacrificial love saved a sinner like me, despite my not-so-golden choices!

FORWARD

Dionne Bell is a dreamer. In fact, she is the biggest dreamer that we know! Impractical? Not by a long shot! Idealistic? Perhaps. Gifted? Absolutely! Dee's dreams are just that – a gift! She has the innate ability to see things outside the scope of the ordinary imagination. Her dreams and aspirations can be quite overwhelming and even intimidating for someone who cannot comprehend her limitless vision. However, that was never us. The thing is, we could always see her vision because we know that Dee is not only a dreamer, but she is also a doer.

When Dee came to us and said that she wanted to write a book, we had no doubt that it would happen. How could we? After all, this is the same person who said she wanted a YouTube talk show. And guess what? Soon thereafter, *The I'm Just Saying Show* was born! So multi-faceted, this YouTube sensation is a devoted wife, mother, sister, and friend. We can now add "author" to that list of credits!

As you, the readers, will soon see for yourselves, Dee has a keen ability to step deep into character and pull out the many different personalities that we all encounter on a daily basis. Whether it is the naiveté of Melissa Sullivan, insecurities of Kim Stormer, or frustrations of Regina Golden, the intricacies of each character speak to everyone, male and female alike. Dionne has the uncanny capacity to draw in every reader in this captivating novel. You'll find that the characters are people you will either love or love to hate.

Golden Choices has been a true labor of love. We have spent countless hours laughing, crying, and praying together over this masterpiece-in-the-works (even if we did have to take a hiatus from *The I'm Just Saying Show*). Nonetheless, we are so proud to have witnessed the birth of Dee's baby! Dionne's talents are truly a gift from God, and we are so very blessed to have watched that gift manifest into the book you are holding today.

Not only does Dee aspire toward greatness in everything she does, but her infectious and humble spirit also inspires greatness in those with whom she comes into contact. She gives so much to her family, friends, co-workers, and community. The love, honor, and pride that we have for

Dee, not only as an author but also as a God-fearing woman, are immeasurable. We are truly privileged to be able to share her love, passion, and talents with all of you.

One thing's for certain: Dionne Bell is proof-positive that dreams do come true. We cannot wait to see what she has in store for us next! Stars and lights, baby! Stars and lights! ☺

Be blessed and dream big!

Chris, Shawnie & Teek
Co-Hosts of *The I'm Just Saying Show*

PRESENT DAY

"You like sucking dick so much, swallow, bitch!"

Regina could barely catch her breath. With tears streaming down her face, she sensed that one wrong move and Kevin would not hesitate to take her life.

"Close yo muthafuckin lips and suck this dick! That's what makes you happy, right?" Kevin barked.

Regina closed her eyes and said a silent prayer as her lips closed around the gun that Kevin had shoved into her mouth. The metallic, salty taste was making her sick to her stomach. Was it the metal from the gun or the taste of her blood from the front teeth that got knocked loose when Kevin assaulted her in her sleep? It really didn't matter either way, since Regina figured she would be dead in a few moments. What in the world was going on?

"Kewin, pweeasssee. Dwont! Dwont dwoh wis bwaby!" Gina's speech was impaired by the huge gun in her mouth. She could barely swallow, much less talk. But her eyes said it all. Regina Golden was terrified. She had never been so scared in her entire life. Last night, she and Kevin, her husband of fourteen years, had a great dinner, shared a passionate lovemaking session, and fell asleep in each other's arms. Just like they had for the majority of their relationship.

Now, it was 4:09 in the morning, and Regina thought she was having a dream, actually a nightmare, as she woke to the sound of her husband yelling at her—and Kevin rarely yelled—with tears in her eyes, his gun jammed into her mouth with one hand, and her cell phone in his other hand.

"We wuv eash wuther. We get awong, we hab gwate sexth lath nith, an' we werk—"

"Bitch, I wish the fuck you would say *work* up in this piece," Kevin cut Regina off as he cocked the Smith and Wesson 4506. "Go 'head Gina, finish what you was sayin' about *work*!"

Regina gulped as best she could, trying to swallow her terror along with the blood pooling in her mouth. Frantic, she planned what she could say to her husband to keep him from ending her life. Too bad things don't always go as planned.

BOOM!

12 WEEKS AGO

"Thank you for calling Bright Star, how may I help you?" Regina asked her first customer of the day.

She'd worked in the call center for nine years now and was about as bored with her job as she was with everything else in her life. The pay was decent, and the hours were great. However, the work was mundane, the other females in the center were catty and petty, and the management staff was largely inept and detached. The best part of each day was lunchtime spent with Melissa and Kim. All three ladies were hired together and were quite popular in the call center. Mostly, people spoke highly of "the three musketeers," as they were often referred to at work. Where you saw one of the ladies, you usually saw the other two. Melissa and Kim were acquaintances before working at Bright Star. They had attended the same high school and, though they had not been friends at that time, they were aware of each other and knew some of the same people. During the new employee orientation, Melissa and Kim sat together and brought each other up to speed on the happenings with some of their old high school peers. By the third day, both ladies noticed that Regina often sat alone in the cafeteria during lunch. They invited her to eat with them the next day, and the trio had been inseparable ever since.

After five years at Bright Star, Melissa was promoted to a lead position. They all started as customer service representatives. All representatives reported to supervisors, and between the representatives and the supervisors were the leads. Even with the promotion, nothing changed with the ladies' relationship. There was no apparent jealousy, no special favors asked or expected, and none granted. That is why, with the exception of the inherent hater in every job setting, most people liked and respected Regina, Melissa, and Kim.

"It's almost 11:30, Reggie, hurry up and finish that call so we can eat," Kim whispered, sticking her head into Regina's cubicle.

Regina repeatedly tapped her fingers against her thumb to indicate to Kim that she had a long-winded customer on the phone.

"Okay, suit yourself," Kim teased. "I'll go meet Mel in the cafeteria by myself and find out the scoop she said she wanted to tell us."

"Sir, I've looked at your account a bit further and discovered we can in fact get you set up with a payment plan. I'm going to get that initiated for you and you'll be all set. Thanks again for calling Bright Star."

Regina quickly ended her call so she wouldn't be left out of the loop. Melissa was forever telling them not to ask questions about other employees, so if she had some information to share, it had to be big.

"Mmmm, Ms. Vincent, now she can make a good burger. I don't know why y'all tryna be all cutesy and eat from that corny salad bar every day," Melissa said, savoring a bite of her hamburger. "Shoot, I forgot to get salt for my fries, hold up." Melissa acted like she was about to leave the table, knowing it would tick off her friends. They had barely touched their salads, as they anxiously waited to hear the news from Melissa.

"Girl, if you don't sit your narrow ass down and spill it," Kim jokingly threatened her friend.

"I know, right!" Regina agreed. "Got me rushing my customer off the phone and whatnot."

"Okay, okay, but y'all can't say nothing. I mean NOTHING...to NOBODY," Melissa admonished.

"Girl, you know telling us is just like telling yourself, now c'mon," Regina pleaded.

"Okay, y'all know Mike?" Melissa asked.

"Yeah," they said in unison.

"Tell me why I had a pretty lengthy conversation with him after the staff meeting, and come to find out, he gets down with the swirl?"

"WHAAAAT?" again in unison from Kim and Regina.

"Y'all heard me. He likes dark meat, hot chocolate, brown sugar, however you want to say it," Melissa said.

"Aww dang, for real? How did you guys end up discussing that? Like, what did you do, ask him on a date or something?" Regina wanted to know.

Melissa went on to explain that after a staff meeting some people were talking about their weekend plans, and she was complaining that she was the designated babysitter for all her siblings' children since she was the only one without kids of her own. Mike told her she should come with him to see the latest Madea movie, and Melissa had asked Mike what he knew about Madea. Mike proceeded to share how his last girlfriend loved the stage plays *I Can Do Bad All By Myself* and *Diary of a Mad Black Woman*. Melissa shared how she told Mike she'd never really seen many white females at the plays and that's when Mike told her his last girlfriend was a black woman.

"Shut the front door!" Kim exclaimed.

Everyone in the call center always talked about what a nice guy Mike was. He was handsome, friendly, and unlike most of the other leads and supervisors, he treated the representatives like human beings worthy of respect, not underlings who should be held in contempt.

"Dang, Mel, guess that blows your chance. Too bad you white. He woulda been a good catch for you," Kim taunted.

"Girl, please, I am not hardly interested in Mike. I told y'all a million times, I like to date guys that are different than me, so no white men. I like Hispanic guys, Asian guys, Black guys, Arab guys, anyone who has a different background and culture. It is interesting and fun that way."

Kim looked at Melissa like she had lost her mind. "Okay, Ms. United Nations, when you run up on something you can't handle, don't come crying to us."

"Whatever. That's not the biggest scoop. The real scoop is who Mike said he thinks is hot," Melissa reported.

"Who?" Regina and Kim again asked together.

"Never mind, I'm not even trying to get something started. Just forget I said anything. And like I said, neither one of you better utter a single word," Melissa rose to leave.

"Really, Mel? You just gon' play us like that? Dangle that juicy steak in front of us then snatch it away?" Kim was starting to get pissed.

Kim saw this as an opportunity. Shoot, Mike was an excellent catch. He was a gentleman, single, made nice money, had no kids, was sexy as heck, and come to find out his freaky butt liked the sistas. That made her the perfect candidate. Mel was white, Regina was married, and none of the other ladies in the call center could hold a candle to Kim. Kim could easily be on a runway or in a magazine, she was that beautiful. Skin the color of sand, light brown eyes – no contacts – and long, straight, gorgeous hair flowing down her back. Shoot, Kim paid good money for that hair every six months, and it was worth every single one of the $800 she spent on her weave. Men and women alike constantly complimented Kim on her hair. Except for family members, Mel, and Reggie, nobody even knew or suspected it was a weave. Most people had a hard time guessing her ethnicity. Some thought she could possibly be Hispanic, some thought biracial, and others thought she might be Middle Eastern. All were incorrect. Kim would enthusiastically tell anyone who stared too long, or dared to ask, that she was a Fine-Ass Black Woman and that black women "come in all shades and sizes, even if not this fine." Kimberly Denise Stoner was not lacking in confidence or self-esteem.

Kim started wearing high-end clothes and shoes and spending large amounts of money on her hair and makeup about six years ago. That's when she was unexpectedly abandoned by then-husband, Robert. Robert and Kim had been married for ten years. They had been high school sweethearts and had gotten married one week after they graduated college. Even with all their immaturity and occasional infidelities, they still managed to hold on to their love for each other. Never in a million years would Kim have believed that Robert was not happy or fulfilled in their marriage. As far as she was concerned, Robert had a beautiful, loyal wife, a lovely home, and they owned the four luxury cars in their massive garage. To say it was a shock when Kim came home from work one day and found a letter from Robert saying that he needed to "follow his heart" would be a huge understatement. The pain was deep and the grief was long-lasting. Slowly though, Kim began to dig her way out of that deep, dark pit, and she emerged a new person. Chuckling to herself, Kim recalled the first day she came to work after she'd gotten her weave.

"Hey, Kim," Cassie had greeted as they were at the bathroom sinks. "Did you do something different with your hair? I don't remember it being that long yesterday."

"Yeah, Cassie, I just put fertilizer in it, sat under a light for ten minutes and voila!" Kim had replied as she exited the bathroom, shaking her head. She then headed straight to Regina and Melissa's cubicles to tell them that stupid exchange.

"Oh hell naw!" Kim heard Regina exclaim, jerking her back from her trip down memory lane.

"What? What I miss, what she say, Reg?"

"Girl, nothin'! Mel just talking crazy, that's all."

"Okay, don't believe me, Reg. But I'm telling you what the man said from his own mouth. He said if he could have a chance with anyone in this office, he would want it to be you," Melissa excitedly reported. "Alright, girls, we better get back. I'd hate to have to give one of you tramps a written warning for being late," Melissa playfully chided as everyone cleared the table.

As they headed back upstairs, Melissa chatted about the rest of the day, the upcoming weekend, and how her sister had the nerve to ask her to babysit for the second weekend in a row. She was so absorbed in her own conversation that she didn't notice how quiet the other ladies were. Kim was in shock. She could not believe that Mike was not interested in her. She immediately began plotting a strategy to correct that little oversight on his part.

Meanwhile, Regina was focused on the fact that Mike thought she was attractive. She was trying to figure out why that pleased her so much.

11 WEEKS AGO

"It's been real, ladies, but I'm going to have to call it a night," Regina announced as she began to reach for her purse. She had met Kim, Melissa, and her sister Regan out for one of their regular girls' night out sessions.

"Yeah gone and run home before Kevin starts blowing up your phone," Regan playfully teased her sister.

Regina got up and hugged everyone goodbye, thankful that she'd decided to meet everyone there instead of riding with the group. Each time they got together, which was usually about every week or two, there would be at least one designated driver, except for Kim, who never accepted that role. They would spend time at a restaurant, bowling, one of their houses, a concert in the local park, just whatever they all decided to do. It was always a fun time to catch up on things that they did not have time to discuss at work and to hang out with Regan. Regan was four years younger than Regina and, by default, the baby sister of the entire group. She was a teacher and was actually the one who had introduced Kevin and her sister to each other about fifteen years ago.

Kevin and Regan were teachers at the same high school and became fast friends. Not having any sisters of his own, Kevin quickly became fond and protective of Regan. He was the only black male teacher in the school, and Regan was one of only three black female employees in the school. There was Mrs. Langford, the one other black female teacher, Ms. Robinson, who worked in the cafeteria, and Ms. Emma, one of the custodians. Although the other three ladies were older than Kevin, he felt it was his job to look out for them. It became known very quickly to all of the students that any disrespect, teasing, or misbehavior toward any of the ladies would mean a visit with Mr. Golden.

A few boys made the bad choice of kicking over trash cans as Ms. Emma was trying to make her rounds after school one day. Kevin got the principal to agree to let him deal with the boys instead of just suspending them from school. Each of the boys had to write a letter of apology to Ms. Emma, they had to assist Ms. Emma with her cleaning duties for one week for each trash can they kicked over – four total -- and they had to submit a paper to Kevin describing how they would have felt had other young boys treated their grandmothers the way they treated Ms. Emma. The principal, Ms. Emma, other teachers, and even the boys' parents noticed how Kevin's alternate form of discipline impacted the boys. It was something different than the same old tired, noneffective approach used to supposedly correct misbehavior.

Regan viewed Kevin like the older brother she never had and figured he might hit it off well with her hardworking, yet fun-loving older sister. At the time, Regina was working as a case manager at a chemical dependency agency. The hours were horrible, and the pay was far less than desirable, but Regina enjoyed her work. She felt fulfilled and like she was making a difference in the lives of others. She enjoyed working with a population which society had given up on because she believed that with each new day bloomed new hope. Both Regina and Kevin were great at their jobs, had hearts as big as Texas, and needed someone special in their lives. Regan and her then-boyfriend met Regina and Kevin at Red Lobster one Friday evening, and the rest is history. They hit it off immediately. About a year after meeting Kevin, Regina Washington became Regina Golden. And that was how she always described her husband and her marriage – golden.

Lately though, Regina had begun to wonder if her marriage was solid gold or gold plated.

*****

"Hey baby, how was girls' night out?" Kevin looked up from the table where he was working when Regina walked in.

"It was fun. Actually, we had a good time. But Kim was starting to get liquored up, and I was starting to miss you, so I figured that was my cue to leave and get home to my baby. What's going on with you, how was your day?"

"Today was cool, just busy as hell, as usual."

"Did you eat? You want me to whip up something for you, or do you want to just go straight to dessert?" Regina suggestively asked her husband. In almost two weeks, she and Kevin had not made love, and Regina was starting to feel tense and frustrated.

Kevin's attention was on the paperwork he was poring over at the kitchen table, and he barely mumbled a response to Regina. Refusing to let this night pass without her and Kevin being intimate, Regina went over and started massaging her husband's neck and shoulders. She knew that always got his attention. Kevin grabbed his wife's hands and tenderly kissed each of her knuckles and led her around the chair to face him.

"Baby, I know I've been so busy and distracted lately. I'm sorry. It's just this one kid at the center is really testing me, Gina. He's smart. He's athletic. He can draw anything or anybody. But he just keeps making dumb decisions that land him in trouble. Now, he is facing expulsion from school and possible criminal charges for supposedly having inappropriate contact with some young lady."

Ah, the center. Regina now understood perfectly why her husband had been so preoccupied lately. About five or six years after they were married, Kevin became more and more dissatisfied with how black students, particularly males, were treated by the teachers and administrators at the school where he taught. There were only a few blacks who worked in the high school, and even fewer teachers. Worse yet, he was the only black male. Kevin's was the only face in that school that looked like those young boys. He was the only person with whom they felt they could relate. There was no way they could convey to a white teacher, male or female, what it felt like to be the first one looked at suspiciously when something was missing from class – just because of their skin color. There was no way they could get their white teachers to understand the intricate balancing act between acting and talking a certain way at school and having to switch into another mode in the neighborhood for fear of being ridiculed or even attacked.

When white kids gathered in the hallways, they were considered a group, yet more than two black kids in the hallway were considered a gang. When a group of white kids vandalized several cars in the school parking lot, they were punished with an in-school suspension and said to have been letting off some steam. When a group of black kids spray-painted one vehicle in the same school parking lot, they were each suspended for five days. The examples of unequal treatment were frequent and seemed to worsen each year. It was so frustrating for Kevin to hear his peers and superiors assign different motives for similar behaviors exhibited by students whose skin color was different. White kids who got high were simply experimenting, going through a phase, or crying out for help. Black students who got high were degenerate addicts and troublemakers, just like their parents. After some years, Kevin decided he had to do something. He loved being a role model for the kids, but he believed his hands were tied by the administrators. Kevin quit his teaching job and founded a tutoring and mentoring center for black, often troubled, young men.

Regina was reluctant when Kevin first came to her with his idea. At the time, she was working at the drug agency, and Kevin's salary was the higher of the two. However, it did not take long for Regina to see Kevin's passion for helping these young men. Not only did she get on board with his idea, but she helped as much as she could with getting the center started. She even left her job at the drug agency to work at Bright Star. The hours were more stable and the pay was almost twice as much as at the chemical dependency agency. Regina had become quite proud of Kevin and knew he had made the right choice.

"I know you have a lot going on at the center, baby, but you have worked hard all day and it will not hurt you to take a little break," Regina purred as she sat on Kevin's lap. She began to plant tender kisses on Kevin's forehead, cheeks, nose, and chin. By the time she made it to his mouth, Regina was starving for her husband. She felt as if she would explode both physically and emotionally if she did not connect with her husband. Her tongue found Kevin's, and they danced a passionate tango that was sure to end with a final bow right there on the kitchen table.

"Mmmm, baby, take me now, right here, Kevin. I need you so much. You know you want this as much as I do, baby," Regina moaned. She unbuttoned Kevin's shirt and began to massage his nipples as her tongue continued to assault Kevin's. Regina quickly felt Kevin's hardness begin to rise against her thigh. Encouraged, she let one of her hands make its way to Kevin's pants and she released the now stiff and ever-growing prize she was aiming to win. She slowly stroked up and down her husband's shaft, while still passionately kissing him, muting the low groans coming from his throat.

Kevin was ready to put in work, almost. "Okay, baby, gimme five minutes. You go upstairs and get ready for me. I'll wrap things up down here, then come upstairs and feed you some of this golden rod," Kevin teased as he playfully swatted Regina's backside. The same focus and drive that Regina often admired in her husband could also sometimes be her greatest source of frustration. Regina hesitantly got up from Kevin's lap and walked backward toward the steps, winking at Kevin and excited that they would finally get back to their usual intimacy.

Two and a half hours later, Regina was lying diagonally across the bed, knocked out. She'd fallen asleep waiting, yet again, for her husband.

*****

Regina had to call her sister from work the next day to vent. "Girl, I'm telling you, something is going on. I'm not saying Kevin is cheating on me, but things are very different between us. Regan, you know how you guys always tease me and Kevin about how often we you-know-what? Well it's been over two weeks now."

"Reggie, you know good and well Kevin is probably just busy with work. Why don't you try making the first move, do something romantic, plan a special date night or something?" Regan offered.

"Check, check, and check. I've tried all of those things. Whatever Kevin's beef is, he better grill it up and eat it," Regina stated.

"Aww, fool, quit trying to quote Dr. Lee. This ain't *Drumline*; this is your marriage. We gotta get you and Kevin back on track so that you can quit being grumpy. You and my brother will be okay, just be patient with him. Okay, sis?"

"I guess, but he is getting on my nerves and this mess is for the birds. I'll call you when I get off work. I gotta run." Regina hung up with her sister so she could continue her work day.

"Regina, are you mad at your husband?" Cassie, who sat in the cubicle next to Regina, stood up and asked.

Regina knew she had to be hearing things. *There is no way that nosey-ass Cassie just asked me about my personal conversation!* With Cassie's cubicle being right next to Regina's, it seemed that at least once a week, she was on the verge of being cussed out. She was always in everyone's business and running her mouth. Even worse, Cassie had no tact, manners, or discretion. *Eavesdropping is bad enough, but to have the gall to ask about it? Oh hecks naw!*

"What did you just ask me, Cassie? As a matter of fact—you know what? Let me step away for a moment," Regina hissed.

As wrong and ignorant as she was, Cassie would never get it, no matter how many times people had to check her. Instead of wasting her time and energy on a lost cause, Regina went to Melissa's office, but she had an employee in there. She went to Kim's cubicle and, seeing it empty, figured she must be in the small break room across the hall. She needed to talk to one of her girls because the situation with Kevin was bad enough, but now Cassie had Regina ready to spit nails.

"Hey, hold up, where's the fire?" Mike teased Regina as she ran into him in the hallway.

"I am so sorry, Mike. I was distracted and not even paying attention. Please excuse me." Regina now wished Mel had not shared what Mike had told her. For the first time since they'd worked together, Regina was nervous in front of Mike, and she felt awkward.

"Not at all, you're fine, Regina. And I do mean fine." Mike licked his lips and leaned against the wall. He was encouraged by the smile flirting at the corners of Regina's mouth. "So were you going to get some coffee or water or something? Are you okay?"

"Actually, I was looking for Kim. I'm not having the greatest day, and I thought she might have been in the break room."

"I didn't see her in there. But I'm glad we ran into each other. Well, you ran into me," Mike teased. "Seriously though, I was wanting to tap into your expertise in the chemical dependency area. My brother is ready to wring my nephew's neck. He thinks he may be experimenting with drugs, and it has him at his wits' end. He has no idea where to even begin. I told him that I worked with someone who may be able to help or at least point him in the right direction."

"Oh my goodness, Mike. I'm so sorry about this situation. I know it must be extremely hard for your family right now. Your brother has done the most important thing he can do, though, which is not ignoring that there may be a problem. Yes, please, by all means, if there is anything I can do to help, please let me know." Regina was genuinely concerned. "Here, put my number into your phone and let your brother know he can call me anytime. His name is Brian, right?"

"Yes, Brian is my brother and his son's name is Matt. Thanks, Regina. This really means a lot. I think it will help just for Brian to have someone to talk to on a professional level. And like I said, even if you can just point him in the right direction toward possible resources, it would mean a lot."

Mike stood there, starting to feel awkward because he had never before talked to Regina about anything other than Bright Star. Also, he did not know if Melissa had told Regina what he'd said about her being hot. He was not ashamed of what he'd said. In fact, Mike wished he'd had the courage to say something to Regina himself. But he considered her to be a classy woman, and he did not want to disrespect her or be inappropriate at work.

"Hello. Earth to Mike. You okay?"

"Huh? Oh yeah, I'm cool. Well hey, thanks again, Regina. I'd better get back."

Regina had not gotten to talk with either of her girls, but she felt a lot better as she headed back to her cubicle.

The rest of the work day seemed to fly by for Regina. She was both saddened by the news of Brian and his son, Matt, and at the same time excited about having talked to Mike. For the life of her, Regina did not understand why she was excited about her encounter with Mike. Their conversation had been very general and was not inappropriate, sexual, or suggestive in any way. Maybe it was just nice to know that someone thought of Regina as an expert, at least a resource.

Mike was a cool dude. He was a well-built and handsome man, at six feet five inches and 220 pounds. Mike had dark brown hair, brown eyes, a natural tan, and personality for days. He could easily be arrogant because of his good looks and intelligence, but he was just the opposite. Mike was the supervisor for whom all the employees wanted to work. Most of his peers were secretly jealous of his relationships with his direct reports. The other three supervisors, especially Alicia, often made remarks about Mike being the "pet" of the senior management team.

None of the other three supervisors understood why Mike was thought of so highly. He was the youngest of all four of them, the newest supervisor to Bright Star, and the least adept at mastering the computer system and databases. Mike was well aware of the way Alicia and the others talked about him. He could not have cared less, though. Mike had a strong sense of teamwork, but it was more important to him that he was respected and trusted by his subordinates and his superiors than by his petty peers. As far as he was concerned, there was no special secret to his success. He simply respected the people on his team and treated them as such. He believed that his role was to develop the folks on his team, which would produce happier employees, satisfied customers, and more productivity for Bright Star. Unlike his peers, Mike did not believe his position should be relegated to just producing reports and nit-picking team members in an effort to find more negative than positive. It made sense to Mike that in order to support an employee's growth and development, the effort had to be made to get to know the employees; what their strengths and weaknesses are, what is it they aspire to do, and what motivates them. Mike applied what his mother told him the day he got hired as a supervisor; people will never care how much you know, until they know how much you care. He didn't know where she'd gotten that nugget of wisdom from, but it had served him well as a supervisor.

As one of the few males in the call center, Mike was the benefactor of a lot of female attention. It did not matter if a female was younger, older, or around the same age as Mike, there seemed to be a natural attraction toward him. Mike was always friendly and professional, even to the women who didn't stand a chance with him. He was never mean, rude, or condescending. Still, as professional a man as he was, he was still a man. He had eyes, and they often roamed to and fro, seeking whom he would like to have his way with. Usually it was pretty easy, too. Mike had had sexual contact with a fair number of the women at Bright Star. Still, there was never any drama. He was always a gentleman, never one to kiss-and-tell and always up-front with his intentions. Mike did not consider himself a player, but he did like to play – often.

Usually Mike was confident and self-assured, so it perplexed and frustrated him that he had felt so nervous when he talked to Regina earlier. Mike felt like a freshman towel boy asking the senior head cheerleader to prom. He was used to being the one to have ladies flustered, stammering, and stuttering when he engaged them in conversation.

Something about Regina Golden was different, though. He had seen her with her friends at work, and she always seemed to be making people laugh, giving someone a hug, or just listening interestedly to a story. Regina was smart, pretty, kind, and easy to talk to. Although she had always been friendly toward Mike, she never flirted with him or tried to drop hints that she available, unlike the other women in the office, both single and married. He respected that about her…to a point. Mike also took it as a challenge. He couldn't be sure if Melissa had told Regina that he thought she was hot, but in a few moments, it wouldn't matter whether she did or not. Mike fired off a text as he was about to leave his office for the day. He'd already seen Regina leave about five minutes prior.

Hope u have a good evening. Tks again 4 ur help. Btw, u looked very nice 2day.

Regina could not believe the text she was reading. She knew full well who it was from.

Who is this????

Its me, mike.

Oh ok. No problem Mike. Have ur bro call me. U have a good nite

Did she read that right? Did Mike slide a compliment in there, telling her that she looked nice? More importantly, why was she smiling so hard?

10 WEEKS AGO

"I know you lyin'! She went back to that fool after all that drama?" Regan had missed the last episode of *Love and Hip Hop Atlanta*, and Kim was updating her on the latest between Stevie K. or J. or Ray or something. Melissa could not keep the names straight, but more than that, she couldn't understand why her friends wasted their time by watching so-called reality television.

"How much educational value is in that show, Regan? Kim, what did you learn during the hour you spent watching that silly show?" Melissa couldn't hold her tongue any longer.

Regina just shook her head. She'd missed the discussion during the last girls' night out, as she wanted to hurry home and get some lovin' from her husband. Thinking back, she'd have done better to stay with the girls, as their conversations were often intense and certainly more heated than the response she had gotten from Kevin a week ago.

Sometimes the girls all got together after a long work week, and sometimes they decided to meet in the middle of the week. No matter when they met, it was always a time for good food, tasty drinks, and interesting conversation. Since they were meeting on a weeknight this time, nobody ordered any drinks with alcohol, except Kim. She swore that 1800 would clear her mind for work the next day.

"Mel, why you acting all *stank-uh-dank-dank?*" Kim did her best impression of Cleo from the movie *Set It Off.* "You always looking down on us and shit, like we are wrong for wanting to have some fun."

"I'm not looking down on anyone, Kim. I am simply trying to get you all to see that it's a waste of time watching these shows. Not only do those type of shows lack educational value, they don't even represent us in a positive light. Where is the *reality* in that type of television? When it was an election year, I didn't hear anyone at this table mention an episode of Washington Watch or Fox News, any of the debates, or anything that had to do with the *reality* of this nation and its well-being."

Regan had to intervene as she could see Kim's blood beginning to boil. "Mel, you are right in that we should have been more concerned with the election and news pertaining to it. You are correct that we should be educated about current events and knowledgeable about what is going on in our cities, states, nation, and world. At the same time, we like to be entertained sometimes, and if reality television provides that entertainment, why is that a problem?"

Regina nodded in agreement.

Kim washed down her last bite of food with another shot. "Right! We are not in school 24/7. Well, Regan damn near is, since she the teacher… but still. Just because we enjoy *Basketball Wives, Housewives of Atlanta, Bad Girls Club*, and *Love and Hip Hop* does not mean that we are not interested in what's going on in society. And as far as those women representing us in a positive manner, I disagree. Those women show the struggle women face when dealing with these men who claim to love them, yet play all these mind games. Almost all of those women are working moms, and even if I'm not inspired all the time from watching them, I'm at least entertained. What's wrong with that?"

"I just think we dummy-down for these reality shows. For example, how is a show called "Real Wives" of anything when none of the characters are married? That's not reality. You talk about them being working mothers, but you guys have never discussed any of these people in a work setting or helping their children through a situation. It is always who slapped who, who slept with who, and whose car, house, shoes, and purse cost what. The black women that I know don't resolve their conflicts by yelling and screaming obscenities and throwing things at each other." Melissa could see Kim relating to a lot of the people on these shows, but Regan really surprised her.

Regina could not believe what she was hearing. "Mel, you are being so judgmental, I'm actually surprised at you. The other day you were watching a reality show about famous ex-wives, and you also told me at work that you watched and actually liked that show that Tia and Tamara have. So how is it okay that you watch the shows you like, but you condemn Regan and Kim for watching shows that you don't like? How is that right?"

"Yeah," Regan agreed. "We don't knock your boring shows, so don't knock what we like to watch."

"Okay, point well made. I do watch shows that would be considered reality television. However, they are, you all would have to agree, more positive shows. There is not all the fighting and profanity and people intentionally plotting against each other. Reality TV is not bad or wrong just because it is reality TV. I just think it becomes negative and wrong when the shows only display or mostly display people on their worst behavior. There are reality shows about everything from towing cars to taming animals. Admittedly, when I'm watching what would be one of the more positive reality television shows, I'm not necessarily stimulating my mind. It's a form of entertainment. We don't have wholesome, funny sitcoms like we used to, so it seems like reality television is everywhere. We should just be responsible about what we choose to watch because that time we spend can never be recaptured. You guys feel me?"

"Yeah," Regan and Regina answered together.

"Hell naw, I don't feel jack! You want us sittin' up here watching *Happy Days* and *Leave It to Beaver* and shit. That ain't reality either, Melissa! That is not our reality, anyway. You said we, what, *dummy-down* to watch these shows? Oh well, so be it then. Look, by the time people get done dealing with crazy coworkers, badass kids, heavy traffic, annoying bill collectors, whatever the case may be, sometimes we don't want to think or be logical while we watch television. Sometimes people just want to be entertained. To your point about the various reality shows, even the show about towing cars is most interesting when there is a conflict. If it was all blue skies and sunny dispositions, nobody would watch." Kim was feeling a little buzzed and ready to go. Since Melissa was her ride tonight, she wanted to squash this mess now so they wouldn't have to discuss this crap the entire ride home.

Looking at her watch, Regan knew it was time to get this night wrapped up. "Well, ladies, we can all agree that when we watch anything on television, that time could be spent doing something else. However, we all want to be entertained, and we all have a right to be entertained by the shows that we prefer. Television shows are as varied as foods or cars, and with good reason. Different people like different things, so there are choices for everyone."

Kim stood up. "I'll drink to that."

"B, please, you will drink to anything; let's go." Melissa quickly hugged everyone and headed toward the door.

*****

"Good morning, ladies," Mike greeted Kim, Regina, and Melissa when he saw them in the cafeteria. "Regina, green is really your color. That dress looks great!"

Regina just smiled, feeling nervous and unsure what would come out of Mike's mouth next. Nobody spoke for a beat.

"Alrighty then, guess I'll see you upstairs!" And with that, Mike left the cafeteria.

"Bye, Mike," Melissa replied. Regina had not spoken a word.

Kim stood there with her mouth open. "What the hell?!? So that's how it is now? Y'all just out in the open, huh?"

"Kim, please! What are you talking about? I am a happily married woman and ain't hardly thinking 'bout no Mike," Regina defended.

"Well apparently he thinking about you," Kim said as they sat down with their morning beverages. "He is so whack, anyway. Mike knows good and well he has been with half the women at Bright Star. Up there talking about he prefers black girls. Please! He prefers *any* girl. Me personally, I wouldn't give that nigga the time of day."

Melissa rolled her eyes. "Kim, why do you always have to say that word? And Mike is white, anyways."

"We are not going there again. I told y'all a million times that 'nigga' does not describe a race, ethnicity, or color; it describes a mentality. That's the one thing. The other thing is that n-i-g-g-a is more of a casual, friendly term. Like saying *homie* or *girlfriend* or something like that.

Whereas n-i-g-g-e-r is a racist, demeaning term used to break and keep people down. I never have and never will use the word 'nigger.' That is foul and offensive. But 'nigga'!?!? Please, nigga you already know, and if you don't, you better ask somebody. Y'all can bury the word, cremate it, shoot it into outer space if you want to, but I'll always say it. No disrespect…nigga!"

Regina just sat there shaking her head as she watched her two friends go at it for the umpteenth time. Melissa and Kim were the two who had known each other the longest, but it seemed like Regina was the center of the relationship between the ladies.

"Melissa, just ignore Kim's crazy butt. Kim, finish what you were saying. You wouldn't give Mike the time of day because what?"

"Well, it's just the fact that he walks around here like he is God's gift. And these silly rabbits fall for it. Why the rush to be with someone that anybody could have? What's special about that? Where is the challenge?" Kim reasoned.

"Apparently, not just anybody could have him because he didn't say you were hot," Melissa reminded Kim. "I think it's cute that he has a crush on Regina. Maybe he sees her as a challenge because he knows she is married and off-limits to him."

"Naw, it isn't that. I'll tell you guys what it is. Mike just knows he could never have me, but since me and Reg are cool he would be willing to hook up with her. That would be as close as he could get to me," Kim offered.

Regina and Melissa looked at Kim like she'd lost her mind. They were well aware that their friend had some peculiar and selfish ways, but now she was really reaching. Physically speaking, most people, at first glance, would consider Kim the prettiest between her and Regina. Regina's complexion was darker, like a rich cup of coffee, compared to Kim's lighter brown skin color. Regina always wore her hair in a short cut hair style, whereas Kim's was always worn in a long, weaved style. Regina dressed in a manner that was classy and stylish, never tasteless or tacky. Kim's attire reflected her "if-you-got-it, flaunt-it" attitude. She left very little to the imagination and often pushed the envelope with how she dressed for work.

Kim often talked about how much better she looked than other women, but she'd never said anything to indicate that she felt that way about Regina as well.

"You are such a hater, Kim...and rude," Melissa was ticked.

"What? No I'm not, I'm just saying —"

"Yes you are! You always have something negative to say when someone says something positive. And heaven help us if someone says something that gives attention to someone other than you. You always have to point the conversation back to yourself," Melissa was getting fired up. "Remember the other day at my house? We were talking about that one R. Kelly song, "Sign of a Victory," and I was saying how it was a great and inspirational song. I said that R. Kelly was asked to write that song for the World Cup. When I asked if you agreed that it was a huge honor, your hater self said, 'I mean. it's *okay*. It ain't like he got asked to write for the Olympics.' What the heck, Kim? You just never believe anybody should get credit for anything, unless it is you."

"Aww, Mel, stop trippin' and lighten up. Girl, Reggie knows I don't mean any harm, so chill. Regina, I'm sorry if I came off rude. You and Mother Melissa are my only real, true friends and both of you mean everything to me."

After hugs all around, everyone headed upstairs to start the work day.

When Regina got to her desk, her cell phone was blinking to indicate that she had a text.

Sorry if I made u uncomfortable downstairs. U have 2 know that I think u r hot. Does that bother u?

Hi Mike. Doesn't bother me. Just confused where this is coming from. 4 the record u r not so bad urself

Tks ms golden. I better get back 2 work b4 I say wut I really mean & u would think I was out of line

O? do tell mr scott. Wut do u really mean 2 say?

No way can I go there. U r married and I don't wanna disrespect u.

Yes I am married. I'm also a big girl & can handle a friendly, harmless text from a coworker. So again wut do u really want 2 say 2 me sir?

This was actually getting interesting to Regina. The idea that a man other than her husband, who also happened to be younger than her and of another race might possibly find her desirable, actually intrigued Regina.

Well I am attracted to u regina. U r beautiful n classy n I would like to show u things

Mike r u texting me from ur personal phone or ur work phone???

My own personal cell, cmon gimme some credit will ya LOL

Ur right, my bad. So u were saying…

Ur different than the other females here. U r sexy as hell n I wish…nm, n a sec I'mma send a link 2 ur phone. Open it & that will say wut I wish

About two minutes later, Regina received a message on her phone with a down load. When she opened the attachment, Regina had to hurry and press the volume button to turn the sound down on her phone. Blaring from her phone, sang "Would you mind, if I touched, if I kissed, if I held you tight…" *No this fool did not just send me "Loves Holiday" by Earth Wind & Fire!*

"Stop lying!" Kim squealed as she and Melissa leaned in over the table toward Regina. They were downstairs in the cafeteria during lunch, and Regina was telling her girls about the text exchanges between her and Mike. "Wait, wait, wait! He came with it like *that*, Reg? Dang, I knew he wasn't shy with the females, but that is crazy." Kim was surprised that Mike had some game.

Melissa, like most everyone else, had heard stories about how various women at Bright Star were weak to resist Mike's charms and advances. However, he would never gain an inch with Regina. She was intelligent, logical, had high moral standards, and was in love with Kevin. No way would Regina ever entertain Mike's nonsense. "So what did he say when you told him to kick rocks? Or did you just blow him off and ignore him?"

"Actually, I didn't do either." Regina pulled her phone from her purse.

Kim snatched the phone from Regina and read the texts between Mike and Regina. While Melissa was shocked that Regina had even entertained those exchanges, Kim was actually proud of her friend. Regina was a cool girl, but a little too stuffy for Kim's liking. She always came off like she was above thinking, saying, or doing anything that was questionable. That was whack as hell as far as Kim was concerned, and she was glad to finally see the girl was as human as everyone else.

Melissa shook her head as she gathered the napkins and empty containers onto her lunch tray. "You are playing with fire, Reg, so you need to stop before you get burned."

"I know. Trust me, I got this. Things are not going to get out of control. It's just nice to have something fun and different going on for a change."

Kim rolled her eyes at Melissa. "You always say I'm a hater, but who's hating now? Dang, you need to lighten up, Melissa. Regina hasn't even done anything wrong. I shouldn't have even read the texts to your corny ass." Kim stood to take her tray to the conveyor belt and paused as she was about to pass the table. "You always sweatin' R. Kelly, Mel. What does he say in that one song? 'I don't see nothing wrong, with a little bump and grind...' They ain't even bumped nothing yet, so bring all that noise to a grind."

Regina and Melissa both had to chuckle at their crazy friend. They could always count on Kim to lighten the mood with a crazy comment.

"I do hear what you're saying, Mel, and I appreciate you for caring." Regina hugged Melissa before gathering her things and heading back upstairs to finish the work day.

"How many minutes are allotted for lunch?" Alicia was standing at Regina's desk when she got back upstairs.

"Excuse me?" Regina figured Alicia must have mistakenly stopped at the wrong desk because she knew better than to talk to her in that manner.

Cassie stood up from her cubicle. "She asked you how long lunch is supposed to be. When I was coming out of the restroom a few minutes ago I heard her ask Kim the exact same question. I bet you guys were downstairs at your normal table in the cafeteria and just totally lost track of time, huh? I told Alicia that's probably what happened. Yeah, she was asking where you were."

Both Regina and Alicia glared at Cassie, who simply shrugged her shoulders and sat back down.

"As we both know, Alicia, lunch is forty-five minutes." Unlike many of the other employees, Regina was not intimidated by Alicia. She was an ill-tempered bully, and Regina usually tried to kill her with kindness or simply ignore her. Today she chose the latter. Regina slid past Alicia into her chair and logged onto the computer to resume her work.

"Since we both know that lunch is forty-five minutes, maybe you can clue me in as to why you were gone for forty-nine minutes? If you can't make it back in the forty-five minutes allotted for lunch then maybe you need to eat lunch at your desk. I'm being nice because I could —"

"Thank you for calling Bright Star, this is Regina. How may I help you, please?" Regina would never give Alicia the power to ruffle her feathers or draw her into a negative exchange. Unlike Kim, who often engaged in heated conversations with Alicia, Regina felt that Alicia was to be pitied more than anything. It seemed that anyone who spewed that much venom had to be filled with nothing but poison. Just as she could not expect to squeeze orange juice from an apple, Regina knew that sweet or kind words could not be squeezed from a bitter heart. Her low expectations resulted in low disappointments when dealing with Alicia.

Regina struggled to remain focused through the rest of the work day. She kept replaying the lunchtime conversation in her mind, and she knew that Mel was right. It was foolish to think that she could play with fire and not get burned, or at least singed. But what if she could just get a little warmth from the fire? There was no harm in that.

A few days later, while getting coffee in the break room, Regina's cell phone buzzed, indicating that she was receiving a text message. Before work that morning, she and Kevin had an argument. After they had finished making love, Regina made a comment about how distracted Kevin appeared to be. He apologized and admitted that he'd been focused on DeShawn, the young man from the center who could possibly be facing a rape charge. They went back and forth about it, with Regina reminding Kevin how very accepting she was of Kevin's dedication to the center and its clients. She even applauded it. But carrying that into the bedroom and allowing clients to be a distraction during their intimate time was more than she would accept. Regina ended up storming out of the house, slamming the door on Kevin's pleas for her to hear him out. She felt bad on the way to work because she knew Kevin was a good man, and he really loved those kids. If DeShawn was weighing that heavily on Kevin's mind, then it must be pretty serious. She was already thinking of her reply to what she knew would be a text from Kevin, apologizing yet again for the way things had transpired this morning.

cat got ur tongue? haven't heard much from u 18ly. wuts up?

just a lot goin on. all gud tho. wuts up wit u?

wondering if u like music? i sent u a song a lil
while ago n wanted ur response.

Regina smiled.

i luv music & chaka n whitney said it best…im
evry woman its all in me…

Now it was Mike's turn to smile. Those last four words were the exact ones he wanted to have Regina Golden saying in the very near future.

9 WEEKS AGO

i bet u neva had a guy wine n dine u

excuse me but i have. u r smooth wit these kids up n here at bright star but im not impressed by a dinner date mike

who said anything about dinner? i said wine and dine YOU. we go 2 my place where we open a bottle of my fave wine n i take my time pouring n lickin it from ur tits ur navel the small of ur back n that sweet vessel n between ur sexy chocolate legs. dats my wine...ur whine is da purring n moanin u do as i nibble and dine on ur honey pot....again regina, i bet u neva had a guy wine n dine u!

Oh hell naw! Regina was not about to engage in this texting—actually more like sexting—match with Mike today. Ever since last week, their texts had been getting more frequent and more explicit. How did it get to this point so fast? And why the heck was this so exciting to her? Regina knew she would have a country-fried fit if someone was texting Kevin the way Mike was texting her. Yet, their exchanges reawakened feelings in Regina that had been lying dormant for years. *Ok, Regina, snap out of it,* she coaxed herself. She would send him a quick text to let him know they were not going to do this today. Then she would focus on returning the calls on her voicemail. Regina began texting…

cant say i had that kinda wine n dine b4, sounds gud tho. b careful wut u wish 4 tho cuz this is most def the sweetest huny & u can mess around n get hurt tasting somethin so pure when u only used 2 imitations. im more of a dog n pony show girl myself tho. after u wine n dine we can rinse off n ur shower n i will stride that lil pony of urs like a champion rider, just as u buck n grunt i slide off n back this ass up on u doggy style. can ur pony dog this huny pot mike

"...Isn't that right, Regina? Regina, are you over there? I sure hope you aren't ignoring me." Cassie was saying something as Regina was finishing her text to Mike.

Regina rolled her eyes and forced the most patient and calm voice she could muster. "Girl, no, I'm not ignoring you. Was just pulling some messages, I'm sorry."

Cassie came from her cubicle and tried to peer over Regina's shoulder. "Oh, you are pulling messages from your personal phone. That's why you didn't hear me, huh? I bet that nice husband of yours was leaving you a message, wasn't he? I know—and this is just between me and you—I know Alicia was having a nasty conversation with her husband this morning. Yeah, I walked into her office to let her know that people have been missing the trash can in the restroom and that there were paper towels on the floor. I saw two of the employees that did it too. I almost said something to them, but you know how I hate to stick my nose where it doesn't belong! So I went to tell Alicia, and she was going on and on about not being happy with the ingrates at home or the ingrates at work. She just gave me this sort of look, so I took my cue and came back to my desk. I have never heard you talk to that handsome hubby of yours like that. You are one lucky lady, Regina, and a nice one, too."

"And a busy one too, Cassie, so I'd better get back to work, and you, too, if Alicia is not in a good mood." Regina quickly picked up her phone and started dialing numbers before Cassie could say another word. *Dang!* Regina thought. It never ceased to amaze her how nosey that woman was. And she was bold with it, too. She didn't even seem to realize how many times she came close to getting cussed out. *Imagine if Kim sat here instead of me. Whew! Cassie wouldn't stand a chance.*

"Wait, wait, wait! So you actually saying you believe that mess? C'mon, Reg, you know good and well that dude is lying." Kim almost choked on her drink when she heard Regina agree with what what Melissa was saying. They were discussing the story of an Olympic track competitor who had been charged with the murder of his girlfriend. Melissa, with her bleeding heart, was saying she believed the guy, that it was an accident. And Regina actually agreed with her.

"I mean, I can see his story making sense. He thought it was an intruder. She didn't answer when he called out, so he protected himself," Regina defended.

The food was always good, but the very best part of their girls' nights out were the spirited conversations. Regina always felt like she could unwind and just be herself, have a good time, and let herself be entertained by Kim's crazy antics whenever they went out. Nobody could ever predict what would come out of that girl's mouth next.

Melissa spoke up. "Look, all I'm saying is there is no motive on his part. He is already rich, plus they are not married, so it's not like he killed her for insurance money. He is a good-looking man, so even if she left him or something, it isn't like he could not get someone else. And let's not forget that the victim tweeted earlier that day how she was looking forward to her Valentine's Day with him. Why would he want to kill that girl, destroy all he has worked for, and destroy his family, too? It doesn't make sense."

"You don't make sense either," Kim teased. "Listen, the neighbors said they heard yelling shortly before the shooting. I know he said it was the television, but people can tell the difference between TV voices and real live voices. Also, if he thought it was a burglar, why did he have to shoot into a locked bathroom? The burglar was trapped in that bathroom, and all Tink Tink had to do was slide his ass in his room and call the cops. But no, he wanted that girl dead."

Usually the quietest one at their outings, Regan spoke up. "Dang, y'all, I can see both sides. On the one hand, it just seems like he could've been calling the police before he even got to the bathroom. Plus, if she was not in bed with him, it seems like his first thought would have been to question where she was in the house. If they did argue that night, maybe it got out of hand and he shot her. They did say that he had a temper. On the other hand, though, Kim, even though the could-be burglar was trapped in the bathroom, if a person is in fear of his life, he is not going to risk an attacker coming out at any moment. What if the burglar just went in there to load a weapon or something? With seconds to think, he may have just shot as a way to protect himself. And why would he want her dead anyway?" Regan was enjoying this. Usually she was content to just observe while her sister and friends had their lively discussions. She was entertained by their vastly different views and ability to never be bitter, even when they disagreed and made each other upset.

"Oh my goodness. Do I have to spell everything out for you guys? Number one: he had a history of aggressive behavior. Two: he was jealous. His girl was a beautiful model, and he didn't want her running off with a nigga with legs. And three: it is in his DNA." Kim ate another forkful of food, slowly shaking her head at how dense her friends were being.

"HUH?" everyone gasped at once.

Kim stopped with another fork full of food midway to her mouth. "Y'all don't know? Yeah, that nigga's—"

"Kim!" Melissa growled under her breath. "Really?"

"Yeah, Mel; really. Don't start. So anyway, this nigga's brother is also in trouble for killing someone too. I think he killed someone with a car. So yeah, it just runs in the family. That's a shame, too, because they may both go to jail. But at least if they share a cell, the brother can have the top bunk, 'cause Tink Tink ain't gettin' up there."

"Wow, Kim, you are so dang gone ignorant. And why do you keep calling that man 'Tink Tink'? He has a name." Melissa didn't know why she continued to be shocked by the things that came out of her friend's mouth.

"Girl, you know Katt Williams, the comedian? Well, that's what he called him in one of his specials. That mess was funny as hell. And when Tink ran in the Olympics, I could have sworn I heard his little blades making the *tink tink* sound when he was running around the track."

Regina shook her head as she motioned for the server to bring the check. She had agreed to pay tonight and wanted to let the girls know it was time to call it a night. Although Kevin had been wrapped up with things at the center, not the least of which was the case with DeShawn, she did miss their friendship. She was, in a weird way, grateful for the distraction that those silly texts with Mike provided because she didn't focus as much on how distant she and Kevin had become.

"Well, I guess we will just have to wait and see what happens with that case. I know one thing that doesn't need a jury to decide though; Kim, you are a fool. You do give us food for thought though, and you cute as a button, so I ain't even mad at ya." Regina high-fived her friend.

With that, everyone hugged, said their goodbyes, and went their separate ways.

Regina couldn't help but shake her head and smile as she got into her car to go home to Kevin. Even as tense as things had been between them the last few weeks, she did still love and care for him which is why she ordered him a to-go dinner from the restaurant. She figured he had not taken the time to get himself anything to eat.

Just then, Regina began to reflect upon the miracle of her and Kevin's relationship. They were an unlikely couple to say the least, and Regina used to doubt that she was even good enough for Kevin, much less worthy of the love and affection that he showered upon her – well, that he used to shower upon her. Now the only showering going on was early mornings as they brushed past each other on the way out of the house. Maybe Kevin's parents were correct when they told Regina that she would fit into Kevin's life only as a friend, a very distant friend. His mother made it very clear that her only child was used to having the best, and marrying a – how did she refer to Regina? Oh yes – "a poor ghetto rat from a single-parent home" hardly fit the bill. Poor Regan was more hurt by Mrs. Golden's words than Regina was. Regina's mother,

Mrs. Washington, on the other hand, was more angry than hurt and she'd wanted to slap Mrs. Golden.

*****

Regina's mother, Judy Sheldon, had married Regina's father right out of high school. Judy was very smart, popular, and beautiful in high school. She'd come from a large, loving family and was wary when she first met the charming and cocky Jason Washington. She was a junior when he was a senior in high school. Jason had a reputation as a player and easily could have had his choice of any of the girls in school, but he thought there was something different about Judy. She didn't seem as easily impressed by his antics and bragging as the other girls did. After he graduated high school, Jason finally managed to convince Judy to give him her telephone number. After meeting her family and getting permission from her parents to officially date Judy, Jason seemed to settle down some of his bad boy behaviors. They spent a romantic, fun-filled summer together, and Judy confided that she was a virgin. That may have been why Jason thought she was so special. He decided from that moment that the first man that Judy Sheldon had sex with would be the last man that she would have sex with - Mr. Jason Washington.

Not only was Judy a smart girl, but she was a good girl, too. Not in the goody-two-shoes way, but in the most real and pure way. She was helpful around the house, respectful to her elders, and very trusting, to the point of sometimes being naïve. So it was little wonder that before the beginning of her senior year, Judy gave her most valuable possession to Jason. She did not enjoy it, and she felt as if she looked, walked, and talked differently. She could not look her mother in the eye for a week afterward. Soon, Judy learned news that would alter her life forever. She was pregnant. It was the '60s. Judy would have to give up her position as head cheerleader and leave school when she began to show. She didn't know how she would be able to go to college to realize her dream of becoming a teacher. Even worse, how on earth would Judy tell her family?

Jason was popular and athletic in high school, but he never showed academic strength, so he never planned to attend college. Instead, he went to work at a local department store. Like Judy, Jason also came from a fairly large family. Although he was an only child, he had a large extended family, including several aunts, uncles, and first cousins. Also similar to Judy's family, Jason's family was a loving one. Even if unspoken, everyone knew and accepted that Jason was very indulged by his parents, especially his mother, Mrs. Washington. Despite several school suspensions, run-ins with neighbors, and a few arrests for minor things like curfew violations and vandalism, Mrs. Washington refused to acknowledge any wrong on her son's behalf. In fact, she considered Jason the victim during most of those situations. When Mrs. Washington first learned that Judy was pregnant, she insisted that the baby could not possibly be Jason's. Then, after finally accepting that Judy had been a virgin, Mrs. Washington was convinced that Judy had purposely gotten pregnant to trap her precious son.

During her senior year, before she started showing, Jason Washington married Judy Sheldon in her grandmother's living room. Jason very soon stopped being a bad boy and very quickly turned into a brooding bully. He and Judy moved into a small rental property that his family owned and officially became a family. Judy did manage to graduate with honors, but college was out of the question. Though she was a young mother, she was loving, dutiful, and attentive. Judy seemed to fall very naturally into her new role, and it was amazing to see this seventeen-year-old girl keep a clean home, well-cared-for baby girl, and positive attitude. Jason was not so positive. He resented Judy the day he married her. As he was saying "I do," he was thinking "I won't." If he resented Judy, he outright hated the thing that came screaming from between her legs, causing his world to turn upside down. It seemed like with the birth of this child came the death of his freedom and fun. Jason could not walk into his parents' house without everyone clamoring to see the new baby. Even Judy had changed. Once thin and pretty and sweet, she had become fat and tired all the time. That was the reason Jason started cheating on her; she just had not kept herself presentable. For her part, Judy was far too busy to be concerned with Jason's antics. At the beginning, she questioned him about coming in with the rising sun, but he was so cold and distant that she stopped caring. Judy was determined to be the best mother possible. She did not work outside of the home, so financially she was dependent upon Jason and the periodic help and blessings of her family members. Of every dollar she did manage to get, Judy saved 20 percent. She was determined to make a good life for her new family.

Although she often felt like a single person, Judy did hope to have a happy family with Jason and baby Regina. Those hopes were smashed like an iron fist to a porcelain jaw when, two years into their marriage, Judy told Jason she was pregnant again. Initially, Jason tried to convince himself that he was justified in breaking Judy's jaw because she had to have cheated on him to be pregnant. He was so disgusted with her that he knew he'd barely touched her in the last year and a half to two years. Then he remembered the time he had been unable to have sex with his side chick because it was her time of the month, so he'd had to settle for Judy. Damn, he couldn't divorce her (his family was too religious for that), and he did not want to hear his mother's nagging and preaching. Jason just pretended as though Judy, Regina, and later Regan did not exist. Whenever any of them got in his way, he literally kicked them out of the way. He ensured that all the bills were paid. After all, he was a "good man," but he never again had sex with Judy. And he never, not once, held, hugged, or showed affection to either of his daughters.

Regina felt the sting of both happy and angry tears burn down her cheeks. The happy tears were produced by memories of how much love, support, and encouragement Mrs. Washington poured into her daughters. The angry tears were produced by memories of how cruel, aloof, and selfish Jason was. Regina and Regan only referred to their father by his first name. That was at his insistence. He was rarely seen with his wife and children in public, but even at home, he made it very clear that he did not want to be known as anyone's father. It amazed Regina how different her and Regan's attitudes toward men were. Regina was more inclined to be a pleaser and worked really hard to win affection from men. Regan seemed to shun men, rather burying herself in her school work and later her career. Regan used to always say that the best way to avoid drowning was to stay out of the pool. The only date Regina ever remembered Regan going on was her senior prom, and Mrs. Washington had to practically force that to happen. It really bothered Regina that her sister had closed her heart and mind to the possibility of love and companionship because of the way Jason treated their mother. At the same time, though, Regina had to wonder if Regan might be the wiser of the two because, until she met and married Kevin, Regina never felt loved, respected, or valued by a man. Now, Kevin seemed like he was losing interest in Regina, too.

"What color green you want, lady?" someone yelled out of the window as his car passed Regina's. She hadn't even noticed the light change while she reflected why she almost believed Mrs. Golden's words that she was not good enough for Kevin. Look at the hell Regina had been born into! Yes, Judy had managed to put both of her daughter's through school and had even earned an Associate's Degree of her own. But if Regina was not worthy enough to be loved by her own father, she wondered how she could possibly be worthy of Kevin's love. Everything just seemed so easy with Kevin. From the beginning, he seemed to only want to protect and nurture Regina, accepting her for who she was, while encouraging her to be all that she could. No man, not even the one who was supposed to be her father, had ever shown that type of love to Regina. She made up her mind, as she was turning onto her street, that she would stop the nonsense with Mike and focus that same energy and attention toward her husband. Before she got out of the car to take Kevin's dinner into the house, Regina decided to send him a text and give him some food for thought.

hey mr golden. ive been a bad girl n need 2 serve detention. might need sum swats. u want me 2 cum get my licks???

One minute. No response.
Ninety seconds. No response.

Two and a half minutes. Still nothing.

Three minutes later:

Gina girl what are you talking about? Have you been drinking with that crazy Kim?

Shaking her head, Regina exited her car, entered her home, kissed her husband on the cheek, and plastered a fake smile on her face as she sat down to inquire about his day.

*****

"I don't doubt that he loves me, and I certainly don't think he is cheating on me. It's just…I don't know, I just feel…" Regina couldn't find the right word as she tried to express her feelings. She put her head in her hands and released an exasperated sigh.

"Neglected? Is that it? You feel neglected?" Melissa rubbed her friend's shoulder and wondered what had Regina so upset all day at work. "Reggie, you know Kevin is busy with that case, trying to help DeShawn. That kid has a lot of people against him, and your husband is one of the few people that DeShawn can count on. So just know that it is not you, honey. It is this crazy situation. Kevin isn't neglecting you. In fact, he probably needs your support now more than ever. Be patient with him, Regina. And don't get distracted!" Melissa knew that Regina was probably still texting Mike, although they had not discussed it since that time in the cafeteria.

Regina peered over her hands, raised an eyebrow at Melissa, and again rested her head in her hands. *Dang, does Mel have a hidden camera in my phone?* Regina wondered. She had intentionally not shared any of the texts or conversations she'd been exchanging with Mike. As things got a bit more heavy and edgy, Regina just felt like she didn't want to have to explain or defend herself.

"Who distracted?" Kim had found her girls in the break room to tell them how Cassie's nosey-ass had just pissed her off. But she temporarily tabled that discussion when she heard Mother Melissa telling Regina not to "get distracted." Head still down in her hands, Regina rolled her eyes before looking up to greet her friend.

"Nobody, Ms. Johnny-Come-Lately. Melissa was just being her normal overly concerned self."

Kim twisted her lips and made that "umm-hmm" face because she knew something was going on, but she would get to that later. She had to bring the girls up-to-speed on the way she just had to, yet again, put Cassie in her place. "So you know how I have been planning the potluck lunch for Julie and taking the collection for a gift card, right? Well, I turn around at my desk and see Cassie reading the names on the envelope of all the people who contributed. I asked if I could help her with something and this heffa had the nerve to say yes, I could help her understand why I was doing all of this for someone who was unmarried and having their second child." Melissa and Regina were horrified, but not surprised. "Yes, y'all. She asked me if I felt like I was promoting promiscuity. I promise it took everything I had not to knock the mess out of that fool. So I told her I was not promoting anything, that I was celebrating the life that a coworker was about to bring into the world. Then I reminded her that Julie's personal life was none of my business, and certainly none of hers. It just makes me so mad that she acts like she doesn't know how offensive and rude her dumb ass is. So Cassie went on about how she didn't mean to offend me, but she would not be contributing for Julie's gift card or bringing anything to the lunch. I told her that was probably best because nobody would likely eat her food anyway."

Melissa's mouth was open, and she couldn't do anything but shake her head. She knew that Cassie was nosey, but this was the first she'd known her to be rude and judgmental like that. "Well, she was definitely out of line. Who is she to judge Julie or anyone else for that matter? But, Kim, really? You had to go there about her food? You know Cassie thinks she is the Bright Star Baker." Melissa knew better than to expect Kim to correct Cassie without getting in a personal dig.

"Yes, Mother Melissa, I did have to go there with Cassie. I didn't even tell you guys the best part. So after all of that, she had the nerve to kneel at my desk and ask me if I had heard that Julie had gotten pregnant by a black man."

"Girl, STOP!" Regina was getting mad now and halfway wanted to check Cassie herself. But she knew it wouldn't do any good. That woman had been the same way since they started at Bright Star, and she would likely be that way when they left.

"Oh, it gets better," Kim continued. "This dumb B gon' say 'I mean, I don't have a problem if the baby has a black father. After all, I even voted for Obama…well the first time anyway.' I couldn't take it, y'all. I told Cassie she had to the count of one to excuse herself from my desk." Kim was getting angry again just thinking about what Cassie had said.

Melissa took off her friend hat and replaced it with her Bright Star management hat. "Kim, what do you think about talking to HR, or to Cassie's supervisor about her comments? I'm thinking that maybe she could benefit from some sensitivity training."

"Uhhh, NO! I don't need to talk to anybody about anything. Trust and believe, I will give Cassie the training she needs. People need to quit excusing her mess by saying 'that's just how she is.' That is unacceptable. Keep messing with me, she gon' learn today!"

u ok? cat got ya tongue today? wish i was dat cat

Dang. Just what Regina did not need; a text from Mike. But she had to admit, his texts seemed to always come at the perfect time, when she was either upset or down about something. And his silly texts never failed to put a smile on her face. She had decided, after talking to Melissa, that she was going to stop interacting with Mike on that level. She really did feel like she was being sneaky, and Kevin did not deserve that. Yes, he had been distant and distracted lately, but his distraction was due to helping a person in trouble. Her distraction, on the other hand, was totally selfish. There was a time, years ago, when Regina would have loved the attention from Mike. In fact, she would have initiated the flirting, as she was prone to seeking male attention to feel better about herself. However, after getting to know Kevin, Regina began to feel okay with who she was, flaws and all. She did not feel like she had to do or be anything other than herself. Being with Kevin actually made Regina want to be a better person. Aside from being her husband, Kevin would be disappointed as a friend if he knew how Regina had been flirting and texting with Mike. She decided to put an end to this right now.

nope. cat don't got my tongue & u won't either. and i need u to plz stop texting me

i cant have ur tongue? well can i have ur cat...i just wanna hear her purr

that's not funny mike. i'm serious. i don't want anyone to get hurt so plz. i neva shoulda gone there wit u in the 1st place

wow didn't know u were serious. hey im sorry i thought we were both enjoying this back n forth thing. like I said b4 u r a classy lady n i dont wanna disrespect u. ill back off

Mike felt like an idiot. He had never had a female cut him off like that. In fact, most of the women at Bright Star, married or not, made it clear to him that they were available to anything that Mike wanted. At first, Mike was uncomfortable with the female attention, and he did not want to do anything to put his job in jeopardy. Then, several years ago, Mike went on a date with someone around his own age at the company. She was single, not his direct report, and fun to hang out with. After they had sex, though, she became clingy and found reasons to come into Mike's office several times a day. One time, all of the leads and supervisors were sitting in the cafeteria after a working lunch, and she stood behind Mike, waiting for him to get up and talk to her. Although he was angry, and more than a little embarrassed, Mike did not want to be mean or hurtful to the lady. He told her that if she wanted to continue to hang out, that was fine, but make no mistake, he was not looking for a relationship. He apologized for not making that clear in the beginning, and from that point on, they did not have any other problems. They continued to get together for about a month or so after that, but she admitted to wanting more than a physical relationship, so they agreed to stop seeing each other. Soon, word spread that Mike was a perfect gentleman in the workplace, and a beast in the bedroom. And most importantly, he always used protection.

There were several women at work who Mike thought were attractive, but he never said a word or gave any indication of this attraction. He treated all of the females, including those he had been with, the exact same way. He was always professional, friendly, and easy to talk to. That could be why so many of the women at Bright Star wanted what had come to be known around the office as the Memorable Mike Experience. Mike was always discreet, never telling anybody at work anything that he had done with anyone. When we was with a female, he worked hard to make her feel beautiful, special, wanted, valued. He was sincere in the compliments he gave. He opened doors, gave foot and back massages, cooked and served meals, and never failed to produce multiple orgasms from his date before his own climax. It was true, Mike had bedded his fair share of women at Bright Star, but he did not consider himself to be any type of playboy or womanizer. He promised himself to not cross a certain moral line by being with anyone who was married. In fact, that promise was part of the reason for the tension between Mike and one of his peers, Alicia. When Mike was first promoted to the supervisor position, Cassie came to his office and told him that she'd overheard Alicia telling someone that she wanted to be the next one to have the Memorable Mike Experience. Cassie relayed how she went up to Alicia and told her that was not likely to happen, since Alicia was married and Mike was a good guy. Like everyone else at Bright Star, Mike knew Cassie's propensity for eavesdropping and running her mouth, so he took her words with a grain of salt. Maybe he should've used sugar instead, because not two weeks later, Alicia started coming to Mike's office quite frequently.

Alicia had a reputation for being curt, even rude, with employees, so Mike was surprised with her offer to "do anything" to make his transition a smooth one. Alicia offered to give Mike a "blow-by-blow" of the Standard Operations Manual and critiques of each of his subordinates. Ever the gentleman, Mike thanked Alicia for her offers and promised to let her know if he needed any help. He did not want to make her feel embarrassed, so he redirected her conversation instead of ignoring her or telling other people about it. The last straw, though, was one day when Alicia walked into Mike's office and reached across his desk, revealing her breasts in the process. When that failed to get the desired response from Mike, Alicia stated she needed to excuse herself and go home for a moment, as she'd forgotten to put on panties that morning before work. She made sure to emphasize that her husband was away on a business trip. It was then that Mike told Alicia that her husband was a lucky man to have such a beautiful and loving wife and that he would be fine learning the ropes as a supervisor on his own. From that day to this one Alicia never looked at Mike without glaring nor spoken to him without hissing.

Needless to say, it baffled Mike when he found himself so attracted to Regina Golden. He had always known that married women were off-limits. And for some reason, Regina intimidated Mike. She was never mean or rude, nor was she intimidating in a bully-type manner, like Alicia tried to be. She was just different from any of the other women in the building. Her friend Kim was a looker, outgoing, and popular. Yet it was Regina's quiet reserve and understated beauty that captivated Mike. He had been nervous when approaching her to inquire about his nephew, but Regina was easy to talk with. Mike knew he was taking a risk when he first texted Regina on a personal level. But she responded in kind and never indicated that she was offended by Mike. In fact, she seemed to enjoy their back-and-forth banter. So it was puzzling as to why she suddenly wanted to stop. Of all the women that he had dealt with at Bright Star, Regina was the one he respected most, so he would respect her wishes and not text her anymore. He still thought she was fine as hell, but he would back off.

Kevin was beginning to get the sense that something was wrong with

Regina. They had argued about the amount of time that he was spending at the center and the fact that she felt like Kevin was not giving her attention. That was crazy! Kevin loved Regina with all of his heart, and Regina was a fool if she didn't know that by now. Kevin practically disassociated himself from his mother in order to be with Regina. Mrs. Golden never seemed to approve of Regina, always telling Kevin that he could do better and needed to be with a woman worthy of the son of the Honorable Judge Golden. Kevin loved his parents, was respectful toward them, and never wanted to be a disappointment. However, as he grew into adulthood, he realized that he had to live his own life and make his own decisions, sink or swim. Mrs. Golden had told Kevin a part of her died when he finished law school then pursued a degree in education. When Kevin told his mother he wanted to make a difference, she told him that he did not have to be broke to do it. It amazed Kevin how snobby his mother was, considering the fact that her own background and upbringing was so close to Regina's.

Kevin never regretted his decision to marry Regina. He loved her carefree, honest, positive outlook. He loved the dedication and support she demonstrated when he wanted to leave teaching to open the center, especially knowing how important the security of a steady paycheck was to her. He relished their sex and intimacy. They were perfectly compatible when it came to the bedroom, and never, until recently, had one of them denied the other's requests for sex. Kevin felt bad about being so preoccupied with Deshawn's case. He understood that he had been focusing a lot of time on DeShawn and meeting with his family and his attorney. Kevin reasoned that he and Regina would always be there for each other; that she would still be in his corner when the entire ordeal with DeShawn was over. DeShawn's situation was current, though, and required Kevin's immediate attention and time. Still, he did not want Regina to feel alienated, so Kevin decided that he would make a better effort to remind her how special, beautiful, and important she was to him.

hey baby i know u been busy l8ly so how about when i get home u sit back relax & watch me play wit that new toy. sound good?

Perfect timing. Kevin couldn't help but smile as he read the text from his wife, thankful that they seemed to be on the same page. This time, he wouldn't disappoint Regina. He picked up the phone to text her back but got distracted when the home phone rang. It was DeShawn's mother saying DeShawn had locked himself in his bedroom, and she was scared he might hurt himself. Kevin agreed to come right over. Grabbing his keys, he rushed out of the door, leaving his cellular on his desk.

One minute. No response.
Ten minutes. No response.
Thirty minutes. No response.
One hour. No response.

Regina was on fire. She had decided to pour the energy into her husband and marriage that she had been pouring into Mike. There was a time when Kevin wouldn't let sixty seconds pass without responding to a text or call from her. Now Regina couldn't get a response in sixty minutes. Her feelings were hurt and she felt ignored. Wanting to feel received instead of rejected, Regina sent another text.

so…exactly how many strokes would it take 4 u 2 make this cat purrrrrr

When Regina returned to her desk from lunch, she saw the familiar yellow flag on her computer screen indicating that she had a message. It was about one of the business accounts that Regina was managing, and apparently there was an issue because Regina was being summoned by a supervisor. When she reached the far side of the building, where each supervisor's office was located, Regina nervously knocked on the third door on the left.

"Come on in."

Regina peered inside, unsure of what this was about.

"I'm not going to bite your head off. Please, come in, close the door, and have a seat." Mike wondered if Regina was even half as nervous as he was.

"Hey, Mike, I got your message. What's going on?" Regina was puzzled, as she had no idea what could be wrong with one on her longest-held accounts.

Mike figured he would get right to the point. "You have a puzzled look on your face, Regina, but I must admit that I am the one who is confused. I called you in here to ask you precisely what you just asked me...What *is* going on?" Mike tensely leaned forward in his chair, but his face relaxed as he patiently waited for Regina to shed some light on her 180-degree change.

"I'm sorry, Mike. I know I was being confusing and misleading so I apologize for that. Boy, this was much easier when we were just texting instead of looking at each other face-to-face. I was just tripping because...well...to be honest, I was flattered by your attention. So I allowed myself to respond to it, and that was wrong. You have always been a nice guy and probably the best supervisor in this place, so I don't want anything to interfere with the good working relationship that we have. That being said, please accept my apology, Mike. This is neither the time nor the place to be discussing this, anyway."

Regina fidgeted with her hands as her eyes darted around Mike's office. She was trying to focus on anything other than his perfectly groomed hair, inviting eyes, and sexy lips. Regina was glad that Mike called her into his office so that she could stop these text exchanges with him. Even though she was feeling neglected, ignored, and unappreciated by Kevin, Regina did not want to hurt him by betraying him. She was no longer the same girl of years ago, who needed the attention and affection of men in order to feel valid and worthy. Standing to leave, Regina stretched out her hand to offer a good-natured shake to Mike.

Reluctantly, Mike accepted Regina's extended hand. His mind was flooded. His logical thought of keeping his professional relationship with Regina intact and letting Regina walk out of his office was drowned by his desire for and attraction to this woman. Mind flooding, emotions swarming, desire cascading, Mike grabbed Regina's outstretched arm like a welcome lifejacket. He pulled her in and practically strapped her onto himself as he held on tightly. When Regina rested her head on his chest instead of pulling away, Mike let his arms loosen as his hands found and rested upon Regina's ample behind. Mike's excitement at the touch could clearly be felt through his clothes. It had been years since Regina felt that from any man other than Kevin, and it seemed weird. She snapped out of it, quickly excused herself, and ran out of Mike's office.

8 WEEKS AGO

Thank goodness today was Saturday! Regina could not have dragged herself to work if her life depended upon it. The past week had been an emotional roller coaster. She had gone from a texting frenzy with Mike, to a decision to stop it completely, to being more attracted to him than ever. Mike was charming and funny and exciting. Kevin was a good man, and he had a good heart. He just didn't seem to have room in it for Regina anymore. He was not mean or disrespectful. He was just neglectful, which was almost worse. To be mean would have at least meant Regina was getting some sort of attention from her husband.

They had not talked for two days last week because Kevin had ignored a text Regina had sent. He told her the same story about the same thing as always, that there was an emergency situation with DeShawn which needed his immediate attention. Regina still had an attitude when she came home one day and found a familiar white-and-brown box on the dining room table. She couldn't help but smile as she lifted the lid and inhaled one of her favorite aromas of Coach leather. It was the British Tan satchel that Regina had her eye on. Umm hmm, Kevin thought he was slick, trying to buy her back from being angry. Regina shook her head as she walked into the kitchen to get her customary after-work Pepsi and saw yet another white box with brown trim in the refrigerator. It was the matching wallet to the satchel. Ok fine, maybe she couldn't be bought, but a short-term lease in exchange for her new Coach purse and wallet was not completely out of the question. Since that day, there had not been any other incidents, and Kevin had even promised that they would spend the entire weekend doing whatever Regina wanted. So far, he was remaining true to his word because he was downstairs making the egg white-and-tomato sandwich she'd requested for breakfast.

Kevin had to admit that it was fun hanging out with his friend, his ride-or-die, his wife, Regina Washington Golden. They had enjoyed breakfast, cleaned the kitchen together, hit Home Depot for supplies so they could stain the deck together, and were on the way to catch the last matinee at the movie theater. "Baby, I have to admit, I didn't realize how much I missed hanging out with you until today. I promise you that you will not have to feel like you are on the back burner any more. Love you baby."

"I love you, too, Kev. And thank you for saying that. I was feeling guilty for wanting more time with you. I know your work at Golden Choices is important. Shoot, I'm very proud of the effort and time you spend on those boys. Even with the craziness of this DeShawn situation, I was trying to be patient. I didn't want to seem selfish, yet at the same time I needed you, both physically and emotionally. I really felt like I was losing you, Kevin. Still, I'm sorry for any pressure I put on you baby." Regina was gladder than ever that she'd left Mike's office. She had wanted to be made to feel like a woman, and Mike was a cheap substitution. This renewed focus by Kevin proved that she had the real thing with her husband. "Hey, Kevin, I have an idea. Let's skip the movie and go home and make our own."

Kevin grabbed Regina's waist and pulled her in for a long kiss. "Hmmm...lights, camera, action. Let's roll, baby!"

Back at the house, Regina took a couple of frozen margarita drinks out of the freezer while Kevin ran upstairs to start their bathwater and light candles around the bathtub. Heading upstairs, Regina decided to leave her buzzing cell phone downstairs. She did not want any interruptions tonight. If there was an emergency with her sister or her mother, they would call the home phone. As she entered their bathroom, Regina saw Kevin putting his cellular on his dresser.

"Who was that, babe?" Regina was hoping that was not another call pulling her husband away.

Kevin saw the concern on his wife's face and was happy to reassure her. "I don't know, and I don't care. The phone started ringing, and I put it on vibrate. This weekend was promised to you, and I'll be damned if anything gets in the way of that. Now let's get in this tub so I can start directing this movie."

Regina creased her forehead with a questioning look as she began to get undressed. "Boy, please, you can be the producer, but I'm the director and will be calling all the shots tonight!"

Kevin chuckled as he and Regina prepared to step into their pool of love. "Yeah, I got your producer right here, Regina. Now come over here and let me remind you what a Golden production feels like."

Regina was elated. Not only was she going to experience the intimacy she'd long been craving and desperately needing from Kevin, but he was actually looking forward to it as much as she was. She gave Kevin a quick peck on the lips and made sure to rub her behind against him as she sashayed her naked body across the room and into the bathtub. Kevin had stripped down to his boxer-briefs and was in the process of peeling them off when the home phone rang.

*****

"Hell yeah, I was devastated. I've been crying since he left over an hour ago," Regina shared with Regan, Kim, and Melissa during their emergency girls' session.

When Kevin left the house after getting yet another call about De-Shawn, Regina was livid beyond description. Her first instinct was to text Mike, but she did not want to deal with any member of the male persuasion. Instead, she called her sister. When Regan answered the phone, Regina broke into a guttural wail that was barely recognizable as being human. Regan immediately got into her car and headed to her big sister's home. She called Kim and Melissa while she was en route and explained that something was going on with Regina. She did not have much information to provide, as Regina only managed to howl, cry, and something that Regan had rarely heard from her sister, use profanity. The three ladies had arrived at Regina's house at the same time, and Regan used her key to get in. They followed the sound of pitiful and mournful cries up to the master bathroom. Regina was in a ball on the floor, head buried in her arms. As was typical of the ladies when any of them was hurting or in need, they got on the floor with their beloved sister and friend and quietly stroked Regina's hair, back, and arms.

Melissa had commented that Regina must've been devastated when Kevin left unexpectedly yet again. She hated to see her friend in so much pain. "Reg, you are totally justified to be upset and hurt. Kevin dealt you another disappointing blow. At the same time, you have to believe that he is disappointed, hurt, and frustrated, too. Think about it, he was getting ready—"

Regina glared at Melissa in a way that was almost scary. "Fuck Kevin! Don't you dare try to defend him to me or try to put his feelings on the same level as mine. He made a promise to me. We were on the verge of a great ending to a wonderful day, and he made the decision to let a needy, delinquent, rapist kid come between us...*again*! No, I don't know what Kevin was 'getting ready' to do, but I sure as hell know what he did. Once again, he left me hanging."

Nobody said anything for at least a minute. It was not normal to hear Regina talk in that manner, and it was awkward watching Melissa lick her wounds. Suddenly, Kim jumped to her feet and pointed down in Melissa's face as she stood over her, "Daaaaaa-yummm, you got knocked the FUCK out!" Kim teased in her best imitation of Smokey from *Friday*. Everyone, including Regina, erupted in laughter.

After a little more than an hour, Regina had finally convinced everyone that she would be fine and that she needed them to leave so she could jump into some pajamas, wash her face, and go to bed. She was still angry with Kevin and her feelings were hurt, but she was exhausted and did not want to keep talking about the situation. Melissa and Kim said their good-byes, and Regan told them she would stay with Regina for a little while longer before heading home herself.

"Girl, I do not need a babysitter; I'm fine. Really, go on home, Regan." Regina hugged her sister and was about to head into her bathroom when Regan grabbed her hand and patted the spot next to where she was sitting on the bed.

Regina hesitantly sat, as she rolled her eyes at her little sister. "What, Regan?"

"I'm just concerned about you, Reg. I've never seen you so upset with

Kevin. He has worked long hours at the center, and you always seemed fine with it. Why are you so mad now? Like really, what else is going on?"

"Yes, he has worked long hours in the past. Yes, I have been fine with his unpredictable schedule in the past. That is all the more reason why I'm fed up. Look, I understand…shoot, I even respect and appreciate all that Kevin is doing with those boys and their families, but I'm *his* family. It is a slap in the face for him to be at DeShawn's beck and call when he is nothing more than a two-bit delinquent rapist. Shoot, and I'm over here wasting my time trying to be the good wife."

"What's *that* supposed to mean?" Regan leaned in closer to her sister's face.

"Nothing. Look, it's late, Regan. Just go on home, and I'll catch up with you later. Maybe we can do lunch or dinner tomorrow."

"Okay, I'll leave as soon as you tell me what you meant by 'trying to be the good wife'. What's up with that? Have you done something stupid? You aren't thinking about leaving Kevin, are you?"

"Let's just say that while Kevin is busy looking after some loser teenager, he is leaving the door open for someone else to look after me."

"What the heck!?!? What is that supposed to mean, Regina? And don't lie! I am not playing with you."

Regan and Regina went back and forth like that for forty-five minutes. Finally, Regina had to accept that her sister was not going anywhere unless she got the information she wanted. Regina inhaled deeply and exhaled loudly as she prepared to come clean with her sister.

"Fine, Regan, but this stays between me and you. And I don't want to hear your mouth, either."

"Whatever." Regan folded her arms across her chest and waited.

Regina proceeded to tell Regan how she had been texting with Mike. Regina explained how it had begun as simple flirting, and she had initially brushed off Mike's messages. Then, as Kevin became increasingly absent, Mike's presence was increasingly welcome. At first, Regina was pacing back and forth then she again took a seat on the bed next to Regan. Regan held her big sister's hand, a physical expression of the emotional support she was offering. Regina finished by telling Regan about her meeting in Mike's office, during which she told him that they could not continue to deal with each other.

"So you see, Regan? Aside from being patient with Kevin, I've really tried to do the right thing. I know I was momentarily sidetracked, but I started to feel guilty because Kevin really is a good guy. I just don't know if being a good guy is enough for me. It is not a benefit to me or to our marriage if that 'good guy' is always absent."

Regan was surprised. She had never imagined that Regina would ever give another man so much as a second thought. Still, she felt sorry for her sister and for Kevin, too, actually. Kevin was the only brother that Regan had ever known. Even though it was not intentional, he was causing Regina pain. Not wanting to choose sides or sit in judgment of her sister, Regan hugged Regina. "Honey, I'm so sorry that you are lonely. I'm also very proud of you for ending things with Mike before they had a chance to blow up and make a real mess. I love you, Regina, no matter what."

Regina walked Regan to the front door, thanked her for listening, and finally got into the shower.

The first few days of the work week were a blur for Regina. She knew she had gone to work, done her job, and returned home, but she could not remember any specific details; not even the daily drive to and from the office. She was so angry and hurt that she robotically went through the motions necessary to get through each day. She and Kevin had barely spoken ten words to each other in the last three days. Truth be told, Regina felt sorry for Kevin, which made her even angrier with herself. She was the one being neglected by her husband. She was the one who had rebuffed the advances of another man. She was the one who had been left high and dry sexually several times over the past few weeks. So it was irritating to say the least; the fact that she felt sorry for Kevin as he moped and sighed around the house like a lost puppy made Regina angry. Kevin was a nice guy. He was never mean, judgmental, unfaithful, or selfish. He was a good husband, and she applauded the fact that Kevin cared so deeply about helping young men. Until recently, that is. Working beyond office hours from time to time was acceptable for Regina. However, placing concern for those hooligans at the center above her needs was not something she was able to handle.

Regina never considered herself a snob, but she did have one thing in common with Mrs. Golden. Regina could not figure out why Kevin had chosen to pursue a career in education instead of law. Kevin was really smart and was doing so well in law school that several firms were courting him before he'd even graduated. He could've been a very successful attorney, making quite a bit of money and possibly even a judge like his father, if he'd wanted to. Then, he left a secure teaching job to open the center. As she thought about it, Regina was probably more proud that Kevin had decided to defy his overbearing mother than she was that he was helping at-risk youth. In order to help someone, they first needed to help themselves. As time passed, it became clearer to Regina that the juvenile delinquents at Golden Choices did not want to be helped. If they did, they would handle their business, go to school, stop smoking and drinking, get jobs, and make better decisions. If anyone knew what it was like to work hard in spite of one's circumstances, it was Regina. She was abused and abandoned by a cowardly father, raised by a mother who had to work multiple jobs just to meet the barest of necessities, and taken for granted by every man she ever dated. Life had not been easy for Regina, yet she chose to struggle through college and secure gainful employment. She helped herself!

Okay, Reggie, you better be lucky these thoughts can't be heard by others, or someone might mistake you for the other *Mrs. Golden,* Regina chuckled to herself as she shook her head and snapped out of her thoughts. It was finally time to go home for the day, and Regina was glad this was the night she and the girls were supposed to meet for dinner. She did not want to go home to the tension which surely waited if Kevin happened to be there.

"Hold the elevator, please," Regina yelled down the hall as she raced toward the closing elevator doors so she would not have to take the stairs to the parking deck. Picking up her pace to a slight trot, Regina made it to the elevator just before the doors began to close again. Were she not so tired, Regina would have gotten off of the elevator and taken the stairs to avoid being alone with Mike.

"Hello, Regina. I'd be happy to hold anything you'd like," Mike offered. Immediately feeling foolish and not wanting to be rejected, he tried to clean it up. "I'm sorry, that was inappropriate of me."

"No, Mike, you don't have to apologize. You wouldn't happen to know how to hold a breaking heart, would you? Oh my goodness, now look at who is being inappropriate. I'm sorry; it's just been a rough last few days. Don't mind me."

"Don't *mind* you? Are you kidding me?!? You have been the only thing my mind can focus on. I don't want to disrespect you, Regina, and I definitely don't want to create a bad situation for either of us at work. I'm gonna level with you. You are stunning to me. It's not just because you are hot, either. You walk into the office, and it just seems a little brighter. You are a breath of fresh air in an otherwise dank and stale environment. I have never heard you say one negative thing about anyone, and I'd bet a month of paychecks that nobody has ever said an unkind word about you. If they have, they are a fool. You are married, I am single, and I know I have no right, but I just…"

"You just what, Mike? Want to add me to your list of Bright Star conquests? I'm flattered, but I'll pass. I am a real woman with a real life and real issues, so these little high school games are not really something I'm interested in. I told you, it was a distraction when we were texting each other. Heck, I'll even admit that I was attracted to you. But I don't need distraction in my life right now. Now, Mike, more than ever before, I need to focus."

Regina had never been on such a long elevator ride. If this thing didn't get her to the parking deck level, she was afraid she was going to have to be mean to Mike just to get him to back off. Bright Star had only seen the mild Regina. She sure didn't want Mike to be the first to see that west side girl come out.

"Okay, you win. I'll back off. Come give me a kiss goodbye, and you will not have to worry about me annoying you again." Mike flashed his sexy, dimpled smile at Regina as he stepped toward her with his arms outstretched.

"Boy, please, you must be out of your mind in real life if you think I'm going to kiss you. Have you not heard a word I just said?" Regina fidgeted as she tried her best to sound annoyed. In reality, she was glad that, yet again, Mike had found her interesting, while her own husband seemed to find her anything but.

"Yes, I heard what you said. I heard the words you spoke, and I also saw how you spoke them. I saw how your lips quivered as you pretended to be annoyed with me and how your nipples got erect when I asked to kiss you. So who is playing games now, Regina? Now..." Mike's voice got husky and thick, "Come here, please and kiss me good-bye. Please, Regina?"

Regina was embarrassed and aroused at the same time. She was surprised that Mike had not been able to detect the warm moisture between her legs as he moved closer to her. One kiss would not hurt anything, Regina told herself. Plus, that was the least she was entitled to after being neglected by Kevin. She could not remember the last time she had been so stimulated.

What the hell, she thought to herself. Regina inhaled deeply, closed her eyes, and puckered her lips ever so slightly. She would not move an inch toward Mike. If they kissed, it would be because *he* kissed *her*. Within seconds, Regina felt the most tender little pecks on her cheeks, neck, and lips. Then Mike's lips lingered a bit longer on hers, and before long, she felt the warmth of her mouth inviting Mike's tongue to explore deeper. Her hands embraced his neck, and his hands embraced her behind.

The ding of the elevator reaching the parking level signaled the time to pull away before the doors opened and revealed the scandal within. Despite her best effort, Regina could not suppress the smile that was forming on her face.

"Satisfied?" she sarcastically asked Mike.

"Hardly. But you will be, Ms. Golden. You will be. Goodnight."

"Goodnight, Mike."

They went their separate ways to their respective vehicles, and Regina could not understand why she was attracted to, instead of offended by, Mike's forwardness. Were she to hear someone else talk about that situation, she would have considered Mike arrogant. But he did not come off that way. It was a certain confidence that Regina actually found attractive. As she got into the car and headed to meet the girls, she tried to hurriedly replay that wonderful kiss in her mind. She had to hurry, though, so there would not be any telltale signs on her face when she arrived to meet the ladies.

Although the ladies had agreed to meet at Regina's favorite barbeque restaurant, she barely tasted her food. Her mind was stuck in replay mode. Careful not to be too obvious for her nosey friends to notice, Regina somehow managed to smile and nod during the right places in the conversation. She honestly had no idea what everyone was talking about, just that Kim was, as usual, getting more and more animated with each minute.

"What, Regina, so you agree with this heffa? You sittin' over there skinnin' and grinnin' and shakin' yo head and whatnot." Kim was holding her drink midair in one hand and a partially eaten baby back rib in the other as she gave Regina an impatient look. The entire table was silent as Melissa and Regan, too, waited to hear what Regina had to say.

Regan began to drum her fingers on the table as she looked at her sister with a slight smirk. "I must say, Reg, I am curious to have you *weigh* in on this. No pun intended. Okay, yeah, the pun was intended… but not Big Pun." Regan began to laugh uncontrollably. "Get it, y'all? BIG PUN! Get it?"

Everyone immediately turned and looked at Regan like she had two heads.

"Forget it. Y'all corny. So what's up, Regina? Do you think Melissa is lying when she says she does not see weight when she looks at people? Kim over here all up in arms, so I want to know what you think?"

All heads and eyes swung back in Regina's direction. She had to think quickly since she had not been keeping up with the conversation. Thank goodness Regan had given her a clue about Melissa's comment; that at least allowed Regina to get the basic gist of the conversation.

"I'm not going to go as far as Kim and say that Melissa is lying, but I do think it is hard to look at people and not notice their physical characteristics. I mean, it's like saying—"

Kim energetically interrupted Regina, barely able to contain herself. "You know that bitch…'scuse me, Reg…that B is lying! She sound like those fake-ass prejudice fools who say they don't see color when they look at people. Talkin' 'bout they love black, white, brown, green and polka dot people all the same. This ain't Fantasy Damn Island! When the last time…shit, when the *first* time somebody seen a green or polka dot person? Get out of here with that mess. If that's the case, why are they so quick to call me a nigger or lock their car doors when my brother walks by? I'm telling you, Melissa sees fat and skinny and everything in between when she looks at people, just like the rest of us."

"Oh my goodness, Kim! You are so annoying and rude. And as usual, you happen to be wrong." Melissa was so irritated that she felt like she had to defend herself to her friends. She was a perfectly proportioned size four in high school. Kim should remember how slim Melissa was back then. What Kim didn't know, what nobody at the table knew, was that after high school, Melissa had gone through some tough times. She became deeply depressed, tried to mask her pain with food, and at her heaviest was wearing a size 20. So yes, she chose to look beyond a person's physical appearance when she saw them. She was now a size 8, but still struggled with inner demons to avoid eating when she was in pain. "Unlike you, Kim, I am not so superficial that I see and judge people by their outward appearance. I really don't see color or weight or any of that stuff. I don't judge people by how they look, so don't put your labels on me. I even see myself as being a little too fat sometimes."

Kim nearly scared everyone at the table as she slammed her hand on the table and shouted, "See? Oh my goodness, Melissa! You are such a freaking hypocrite! How are you gonna sit up here and say you are fat and, at the same time, you supposedly don't notice someone else's weight? If you consider yourself fat, then what do you think about that cow at work who sits a few cubicles down from you? Wait, let me guess! You thought that expansive mass under those ugly-flowered moo-moos she always wears was her large and generous heart, didn't you? Bitch, please!"

Regina could see that this was about to turn into yet another heated debate, so she figured she'd better speak up and try to be the voice of reason. "Melissa, I understand what you are saying – that you do not judge people by their physical appearance. That is a good thing. In fact, that is great. With that being said, it is hard to believe that you don't actually *see* a person's weight when you look at them. For example, if you had to give a physical description of a person, one of the things you might specify is their size or approximate weight. You can say that you don't use a person's weight to measure their character, attitude, or personality, but honey, if you have eyes, you have got to see a person's size, skin color, and hair texture, just as you would see their clothing or a tattoo. It is not good or bad; it's just an observation."

Kim sucked her teeth as she sneered at Melissa, "I told yo lyin' ass. So as I was saying, I had to check my delusional cousin when I asked her what she was wearing to the concert this weekend. She had the nerve to say a sweater, some boots, and some skinny jeans. She know good dang gone well ain't nothing *skinny* about a size 18 jeans. No offense, Melissa."

Everyone looked at Kim in astonishment, not simply because of the statement she'd just made but because they knew that she was just as serious as she was oblivious. It probably never occurred to her how rude, judgmental, and superficial she sounded. Worse yet, if the ladies told Kim about the impact of her statements and how they could be interpreted by others, she would not even care. She would simply shrug her shoulders and say that she was "keeping it real," and people only hate on her because they don't want to hear the truth.

Melissa decided not to waste the breath, time, and energy responding to Kim. Regina simply shook her head.

Regan decided to speak up. "Kim, that is so mean."

"Nooo, Regan! That is so honest. Don't hate me because I have the courage to say what other people are thinking or what people need to hear."

Regan suddenly felt like she was the older friend and Kim was the younger one. "Kim, they sell skinny jeans in sizes ranging from 0 on up. So, what was inaccurate about your cousin saying she was wearing skinny jeans to the concert?"

Kim sighed heavily. "Referring to a pair of size 18 jeans as *skinny* is just as much of an oxymoron as jumbo shrimp, original copy, living dead, or virtual reality. Anything that comes in a size 18, just by virtue of that size, cannot be skinny. Now, what she should have said… what would have been more accurate would have been to say that she was wearing *fitted* jeans. That's all I'm saying. I am not criticizing her weight, just the inaccurate description of her clothing. And how did this get all turned around on me anyway? It got all messed up when Mother Melissa said she did not see weight and size when she looked at people. Shit, if you ask me, that is way more insulting than what I said."

"Wow!" was all that Regina could muster. She could understand Kim's reasoning, although her delivery was much less than polished.

Regan spoke up again. "Kim, I think I understand your point. You don't necessarily have a problem with bigger women, just some of their fashion choices. Is that right?"

"Well, basically. I mean, I kind of do have a problem with big girls because y'all can sometimes have a chip on your shoulders. It's like just because I'm a size 4, don't get all huffy and puffy. Shoot, I shouldn't have said *puffy*, but don't be getting all mad when I say I have to work out. Truth be told, we should all be trying to live healthier. It's like you bigger girls take everything the regular people say as a personal attack. Don't take my words about me and try to make it apply to you because it's not intended for you. If I say I need to go to the gym after work, I'm speaking on me, Kimberly Denise Stoner. Now, if you feel some type of way because you know you really do need to be working out too, then that is your issue, not mine. And for the record, just because it comes in your size, does not mean you should wear it. I get tired of seeing skin slipping and sliding out of material that is not adequate to cover it."

"First of all," Regina piped in, "what do you mean *y'all*, Kim? If you think that everyone who wears anything higher than a size 4 is fat or heavy, then you are the one with the problem. Do you happen to know that the size of the average woman is 14/16? Second, 'regular people'? What the heck is that supposed to mean? You can't possibly think that someone is *irregular* if they are a bit heavy. Who are you? Well, we know who you are, and we love you anyway. I guess the question is who do you think you are? And skinny does not mean healthy, my friend. Surely you have heard the phrase that nobody but a dog wants a bone."

A hint of light sparked in Melissa's eyes as she felt supported and understood for the first time all night. "Kim, you should know that better than anyone with all the dogs you get passed around to. It's a wonder there is any meat left on your raggedy bones at all."

Kim glared across the table, looking ready to pounce. But she held her tongue because she was secretly kind of proud of Melissa for her little dig. She would learn yet not to be such a mousey pushover.

"Well, ladies," Regan had to interject before things got completely out of hand. "It seems we can all agree on the fact that being fit and healthy is the goal. And let's be clear, healthy comes in all shapes and sizes. As far as the clothing—skinny jeans, fitted jeans, booty shorts, maxi dresses—all of that stuff can look just as flattering on a bigger woman as it can look unflattering on a smaller woman."

"I can roll with that," Kim said as she stirred her drink with her pointed acrylic fingernail.

Regina was proud of her little sister. She had brought her teaching skills to the girls' table and managed to simmer the World War Three that was brewing between Kim and Melissa. "Very well said, Regan. No matter what the size is on the label, most women have issues with some part of their body. As women, we should be sensitive to each other's feelings. At the same time, if you have the desire and confidence to rock a certain look, then I say go for it. In my opinion, the attitude of the woman is the most important article she will don anyway. More than her shoes, jewelry, or any makeup, the attitude of a woman will build or disassemble her look."

Thankfully, the conversation ended on a positive note, and the ladies managed to enjoy the rest of their evening. Even the tension between Kim and Melissa thawed before the night concluded. Although they did not always agree with each other while discussing different topics, each of the ladies could honestly say that they enjoyed their girls' night conversations. As was customary, there were hugs and kisses all around before everyone headed home for the evening.

Normally, Regina would have ordered a to-go meal for Kevin, but she did not bother this time. Hopefully, he would be in bed by the time she got home, and she would not have to look at him, much less talk to him.

*****

"Look, Ms. Martin, I really did mean it when I said I would do everything I could to help DeShawn, but I cannot come over here every time he is in a bad mood." Kevin was trying to be as empathic as possible with DeShawn's mother, despite the fact that he was quickly losing patience with her phone calls. The last phone call had come at the worst possible time. He had promised Regina an entire weekend to be spent however she wanted. They had a great Saturday morning and afternoon, and just as they were about to get to the happy ending, the phone rang with Ms. Martin frantically screaming that DeShawn was "losing it" and that she was afraid for her son. He had locked himself in his bedroom and refused to talk to anyone except Kevin Golden. Kevin had to admit that De-Shawn was in pretty bad shape when he had arrived at the Martin home. Still, that was little consolation to Regina. In fact, she still was barely speaking to him, and it was almost the weekend again. In an effort to create more defined boundaries with the Martins and hopefully win back the affections of his wife, Kevin had called DeShawn and Ms. Martin to the center so they could come to a mutual understanding.

"Mr. Kevin, I understand that my son and I have taken a lot of your time. I started not to even call you last weekend, but I was at my wits' end. You and the lawyer, Mr. Thomas, said to call anytime. Well whenever I call the lawyer, I get a bill in the mail. Plus, DeShawn doesn't like him. He said the man acts like he does not believe DeShawn's version of what happened. DeShawn is tired of telling Mr. Thomas the same story in a hundred different ways. I apologize for calling on you so much, Mr. Kevin. I guess I just took you at your word when you said you were always available. You are the only positive male role model in DeShawn's life and the only man he respects enough to take advice from. You have been more than kind to us, so we will try not to bother you so much."

Ms. Martin and DeShawn sat across the small circular table from Kevin. Although he had a desk in his office, he did not like to meet with clients while sitting behind the desk. It did not fit with his desire to create a more personal and intimate atmosphere.

Ms. Martin began to sob as DeShawn, her only living son, leaned over and hugged his mother. That hug seemed to touch a secret button because Ms. Martin collapsed into her son's arms as the floodgates that held her tears opened with a vengeance. DeShawn didn't know what to say to comfort his mother, so he just kept apologizing. "Ma, tell me what to do, okay? I'm sorry. I don't know what to do anymore, and I'm sorry, Ma. That's why I locked myself in my room last weekend. I know you are hurting and mad because of me. You put up the house to pay Mr. Thomas. You don't have any friends anymore, and now it seems like all I do is make you cry. I swear I was this close to making all of that better last weekend when Mr. Kevin showed up at the house."

Ms. Martin raised her head slightly off of her son's chest. "What do you mean, DeShawn? How were you going to make everything better?"

"Simple…I was going to kill myself."

DeShawn and Kevin were both shocked at the catlike swiftness and agility Ms. Martin displayed when she suddenly jumped up and slapped DeShawn's face.

"Boy, I know good and well you have taken leave of your senses. You just said it…I'm barely scraping by, haven't had a good night's sleep in over a month, can barely hold down food, and can't walk to the corner store without folks whispering and pointing. And you talk about killing yo fool self? You ever think of something crazy like that again, and I'll kill you myself! How selfish and weak, DeShawn. We are strong people and to even think—"

"Hey, man, why did you want to commit suicide?" Kevin interrupted

Ms. Martin. She was about to go hard on DeShawn, and that was the last thing he needed right now. DeShawn clammed up, looking ashamed and angry at the same time. "C'mon, man, don't act bashful now. We have been through too much in the last month to be playing games and keeping secrets."

"Man, shit is just real hard right now. The struggle is real. And I'm not even talking about myself. I could give a damn—sorry, Momma—I could give a doggone about what these haters say about me. But my momma… man, that's a whole diff'rent thing, know what I mean? So it's like, to get some of this load up off her, I was just gonna take myself out."

Ms. Martin took a seat beside her son again. "Baby, you don't have to worry about me. I need you, DeShawn. You are the reason I'm fighting so hard, son. I believe in you, and I believe that you are innocent. Your room stays a mess, and you can get fly at the mouth from time to time, but you are a good boy. You are my only living child, DeShawn, and we need to have each other's back. If you love me, son, and I believe that you really do, you need to stick around. Momma can't do this without you." DeShawn embraced his mother and promised to never even consider taking his own life again. "As for you, Mr. Kevin, like I said, me and DeShawn will try not to be a burden to you."

Kevin felt like an idiot. How could he have been so insensitive? Yes, this whole incident with DeShawn had taken time away from his wife and home life, but things were not always like this. Clearly, Kevin had underestimated how this ordeal was impacting DeShawn and Ms. Martin. Really, this truly was a matter of life and death. Regina would just have to understand.

"Listen to me, Ms. Martin. I'm the one who should be apologizing. I promised to be available to you and DeShawn, and I intend to keep that promise. I'm glad that you called when you did last weekend. And D, you have my cell number, man. Hit me up if you feel overwhelmed." It was very important for Kevin to build and keep the trust with DeShawn and his mother. They had very few people they could depend on, and he did not want to fail them.

Ms. Martin had given birth to three children. Unfortunately, before she reached her fiftieth birthday, she had buried two of them. Her oldest, a boy named Deon, had been killed by a drunk driver. As painful as Deon's passing was the fact that the drunk driver was not even charged with a crime. Because he was a judge, the driver was considered to have made a "terrible mistake" and that was pretty much the end of it. Delisa, Ms. Martin's middle child and only daughter, had been plagued with health problems since her premature birth. According to her ex-husband, the constant trips to the hospital were simply more than he had signed up for, so he left when Delisa was just three years old. He did not even attend the funeral when Delisa died less than a year later. If he had attended the funeral of his only daughter, Mr. Martin would have known that his youngest child was not being buried that day, but that he actually had a newly born infant named DeShawn. Ms. Martin never told her ex-husband about DeShawn. Although Mr. Martin knew in his heart that DeShawn was his son, he did not want the burden of knowing or burying yet another child.

Kevin had known about the loss and pain that Ms. Martin had suffered, but he had considered none of it when he'd decided to advise DeShawn and his mother that he could not be available to them all of the time. After DeShawn and Ms. Martin left the office, Kevin felt exhausted. He was hungry and tired, and he missed his wife. He wanted to call Regina but thought better of it. He knew this was the night that she and the girls were getting together for one of their regular outings, and he did not want to disturb her. Actually, that would work out well because when the girls all went out, Regina always brought a meal home for Kevin from whatever restaurant they'd dined. Suddenly, he felt better already. Kevin locked up the office and eagerly headed home to enjoy his dinner and hopefully have a conversation with his beautiful wife.

"Hey, baby! I'm home," Kevin called out to Regina as he stepped into the house. Things had been tense ever since Kevin left unexpectedly to go to the Martin's house. He was initially annoyed at having to leave and break his promise to Regina to spend the entire weekend together, but he thought she had understood. She knew how much he needed to be available to the boys at the center, and she had historically been very supportive. "Babe, where you at? I'm home, and I'm starvin' like Marvin! So what did you bring me back? Did y'all go to that Mexican restaurant or to that barbeque place? Either way, I'm good. Shoot, I could eat this couch right about now."

Still no answer.

Kevin figured Regina must be upstairs in the bathroom getting ready for bed. He headed into the kitchen and checked the microwave where she always put the takeout that she would bring home from her nights out with her sister and friends.

Empty!

Very hungry and a little puzzled, Kevin trotted upstairs to see what was going on. He refused to believe that Regina was still mad at him for going to help DeShawn. Even if her feelings had been hurt, she could not be *that* selfish! They had minor disagreements in the past, but they usually reconciled quickly, and never did either of them carry a grudge or try to punish the other one. Why there was no to-go tray in the microwave was a mystery to Kevin.

Kevin walked into the bedroom and saw Regina reading a magazine. "Hey, baby, you didn't hear me when I came in?" She didn't take her eyes off the page or even respond to him. "Hey, Regina, what's going on? You not speaking?"

"Hey," Regina mumbled, without so much as a glance in Kevin's direction.

"What's going on, Gina? Did you bring me back something to eat?" Kevin was leaning against the doorpost, trying to figure out if he should walk away because his wife was starting to tick him off, or chuckle because she was acting exactly like the woman she least liked…his mother!

Still pretending to read, Regina stubbornly refused to look at Kevin. She briefly wondered if she was still mad at him, or if she actually felt guilty about having kissed Mike earlier that evening. Regina decided to dismiss any guilty thoughts because she felt justified in receiving the attention that her husband seemed too busy to give to her.

"No, Kevin, I did not bring you anything to eat. I was not sure that you would stick around long enough to eat, so I didn't want to waste my money or your time." As soon as she spoke those words, Regina felt like a jerk. Kevin was as much her friend as he was her husband, and she felt bad for being so cold. Still unwilling to relent, Regina lifted her eyebrows and twisted and puckered her lips when she looked up at Kevin, as if to ask why he was still standing there.

"Ok, Regina, I get it." Kevin turned to walk back downstairs but instead went over to the bed and stood over Regina. "Here, baby, this will help you enjoy your reading a little better." Kevin gently took the magazine from Regina's hands, turned it right-side-up, and placed in back in her hands. He lightly kissed her forehead and headed toward the bedroom door. "I'm going downstairs to make a sandwich or something before bed. Would you like anything, Regina?"

"No." Now Regina really felt like an ass.

"I'll be back up in a few, then. Just so you know, Gina, I am very sorry that I let you down the other day. I just found out tonight that DeShawn was going to kill himself that night Ms. Martin called me over there. This situation with DeShawn has pulled me away from home and from spending time with you more than either of us would like. I need to be honest with you though, baby. As much as I love you and don't want to see you hurt or mad at me, I'm going to see this thing through with De-Shawn and Ms. Martin. Those people have nobody else in their corner, Regina. Shoot, they wouldn't have even been able to hire that attorney if the congregation at Ms. Martin's church had not raised the money, and that was after she had taken a second mortgage on her house."

Regina did not move a muscle.

"Look," Kevin continued. "You have always supported my work at Golden Choices, and I need that support now more than ever. I hope you extend that support. That will be your choice, but know this: tonight is the last time that I will apologize for doing my job. No, correction…I'm not doing my job; I'm pursuing my passion. This tension between us is not easy for me. And if I know you the way I think I do, it's not easy for you, either. You miss me just as much as I miss you. I'm going to let you work it out however you need to, Regina. I love you, but you know that already. I don't believe I deserve the punishment or the cold treatment, but I love you just the same." With that, Kevin went downstairs and made a turkey sandwich for dinner.

Knowing that every word Kevin had spoken was true, Regina threw her magazine across the room. She was angrier with herself at this point than she had been with Kevin. Feeling ashamed and wounded, Regina curled into a fetal position and cried like a baby. She was sound asleep by the time Kevin came to bed.

7 WEEKS AGO

Like most people, Regina was not a particular fan of Monday mornings. She usually had no less than ten voicemail messages waiting for her and twice as many emails. Today, she had something else waiting for her. As she approached her cubicle she saw Cassie leaning on her desk. Trying not to express her irritation, Regina greeted Cassie as pleasantly as possible.

"Good morning, Cassie. Can I please get to my desk so I can sit down and put my purse away in my drawer?"

"Well happy Monday. About time you made it to work. Somebody must have taken the late bus to work. Never mind that. Guess what, Regina?"

Regina could not believe Cassie hadn't moved anything but her mouth. Regina was trying to be patient, but she felt like Cassie was bordering on being rude. "Well, seeing as how I don't report to you, it really doesn't matter what time I—"

"You are never gonna guess, so I'll just tell you," Cassie cut Regina off. She was oblivious to the fact that she had completely, yet again, overstepped her boundary. "Look! These pretty flowers were on your desk when I got here this morning." Cassie finally moved out of the way to reveal a beautiful floral arrangement. "Don't bother looking for a card, I already checked. I mean, we both know they are from that handsome hubby of yours, but I was just curious to see what sweet little message he had put on the card."

Unwilling to hide her irritation any longer, Regina bumped into Cassie as she moved to take her chair and put her purse on top of her desk. "Cassie, you do know that curiosity killed the cat, right?"

"Yeah, I guess it's good that cats have nine lives then, huh?"

"Well you are on your last one, Cassie."

Neither Cassie nor Regina saw Alicia, the Bright Star bully, approaching them. "Let me ask you something, Cassie. Does that empty chair on the other side of this cubicle look familiar to you?"

"Yeah, sure. Of course it does, Alicia, that's my chair." Poor Cassie. She had no idea that she had just taken the bait that Alicia dangled in front of her to reel her in and gobble her up. Regina simply shook her head because she knew what was coming.

"Good, Cassie! Now here is what you are going to do: put your ass in that chair, pick up that telephone, and try running your big mouth for what we pay you to do – talk to customers." Alicia was talking through clenched teeth and had managed to scare Cassie to the point of immobilization. "Now!" Alicia roared.

The normally talkative Cassie was reduced to a statue; neither a motion nor a sound escaped her. For a brief moment, Regina almost felt sorry for Cassie. Almost.

As Cassie slid by Regina and Alicia, Regina heard Cassie mumble, "Guess somebody rode the grumpy bus to work."

Fortunately for Cassie, Regina was the only one who heard it.

For once, Regina was actually relieved that Alicia had come to her desk. Shaking her head, she was finally able to get situated at her desk and put her purse into her drawer. When she opened the drawer she saw a small note taped to a chocolate candy bar. The note read:

I put this in your drawer so your nosey neighbor wouldn't get to it. Thanks for the greatest elevator ride ever last week. Hope you enjoy the flowers as much as I enjoy chocolate.

Despite herself, Regina couldn't help but smile. She stuffed the note and candy bar into her purse and answered her first call of the day. "It's a great day at Bright Star! This is Regina, how can I help you?"

That day in the lunchroom, as Melissa, Kim, and Regina were eating lunch, Cassie stopped as she was about to pass their table. "Regina, I'm sorry about this morning. I was just admiring your pretty flowers."

"That's fine, Cassie. Let's just act like it never happened. How are you doing? Are you okay? You seemed a little shaken up." Regina did not want to get into a long, drawn-out conversation with Cassie, but she did feel bad that Alicia had come down on her so hard earlier.

"I – I'm okay I guess. That Alicia sure can be grumpy, though. But I've learned my lesson with her. From now on, if I see her coming, I'm just going to turn the other way."

Kim, being Kim, could not resist. "Isn't that her headed this way now? Yep, I think it is. You better go ahead and take off, Cassie."

As the blood appeared to drain out of her face, Cassie took off to the far side of the lunchroom. She hadn't even bothered to look up. If she had, she would've known that Alicia was nowhere in sight. Kim turned her attention back to the table and, along with Melissa, focused on Regina with an inquisitive look. Regina pretended to eat her food and not notice the two pair of eyes that were boring into her.

"Okay, so there were some flowers on my desk when I came in today. So what? It's not a big deal."

Kim knew better. "If it wasn't a big deal, Regina, you would have told us. But the fact that you did NOT tell us means that it really is a big deal. So what's up with the flowers? Was it a dozen roses…a bouquet…what? Oh, and what did the card say?"

Not wanting to bare her secret and also knowing she would never be able to completely avoid this conversation, Regina decided to give up just enough information to satisfy the girls and keep them out of her business. "There was no card, Lil Miss Cassie, Jr.," Regina joked to Kim. "No, it was not a dozen roses. It was more like three dozen roses with other little accent flowers. The flowers are in the prettiest blue vase I've ever seen."

Kim was almost beside herself with excitement. "Aw shit, you have a secret admirer! Or *is* it a secret? Do you know who it is? Dang, this is about to be good! Girl, who is it? Is he cute? Have y'all done it? What about—"

"Kevin?" Melissa interrupted Kim and looked at her like she was crazy. "What about your *husband* Kevin? We know the flowers were not from him because whenever he sends flowers the whole office knows about it. And he always has a card with some corny, cute little saying on it. I don't really need to know who the flowers are from. I just want you to know that since they did not come from your husband, they are not something to be excited about. Regina, you know better."

"Look, Melissa," Regina began.

That was as far as she got before Kim chimed in. "Oh, hell naw! Heffa, I know you didn't just cut me off!" Kim was ready to let Melissa have it.

"I apologize, Kim. Really. I did interrupt you, and that was rude. I was just saying, though, that we should not be happy or excited that Regina got flowers from some other guy. It will just lead to trouble. No man has any business spending money on flowers or anything else for her unless it's Kevin."

Melissa's apology seemed to soothe Kim a little. "Uh-huh, I guess. But anyways, I'm not suggesting that Regina cheat on Kevin or anything. I'm just keeping it real. It is exciting to have someone send you flowers. Shoot, the way Kevin been all busy and neglectful lately, it's no wonder someone else is paying Regina some attention. My thing is *who*, though?"

Regina really loved Melissa. She just had a way of bringing things into proper perspective. She did not sound judgmental or maternal, but rather like a concerned friend. Regina knew in her heart that Melissa was correct. At the same time, she liked that Mike had thought enough of her to send such beautiful flowers. She couldn't help it, but she was attracted to him. So even though she knew Melissa was giving her sound advice, she did not want to hear it. "You guys are making a far bigger deal out of this than it really is." Regina tried to downplay the situation. She wasn't going to give an inch. She hated they knew anything at all. There was no way in the world she would let them know Mike had sent her the flowers. "Nobody even said the flowers were from a man."

"Come on, girl. Now even I know better than that." Melissa could clearly see that Regina wanted to move on from this topic…and that she was hiding something.

"No, for real," Regina insisted. "Why couldn't the flowers have been sent by Regan or my mom…or even one of my customers?"

Kim sucked her teeth. "Girl, just say you don't want to tell us, but don't play us. You know good and well ain't no damn customer sent you no flowers. And your mom or Regan? That would be the first time! And even if that were true, they would have included a card. So who is this mystery man? And yes, I do believe it was a man."

"Yeah," Melissa chimed in, unable to believe that she and Kim were in agreement for once. "You have never mentioned anything about another guy, Regina. Shoot, the only time I even heard a man mention your name was that one time a few weeks ago when…" Melissa stopped talking. She looked at Kim, and it was obvious they were thinking the exact same thing. Melissa wore a look of shock, while Kim wore a look of delight mixed with something else that Melissa couldn't quite put her finger on.

Kim slapped one hand over her mouth and pointed a finger at Regina with the other hand. "Oooh! You go, girl! It's Mike! Get *OUT*!"

"Shh!" Regina tried to quiet her loud-talking friend. "Will you be quiet, please? This conversation is just like this lunch break…*over!*" With that, Regina hurried to gather her tray and purse and headed to the door. Had she slowed down a bit, she would have noticed the candy bar and note that fell onto the table when she snatched her purse up.

Melissa was so busy trying to get Regina to come back that she, too, neglected to see the candy bar. Never one to miss anything, Kim not only saw the candy bar and the attached note, but she quickly slid it from the table onto her lap and then into her own purse. Kim was beside herself with excitement. Sure, it would have been good if Regina had told them about the flowers, but this was even better. Kim knew that she, not Regina, now had the upper hand. Armed with information that Regina had tried to keep secret, Kim didn't even notice the mischievous smile that had crept upon her face.

"What?" Melissa asked. She certainly noticed Kim staring off into the distance like she was trying to figure out life's greatest mysteries.

"What you mean 'what'?" Kim asked, as she snapped back to reality.

"I mean, why are you sitting there looking like the cat that ate the canary? And why didn't you help me call Regina back? Don't you want to know who sent the flowers? You don't think it really could have been Mike, do you?"

"I think we should respect Regina's wishes and leave it alone. If and when she wants to share, she will. In the meantime, we just need to be supportive friends. Dang, Melissa, yuck! I'm sounding like you. Let's get out of here before Alicia comes looking for me. I'm already ten minutes late, and I would hate to have to cuss that heffa out if she says anything to me."

Melissa stood and started gathering her belongings, puzzled that Kim was actually willing to let something go. Maybe her old high school friend was finally starting to grow up.

"You're right, Kim. Write it down because I'm actually admitting that you are right this time. We will give Regina her space and just drop this until she is ready to talk to us about it."

Kim arose too, and followed Melissa out of the cafeteria doors. She could not wait to see just how much Mike liked chocolate.

*****

Mike was in the small break room getting his morning cup of coffee. His back was to the door, so he did not see the face that matched the voice wishing him a good morning.

"Good mor—" Mike's words got stuck in his throat as he turned around to see two caramel mounds of flesh. Kim had dropped a napkin on the floor behind him so that she would be bending over with her breasts spilling out of her low-cut blouse when Mike turned around. "I'm sorry, Kim. I didn't see you there. Good morning. Can I get you a cup of milk...er, I mean coffee?"

Yes! Kim was thrilled to have Mike just where she wanted him. "No thanks, Mike. I like the smell of coffee, but I don't like the taste of it. I'm more of a sweet tea girl myself. What about you? Do you enjoy tea, Mike, or do you prefer dark, bitter coffee or hot chocolate?"

Mike chuckled to himself as he applauded Kim for trying to be clever. Did this girl think he was stupid? He knew that Kim, Melissa, and Regina were all friends and even hung out together outside of work. He did not know for sure what Regina had told them about her dealings with him, but he'd bet it was little to nothing. He knew how conflicted Regina was about even talking to him, and she certainly did not seem like the type who would want anything to get out about their flirting—not even to her friends. *Nice try, Kim*, Mike thought, *but this is not going to work.* Still, Mike decided to have some fun with Kim. "Surely you've heard by now, Kim. I like all kinds of drinks. And I don't sip either; I chug. Have a nice day." With that, Mike brushed by Kim as close as he could without touching her.

For once, Kimberly Stoner was speechless.

It had been a long and busy day at Bright Star, but Mike had one last thing to do before he left the office.

hey girl. ur friend is crazy

Regina had just tossed her purse over her shoulder, about to head out of the door when her phone alerted her that she had a text.

hey there. what friend? what r u talkin about

ur girl kim. she didn't tell you she BUMPED into me this a.m. in the breakroom? she asked me if i liked chocolate. crazy huh?!?

Panicked, Regina plopped down in her chair. She halfheartedly said goodbye to coworkers who waved and spoke as they passed her desk heading out for the day. Mike might not think this was a big deal, but Regina knew better. She knew that Kim suspected something. And with

Kim, a suspicion was a very dangerous thing.

mike! this is very bad, not crazy. what did you say to her? you didn't tell her we kissed did you? omg do you think she knows something?

Mike was starting to wonder if he should have even said anything. He did not necessarily think that Regina would get as big a kick out of Kim's antics as he had, but he certainly did not think she would be so scary acting, either.

whoa. dude. chill will ya. 1st off i knew wut she wuz up 2. no way was she gonna get me 2 bite. 2nd i dont kiss n tell…. but tell me this…wen can i get another kiss? i have played that n my mind 100 x's n i was hoping u did the same thing

Regina stared at her phone for what seemed like an eternity. Sure, she had replayed their elevator scene in her mind many times. But she did not want to admit that to Mike. She had a hard enough time dealing with the fact that she was even aroused by this man. Regina was still staring at her phone when another text came through.

SNAKES on a plane. incredible HULK. man of STEEL. limitless. ANACONDA. the longest yard.

Regina had no clue what Mike was talking about.

are those your fave movies?

not really. they just describe me pretty well. LOL

LOL is right! i heard it was more like MATCH-

STICK men. FINDING nemo. doctor doLITTLE. 2 FAST 2 furious. LITTLE mermaid. are we there YET.

Mike roared with laughter. Classy, pretty, and a sense of humor. Regina was truly Golden!

ha ha ha. very funny. Maybe one day u can c 4 urself. u can tell me what movie describes me. hell, we can make our own movie if u want

Where had the time gone? Regina was so engulfed in texting back and forth with Mike that she had not noticed that it was getting dark outside. Nor had she noticed the texts that Kevin had sent her over thirty minutes ago.

Regina thought it was strange that the house was completely dark as she pulled into the driveway. She and Kevin weren't completely back to normal, but the chill between them had certainly thawed. As the garage door lifted, Regina noticed Kevin's car was parked in its usual spot. It was unlike him to take naps, especially in the evening, so she was more puzzled than ever as to why no lights were on. Approaching the door leading from the garage into the laundry room, Regina noticed a note taped to the door. She read it aloud:

Hey baby. If you did not grab anything on the way home, don't worry about making me anything for dinner. I had sent you a text asking if you wanted to go out to dinner. Me and Drew wanted to take our beautiful wives out to eat. When I did not hear from you after about 20 minutes, we figured just the two of us would go, and we could discuss some work over dinner. We will be at Flemings so if you want me to bring you back one of those steak burgers you like just hit me up. Love you girl. p.s.- I'm going to have to jack those customers up at Bright Star, making my baby work over like that. Unless you were with the girls, then I'll deal with those heffas later. Peace out."

Regina chuckled to herself. Kevin was always teasing with the girls. He acted like a big brother to all of them, and Regina was glad that her husband liked her friends. Her chuckle turned into an outright laugh, though, because Kevin always had something to say about her friends. He would often say that Melissa was not as polished as she appeared. He said nobody was that positive and squeaky clean all of the time. Whenever she visited, Melissa would just roll her eyes and shake her head when Kevin would accuse her of being an undercover freak or having a family in another state that nobody knew about. Or he would accuse her of being a hustler or something on the side. Kevin had his opinion about Kim, too. He always told Regina that, while Kim was the funny one of the group, she was probably the deadliest. When Regina would say that Kim was harmless, Kevin would tell her not to be so sure. Regina tried to explain to her husband that Kim only said shocking things to get a rise out of the group. Kevin wasn't hearing it. He was convinced that Kim was a cool person to hang with for a good time, but beyond that, Regina would be wise to not let her close enough to break her heart. He believed that Kim was incapable to being a true friend to anyone.

Regina went into the house and set her purse and keys on the kitchen table. Since she hadn't even thought about making dinner, she decided to accept Kevin's offer. She called him to ask that he bring back a steak burger. Kevin picked up on the second ring.

"Hey, baby, what's up?" Kevin asked, as he held up his finger to Drew to indicate that he'd just be a moment.

"Hi, Kevin. I got your note. Can you bring me back a burger the way I like it, please?" Regina felt weird asking her husband to bring her dinner, when the reason she neglected to cook in the first place was because she'd let time get away from her while she was texting Mike.

"Of course, baby. I know how you like that meat in your mouth!" Kevin couldn't help but tease his wife. It had seemed like forever since they'd engaged in any playful banter.

"Oooh, Kevin! No you did not just say that in front of Drew! Tell him I said hello, by the way."

"Gina says hi, man," Kevin relayed to his friend. Drew nodded in return and told Kevin to let Regina know that she was in trouble with his wife because she was at home eating a salad instead of dining at Flemings with the guys.

Now Regina felt even worse. She liked Drew and Del and had known them since shortly after she and Kevin started dating. His full name was Andrew Steele, and she was Rindella. Drew and Kevin's fathers had been college roommates and then went on to law school together. Andrew and Kevin had seemingly been friends since birth. While Mr. Golden was just as happy that Kevin had pursued a teaching degree as he was that Andrew pursued a law degree, Mrs. Golden was enraged. She was so embarrassed that Kevin was *only* a teacher that she refused to hug him when he graduated. She also could not feign happiness for Andrew. Still, Kevin and Drew remained close friends who had mutual respect and admiration for each other. They were as different in looks, culture, and ethnicity as could be, yet they loved each other like brothers. As only children, they relished the times when their families got together for work, as well as social gatherings. The Golden and Steele families even vacationed together. Drew was thrilled that his friend had refused to give in to Mrs. Golden's pressure to follow in Mr. Golden's footsteps and pursue a career in law. Few were more proud of Kevin for following his pursuit of a job in education and, later, his passion for working with troubled youth and opening Golden Choices. Drew and Del welcomed and embraced Regina when Kevin fell in love with her, and she thought very highly of them, as well.

"Tell Drew I know. He just needs to give Del a kiss and let her know we will have our own time together. We don't need you two crashing our party."

"Will do. Well, let me jump off of this phone so we can talk shop before our food gets here. I'll see you in a little while."

"Okay; thanks, Kevin. Can't wait to get my meat! It's been a while," Regina teased before hanging up the phone with her husband.

Damn! Regina thought. *How could I have not seen the texts from Kevin?* She frantically scrolled through her text messages, searching for Kevin's name. Yep, there they were. The first one was received right after the very first text from Mike. Then he texted again when she was on the way to the parking deck. *Oh boy, the parking deck.*

For the second time, Regina had found herself on the elevator with Mike. Only this time, there were no pretenses or games. Regina began to moisten as soon as she felt Mike's hardness rub against her as he pressed the button to close the elevator doors. She offered no resistance whatsoever when he grabbed her to himself and thrust his tongue into her mouth. The lips on her face parted to receive Mike's hot tongue while the lips between her legs parted to receive first one, then two of his fingers. By the time they had reached the level where her car was parked, Regina's knees were weak. At the time, she had not wanted him to stop. Reflecting back, she was glad he did. Everyone at Bright Star knew there were no cameras on the elevators. Every so often, there would be rumors around the office about people who were allegedly "making out" in the elevators. Regina always dismissed those rumors as silly gossip. *There is no way possible that someone would ever conduct themselves so irresponsibly,* Regina had thought; *especially on company property, with such a small window of opportunity.* Regina sometimes wondered if people would really be so careless as to risk so much for so little. Mike had asked Regina why she was so quiet as he walked her to her car. She slowly shook her head as she told him that she had just gotten the answer to something she'd wondered about in the past.

*****

"Dude, I always knew you were a softie when it came to kids and stuff, but this is a bit much. Kevin, there is no way this kid isn't going to do some major time. Why are you so hell-bent on sticking by this lost cause?" Andrew and Kevin had been discussing DeShawn's case over dinner.

Andrew had always been proud of Kevin's work with young, at-risk males. Kevin had a way of relating to those kids that made them listen to him, instead of dismissing, ignoring, or disrespecting him. When Andrew, or anyone else for that matter, would ask Kevin how he got the kids to open up and to listen to him, Kevin would always say, "That's easy; just show them respect". But even Andrew thought Kevin was being a bit ambitious in his support of DeShawn. Usually, Kevin would be the first one to put his foot in a kid's butt for any behavior that was disrespectful, much less criminal. Kevin would not tolerate kids who did not want to work to improve their grades, character, relationships, and situations. Andrew put his fork down and looked at his friend, waiting for an answer.

Kevin ordered another Crown and Coke before answering his old friend. He pulled the cloth napkin from his collar and covered his plate, as he knew the eating part of the evening had just concluded. "Drew, you know me, man. Some of the same 'lost causes,' as you say, have graduated high school, done very well in college, and are giving back by volunteering in the very schools and communities where they got into trouble."

"Yes, I get that, Kevin. What you've done with some of these young men is nothing short of a miracle. But let's be honest. You have dealt with kids with some behavioral problems, kids who were a little mouthy or unfocused. But this time, it's different, Kevin. This guy DeShawn is a criminal. A thug. What are you doing, man?"

Kevin had not seen Andrew so riled up before. He took a sip of his fresh drink before teasing his buddy. "You mean 'alleged criminal,' don't you, Drew?"

"No Kev, I'm not alleging anything. I'm not talking to you as a former prosecutor. I'm talking to you as a friend. This guy is a rapist. He said yes, she said no. Given his background and environment, when someone doesn't give you what you want, you take it. You would do well to distance yourself from DeShawn Martin. And from what Del says, dealing with this kid hasn't exactly helped your marriage, either." Andrew knew that may have been a low blow, but he needed to say something to get Kevin to see how far gone he was with this whole situation.

"Look, Drew. I'm about as surprised with you as I am disappointed with Regina about this. You of all people should know better than to rush to judgment. If background and environment were guarantors of behavior and character, why or how would wealthy people rape, murder, or do drugs? How was a man from a single-parent household elected president of the United States? Using your logic, my dad should have been a criminal instead of a judge. Since when did you become so judgmental? Have you ever had a conversation with DeShawn? Nobody has bothered to listen to anything this kid has to say because…well, I don't even have to say why. You know as well as I do why the supposed victim has been elevated to sainthood in the local media, while DeShawn has been demonized. You know as well as I do, Andrew, why this community is calling for blood from DeShawn, his mother, and anyone who dares to support him. What is the glaring difference between those two families? And keep it one hundred with me."

Andrew expelled a long and loud sigh. He and Kevin had discussed race in the past. They agreed about some racial issues and disagreed about others. Never, though, had Kevin used the race card as an excuse for criminal behavior. "Yeah, Kevin, I know the obvious difference between the families. Anyone with eyes can see the difference. But that is bullshit. And quite frankly, I'm shocked that you would use race to polarize this situation. I mean, everybody—"

"Naw man, it's *me* who is actually shocked." Now Kevin was starting to get agitated. He finished his Crown in one long gulp before continuing. "I don't think race has much to do with the way all of this is playing out. I believe the glaring difference between these families and communities is money. If DeShawn was from the same side of the tracks as the supposed victim, then nobody would even know about this case. It would be a misunderstanding between a couple of bored kids. What was it that rich kid claimed who killed those four people? *Affluenza*, wasn't it? According to his attorney, he was so privileged that he could not grasp the concepts of right and wrong. Drew, that's a bunch of bull, and you know it. That kid stole two cases of beer, plowed through a crosswalk, and hit thirteen people. Of the four who died, what do you know about any of them? What schools do their children attend, or what do their parents do? You don't know. Most people don't know because those victims were not talked about in the media. Hell, as a matter of fact, the thieving, drunk-driving killer was made to look like the victim. So tell me—"

Andrew cut Kevin off before he could finish. "Now wait a minute, Kevin. You and I talked about that case, and I told you then that 'affluenza' defense was a bunch of hogwash. Even without the benefit of a private education, all kids are taught the basics: don't steal, don't drink and drive, obey the rules. Even if not from his parents, that kid heard those principles somewhere, from someone. He knew right from wrong. He just never had to face any consequences. That really made me angry because society says people should not blame poverty as an excuse for committing crimes, and yet this kid got away with using wealth as an excuse. I agreed with you on that. But you can't possibly think that people are biased against DeShawn based on the amount of money that his family has."

"That is exactly what I'm saying. And you know it's true. Bro, there has been daily coverage on the television as well as in the newspaper about this supposed victim being an honor student, having a stellar reputation, and being from an upstanding family. What have you read about DeShawn Martin?"

Andrew ordered another round for him and Kevin. "I'll tell you what I read, Kevin. I read the charges they are planning to bring against this kid. And rich or poor, he took advantage of an innocent girl. He deserves to be punished for that. And it's not because he is not white or wealthy. It's all about choices, bro. And when people choose to break the law, they need to bear the consequence of that choice. It's not a race thing or a class thing. It's a justice thing. And another thing, you need to stop calling her a 'supposed' victim. Why do you keep saying that? You think she's lying or something? Certainly, she wouldn't have anything to gain from that."

Kevin laughed out loud. "You must be more buzzed than I am if you believe that she doesn't have anything to gain. By crying rape, she has everything to gain...or should I say *maintain*. But don't even get me started on that. I call her a 'supposed' victim because I happen to believe that she is lying. In fact, I know that she is. But that will come out later, Counselor. Just know this: money, education, or social status do not directly correlate to or reflect one's character. In this country, you usually get as much justice as you can afford."

"Okay, I'll give you that, partially. Hell, O.J. got off, and so did Michael Jackson. But Martha Stewart did time, and so did Wesley Snipes. So, wealthy people do serve time, Kevin...although I will agree that it is more an exception than a rule. But you still haven't told me why you are supporting this kid DeShawn so strongly. Man, Rindella had me thinking that Gina was on the verge of kicking your butt out a few weeks ago. She told me your wife was complaining that the kid's problems were consuming you. What's up with that, man? Why are you making this kid your problem?" Andrew pushed his chair from the table a bit, folded his arms across his chest, and patiently waited as Kevin explained why he refused to give up on DeShawn.

Kevin explained to Andrew that death had claimed both DeShawn's sister and his brother and that he'd never known his father. He explained that like the alleged victim, DeShawn, too, was an honor student. Unfortunately, DeShawn's academic reports were sometimes overshadowed by his behavioral reports. He never got into any real trouble, but DeShawn did not have any respect for authority, especially male authority. He did not trust any male - until he met Kevin - because DeShawn did not expect that any male would ever have his best interest at heart. If his own biological father did not want anything to do with him, why would any other man? So DeShawn was labeled as a problem in the classroom. From kindergarten through high school, DeShawn excelled academically while at the same time struggling socially. His school work came easy to him, and he actually liked learning. But since he neither trusted nor respected the teachers, he frequently talked back, walked in and out of class whenever he felt like it, and was difficult and uncooperative. In high school, DeShawn's guidance counselor had asked Ms. Martin if she would follow up on a referral to Golden Choices. Believing that she had nothing to lose, Ms. Martin agreed. Before DeShawn met Kevin, Ms. Martin had gone to the Golden Choices Center. She wanted to meet Kevin, get information about the programs and services offered by the agency, and determine if there was anything there that could benefit her son.

Kevin recounted to Andrew how his first meeting with DeShawn was icy at best. DeShawn had sat in Kevin's office with a baseball cap pulled low over his eyes, earplugs in his ears, and a cell phone in his hands. He gave one-word answers to Kevin's questions and made it clear that he would rather be getting a root canal than sitting in Kevin's office. Having been in this situation more than once before, Kevin knew exactly what to do. He turned on the television that practically covered the wall behind where DeShawn was seated. Try as he might, DeShawn could not resist turning around after about forty-five seconds. He could not act disinterested any longer.

"What you know about that Madden 25, man?" DeShawn asked. "And that's the Xbox One?" DeShawn was frantically looking around the office for the other controller.

"Here ya go, man. Maybe you can teach me a thing or two." Kevin tossed a wireless controller to DeShawn.

And so it began. The ice was broken, and DeShawn began to go to the center several days a week after school. Initially, DeShawn only came to play video games. Slowly, their conversation ceased to center around sports and video games only. Kevin and DeShawn began to talk about school, subjects that interested DeShawn, girls who interested DeShawn, and teachers who got on his nerves. Unlike the other adults in his life, DeShawn believed that Kevin was cool because he did not talk down to him or treat him like a second-class citizen simply because he was a teenager. Kevin seemed to genuinely enjoy DeShawn's company, and he listened to DeShawn. After several months, DeShawn began to open up more and more, until he and Kevin shared a mutually respectful relationship. Nobody, not even Ms. Martin, could understand how Kevin had earned DeShawn's trust. Whenever anyone asked how he did it, Kevin simply referred to one of the quotes on his office wall: "People don't care how much you know, until they know how much you care."

Kevin smiled reflectively. "Man, that was four years ago, DeShawn's freshman year. Now DeShawn is a senior, supposed to be having the time of his high school experience, and he is scared to death that he might be charged with rape. That young man is a good kid, Andrew. Sure, he's had some minor behavior problems in the past, but never anything criminal. Ms. Martin is not an educated woman. They don't have much money and even fewer advocates. So that makes me want to help that family and stick by this kid. That, and the fact that I happen to believe DeShawn's story that he did not rape that supposed victim."

Although Andrew could not say that he agreed with his friend, he did respect his commitment. "Alright, brother, whatever you say. Just be careful."

Kevin looked curiously at Andrew. "What is that supposed to mean... *'be careful'*?"

"Just this: while you are so busy professing your commitment to this thug...uh, kid...don't lose sight of your commitment to Regina. Whether this kid is charged or not, you still need a place to go home to. And you had best be sure your wife is still there when you get there. Just a free piece of advice."

Kevin and Andrew both stood up and gave each other that masculine half hug as they prepared to leave. "Thanks, man. But when I want your advice, I'll make an appointment and pay for it like everyone else. So don't do me any favors."

Andrew roared with laughter. "Yeah, right; you can't afford me. So you better hope and pray that you or Dewan don't need my services."

"Man, it's De*SHAWN*, and...never mind, you are hopeless. Let me get out of here and take this food to Gina before she has one more reason to get an attitude. We'll catch up, okay?"

*****

"No way, Regina! Are you saying Kevin never brought your dinner, didn't call or anything?" Regan was questioning her sister as all of the ladies sat around on oversized pillows on Melissa's living room floor.

This week, they had decided to have a girls' night in, as opposed to a night out. An emergency session was called before the weekend, because Melissa sensed that something was bothering Regina at work. She'd sent a text to all the ladies to meet at her house at seven that evening.

"No, Regan. I did not say he *never* brought my dinner. I saw the food this morning when I got up for work. He just didn't bother to bring it when I was still awake and able to enjoy it. It seems like every time I take y'all's advice and try to patch things up with Kevin and not have an attitude, he does something stupid to blow it. I'm getting really sick of him, and mark my words, he is going to miss this water when the well runs dry. Anyway, whatever…I'm not thinking about stupid Kevin. This night is not going to be a pity party for me. Trust me when I say I'm gonna be just fine."

Everyone sat quietly for a moment, not sure if they should move on from that topic and respect Regina's wishes or try to dig deeper into how she was really feeling.

Melissa finally spoke up. "Well, ladies, I have some news. I've been dying to say something for a few weeks now, but since the announcement will come out tomorrow, I guess I can finally spill the beans. I got the supervisor job!"

The room erupted in cheers, screams of congratulations, and jumps up and down.

Regina went to give Melissa a hug. "Come on, Kim. Get over here, Regan. Group hug!"

"Uhhh, I'll pass." Kim was the only one still sitting down. She continued to stir her Tequila Sunrise as she pretended to not feel the heated glares of the other ladies in the room.

"What?" Regan asked as she sat down on a pillow next to Kim. "Why are you acting so mean, Kim? You should be happy for Melissa."

"Well excuse me if I'm the only one in here who can see the big picture. This announcement just perpetuates what is already wrong at

Bright Star – the management. You guys want me to be happy for Melissa? Fine, it is good that she got a promotion if that is what she wanted. But I'm damn sure not happy for us."

Melissa, now feeling like the helium had been let out of her balloon, took a seat in her rattan chair. "That's pretty harsh, Kim. I've been fair, approachable, and helpful as a coordinator. Why would you see it as a negative that I've been promoted to supervisor? If anything, that leaves the coordinator position open. You or any other qualified person can apply for that."

"I am a black woman, Melissa!" Kim sounded exasperated as she let out a long sigh.

"So?" Melissa retorted. "What does that have to do with anything?"

Now Kim stood up. "You cannot possibly be *that* naïve! Melissa, as a black woman, the only type of supervisor that is worse than a white female is a black female."

"Okay, you have really lost it this time. Must *everything* be about race? Or about you? What the heck does the color of a person's skin, or their sex for that matter, have to do with the kind of supervisor they are? I swear, you are always pick, pick, picking! If you have had bad experiences with supervisors, maybe you need to look in the mirror. Better yet, look in the toilet because that's where the crap that comes out of your mouth belongs!" Melissa was hot. By this time, she had gotten on her feet.

Regina, too, stood up. "Well, Melissa, I actually see where Kim is coming from...I think. I mean, I for one can tell you that it really is different having a woman as a boss than having a man as a boss. And as a black woman, it is even worse having a black female as a superior than a white woman, white man, or black man."

"Regina!" Melissa was really astounded. "I never knew you felt that way. I mean, a good boss is a good boss, right?" She had no idea that her friends held such opinions about these things.

"Listen," Regina said as she grabbed Melissa's hands and sat her down beside her on the couch. "You are going to be a wonderful supervisor, and all of us are very proud of you and happy for you. Aren't we, Kim?"

"Whatever." Kim waved a dismissive hand.

"Anyway, Mel, don't be offended by what we are saying. You just have no point of reference because your experience is very different. There are great bosses, male and female, who are white, and there are great bosses, male and female, who are black. That being said, as a black woman, it can sometimes be very hard working for a female. A lot of women feel threatened by other women. Instead of developing and encouraging each other, women can often be petty, jealous, and catty. For reasons that are too numerous and complex to get into now, that goes double for black women. Have you heard of the phrase 'crabs in a barrel'? Well, that is often how it is among black women."

Regan joined her sister and friend on the couch. "It's true, Melissa. It's sad, but it's just the way things are. Women need to realize that other women can be smart, creative, and even beautiful without wanting their position or title or anything from them. From high school through college, and even as a teacher, there have always been times when I've felt like I've had to lessen myself, so to speak, just so as not to be perceived as a threat by some female professor or superior. It's a shame, really. I find it much easier to work for males. As ridiculous as it sounds, there are many black women who perceive other black women as inferior simply because of their complexion, style, or texture of hair. Imagine a female, black or white, who has been made fun of, socially outcast, or even bullied because of her looks. She never deals with those issues, and she eventually obtains a position of authority. How do you think that woman will treat the so-called pretty or popular women who report to her? Even if it is unintentional, those unresolved issues will come out. More often than not, though, there is intentional mistreatment because that woman tends to feel like she has to get revenge. Now she is in a position to punish others and make others feel as miserable as she was once made to feel."

Kim scooted over to where the other ladies were on the couch and sat on the floor in front of them. "You my girl, Melissa. Of course I'm happy for you. I'm sorry; I just got caught up for a moment. I just think about that bitch, Alicia, and it just ticks me off. Unlike Regan, I refuse to back down, dummy down or bow down. One of these heffas is gonna get BEAT down if they get on my nerves. I'm not apologizing for my clothes, my hair, my looks or my brains just because some reject has unresolved issues. You have been warned, so don't roll up in there trippin' tomorrow! Now give me a hug."

The four ladies passed the next several hours eating Chinese, drinking wine, and thoroughly enjoying each other's company.

The next day at work was by far the most bizarre that Regina had ever experienced. She was into her second day of giving Kevin the cold shoulder, and she was in need of a warm touch. Regina had never been much of a flirt, but she poured it on thick with Mike. Before he arrived for the day, Regina printed off a picture of a kitten and placed it on Mike's desk along with a note that read:

I got your candy bar, it was melting and kinda mushy

Wonder if you can be the one to CUM rescue this - - - - -?

Regina picked the picture up and put it down again at least four times before finally deciding to leave the picture on Mike's desk. She felt so weird walking away, like someone had seen her pick her nose or remove a wedgie. Regina felt a tinge of guilt, but that was slowly replaced by the scenarios that danced in her head as she tried to imagine Mike's reaction. She did not have to imagine for very long.

Before Regina could check her voice messages, she received an instant message from Mike asking her to please come back to his office, as he had an idea about rescuing kittens. She felt like a kid in a candy store who was stealing. After setting her phone and her computer to Do Not Disturb, Regina went to the bathroom before she made her way to the opposite side of the building to Mike's office.

"Come on in. Close the door and have a seat, please." Mike tried to sound as professional as possible when he addressed Regina. He was intoxicated by both her scent and her appearance. Mike loved the fact that Regina was very tastefully dressed in a pantsuit which hugged her body in all the right places. Her short, razor-sharp haircut was as perfect as her manicured fingers. Unlike other attractive women at Bright Star, Regina's physical beauty was matched by her personality. She was always courteous and friendly and seemed to not be an attention seeker. That was perfect. Mike had dated several women at Bright Star, and most had been discreet. He did not want the headache of being in that uncomfortable situation which can develop when coworkers are no longer intimate. Regina intrigued Mike because she did not play the hard-to-get game, but yet she was a challenge. When she gave in to her basic needs, she simply left him speechless. "I'll get straight to the point," he continued. Mike had no idea why he was being so forward with Regina. He acted as if he had a sense that there was no time to waste.

"Ok, please, get to the point. I have work to do and haven't even looked at a single account today. Remember, I was summoned at the beginning of the work day." Regina smirked as she let herself be swept away by Mike's cologne. She folded her hands tightly in her lap, just to keep from jumping up and kissing this attractive, sexy, funny man who was giving her something she had not had in a long time—attention and excitement.

"That pretty, sweet, delicious kitty from the other day needs to be rescued, huh?"

Regina blushed. "How do you know she is sweet?"

"I tasted her!" Now it was Mike's turn to blush. He leaned in across the desk so he could speak more softly. "Yeah, when I got to my car, I practically licked the skin off my fingers, trying to ingest your taste. It was the sweetest nectar I've ever experienced. So when would you like this rescue mission to take place? Because I serve at your pleasure, Madam Golden."

Regina swallowed so hard that she felt like her gulp could be heard across the street. She was lecturing herself in her mind. *See? You start this little flirting game, trying to get some attention, and now look...your mouth has written a check that your behind is too light to cash! Think fast! Get out of this man's office and stop playing these games before things go too far.* Regina audibly exhaled. She should have been thankful for the self-lecture. That let her know that she still had a conscience. "I'll have to get back to you on that. I have to be sure that you are the right man for the job."

"Don't be silly; you know I'm the ONLY man for the job. You get back to me as soon as possible. I don't want you changing your mind."

"Okay, I can do that." Regina stood to leave.

"Hey, why are you rushing off?" Mike stood as well and came around the desk to stand between Regina and the door.

"Mike, it's going on nine o'clock. You know as well as I do that we have an office meeting at nine thirty. The e-mail said there is going to be a staffing announcement. I want to at least do one thing at my desk before we head to the auditorium. Is that okay with you?"

Although he was the one who sent the email, Mike had completely forgotten about the meeting. Senior management was going to announce that Melissa had been promoted to supervisor. Also, the coordinator position that Melissa vacated was going to be filled, and management wanted to encourage frontline employees to apply. Mike thought Regina would be perfect for that position. Aside from working more closely with him and the other supervisors, Regina would be an ideal choice because she did great work on customer accounts, was knowledgeable and thorough, and most importantly, had the respect of her peers. Still, he could not say anything about the changes prematurely. He took pride in never crossing the line of mixing Bright Star business with personal business. "Yes, by all means, you better get going. Can I have a quick hug?"

"Uhhh...no! You cannot have a hug, Mike. Do you see that clear stuff in the middle of your door? It's called glass. Funny thing...just like we can look through that glass and see into the hallway, anyone who happens to walk by can look through that same glass into this office. I don't think so. No way. Sorry."

"Okay, step over this way a little. Now, may I *please* have a hug?" Mike did not feel like he was coming on too strong because he sensed that Regina was as excited and aroused as he was. She was just better at keeping it under wraps.

"Mike, you can have a quick, innocent, friendly handshake. That is the best that I can offer." Regina quickly wiped her sweaty palms on her pants as Mike moved closer. Dang, she wanted him to kiss her so badly. Regina clasped Mike's outstretched hand and pressed firmly as she shook. Without a word, she quickly opened the door behind her and dashed into the hallway before Mike could respond.

At the same time that Regina was dashing out of his office, Mike's face lit up like a lightbulb. He opened the hand that Regina had just shaken to reveal a pair of white lace panties. Mike quickly closed his office door and took a seat behind his desk. Unable to stop himself, he simultaneously sniffed the panties and willed his erection to retreat. At that moment, Mike knew that he would not be rescuing Regina's kitty. He knew that he and Regina would end up rescuing each other. And he was going to enjoy every moment of it.

Something was different, and it was *bad* different, not *good* different. Kim knew that something was going on between Regina and Mike. *Ever since Melissa told us that Mike is attracted to Regina, I see a difference in her,* Kim thought. *She now acts like her shit don't stink. Regina is not better than me, and she certainly does not deserve Mike's attention.* It boggled Kim's mind to try to figure out why Mike, or any other man, would find Regina attractive, and not her. After all, Regina had dark complexion, short hair, and was more hard and athletically built. She thought working out and lifting weights was so great, but it actually made her look rugged and unfeminine as far as Kim was concerned. Conversely, Kim's skin was lighter and, therefore, more beautiful, she felt. Her hair was down her back—twenty inches to be exact—and she had ample breasts, a small waist, and hips that begged to be parted. Kim took pride in the fact that she never exercised, and yet her body rivaled any model. In Kim's mind, she was soft and smooth like a woman should be, not hard and ripped. Kim thought, *I just might apply for that coordinator position after all. I don't have any issues that I can think of, and I'm certainly not jealous of any female at Bright Star…hell, of any female anywhere!*

Kimberly Denise Stoner was thirty-eight years old. For as long as she could remember, Kim was always the life of the party. She was known to speak her mind and sometimes even speak what other people were thinking but thought better of saying aloud. In high school, college, and even into adulthood, people often referred to her as rude or obnoxious, but

Kim did not care. Kim felt that most females were jealous of her because they did not look like her or have her charm, or because men were not attracted to them the way they were attracted to her. To Kim, the people who called her rude were the people who could not handle the truth. She believed that her real friends knew her on the inside, and that was all that mattered. Well, in a way. Actually, as far as Kim was concerned, it didn't matter if anybody really knew or accepted her. She was fine either way.

Aside from her physical beauty and outgoing personality, Kim believed that she was better than most of her peers because of her background. Unlike many of her peers in high school and beyond, Kim came from a two-parent household. Her parents were not super rich, but they were considered upper middle class. They worked hard, managed their money well, and lavished every indulgence upon their only child. Growing up, Kim did not have a favorite parent. She could just as easily get her way with either of her parents. She could not remember a time that either of them had ever denied her anything. Once, in elementary school, Kim went to a friend's house for a sleepover. She was shocked when the girl's mother told them it was time to put the snacks away and get ready for bed. Kim was horrified. She had never been told when to go to bed by her parents. Kim suggested that her friend go tell her father what her mother had said so that he could overrule the mother. That was Kim's last time staying overnight at that friend's house for several reasons. Kim did not want to be in a place in which there were rules and structure, and her friend's parents did not want their daughter being influenced by such a manipulative child.

Kim had developed a sense of entitlement which was thirty-eight years in the making. Usually, when she wanted something, she got it. Even worse, as she did not see anything wrong with it, Kim usually wanted what other people – especially women – had. Kim considered herself a healthy competitor. In actuality, she was jealous, petty, and insecure. Kim would argue that she had a healthy self-image and that her esteem was perfectly intact. However, she'd spent her entire life seeking the two things her parents neglected to shower upon her – love and attention. Since they were consumed with their own image, saving a substantial amount of money, and being able to give their precious daughter the best of everything, Kim's parents spent their time either working or social-izing. As Kim moved into adulthood and her parents found themselves bailing her out of more and more situations; they also found themselves blaming each other for their daughter's antics and questioning when her attitude had become so bad. Finally, they came to accept that they were to blame for their daughter's terrible attitude. Sure, as she grew older, Kim, like all people, was responsible for her own choices and behaviors. However, her parents knew that they had not exactly given her the best foundation upon which to build a solid character. As a toddler, when Kim would coo, crawl, or do something funny, her parents were dismissive at best. They were great at making sure Kim's physical needs were met, but they were largely absent emotionally. Too busy working, shopping, or going out with friends, Kim's parents rarely held, hugged, or spent time with her. Instead, they constantly bought material things for Kim. Before she was five years old, Kim had learned to equate love with gifts and getting her way. That lesson stuck for life.

Kim had never been physically attracted to Mike. Like most other women, she thought he was good-looking, but she did not consider him to be anything special. And she never saw him in a sexual manner. That changed when Kim figured out that not only did Mike find Regina attrac-tive, but Regina obviously felt some type of way about him also. Kim was pissed. *First of all*, Kim thought, *how dare Regina walk around like a hypocrite, pretending to be all sweet, innocent, and happily married?* Think-ing back to her own divorce, Kim recalled how Regina told Kim that people's actions came with consequences. *Now this bitch has the nerve to be sneaking around with Mike.* No, she did not have proof that anything had happened between Regina and Mike, but Kim knew that something was brewing. There would be no way Kim would sit back and allow Mike to overlook her in favor of Regina. Kim logged off of her comput-er for the week. She practically danced to her car as she stepped off the elevator into the parking deck. She was anxious to map out her plan for Operation Take Down.

6 WEEKS AGO

Finally, a weekend with no birthdays, graduations, or going in to the office! Regina looked forward to having a few days off to catch up on housework, recorded TV shows, and her ever-growing list of unopened emails. As soon as she finished her exercise video, Regina planned to get showered, make a healthy breakfast, and get laundry started. Heck, she'd tilted, tucked and tightened so well, she might even make enough for that husband of hers. As if on cue, Kevin appeared in the doorway of the den.

"Hey, babe, how much longer you have on your DVD?" Kevin had actually startled Regina. As hard as she tried to ignore him, Regina couldn't do it. One look at her husband in his workout gear, and she had to actually stop moving.

"Why, Kevin? You want me to make you something to eat? I have a better idea. How about I go out and get you something, and wait until you are asleep to bring it back?" Regina was still upset that Kevin had let her go to bed hungry a few nights ago, and they were just barely talking to each other due to his previous screw up. Who was this man, and what had he done with her loving husband?

Kevin refused to back off. He was determined to melt Regina's icy demeanor even if it took the entire weekend. "Well actually, Mrs. Golden, I was going to join you if you didn't mind. You are always saying how I need to work out since I'm getting old now. Then, I figured we could shower together, and you could relax while I fixed us some bacon, eggs, and pancakes. And bacon. Maybe some fresh-squeezed orange juice. And bacon."

"Okay, out of all that stuff you named, I only heard one thing for me." Regina knew what Kevin was up too, trying to break her down so she wouldn't be angry with him.

"Fine, you want to play hard? I will make Kool-Aid instead of orange juice. See, I was trying to be nice, but you had to mess it up with that mouth of yours, didn't you?" Kevin teased Regina as he walked over to the middle of the room where she stood breathing hard, dripping with sweat, and looking sexy as hell while trying to look angrier than she really was. "Look, I'm sorry, baby. You know how Drew is. He just went on and on asking me about DeShawn, and before I knew it, we had—"

Regina wiggled from Kevin's embrace. "You have a lot of nerve mentioning that thug's name in my house. After all the—what is so funny, Kevin?" Regina had to fold her arms across her chest to keep herself from throwing the remote control at Kevin. She was about to fall for his little apology, but he just had to ruin it, bringing up the very name that had been the source of all of their problems lately.

"I'm laughing because you sound exactly like Andrew. He kept referring to DeShawn as 'that thug' just like you always do. That is one of the reasons that I was gone so long. Andrew called himself setting me straight about letting this situation with DeShawn come between you and me. Now, here *you* go. Are you sure you didn't give Drew a script for the other night? Huh?" With that, Kevin began to tickle Regina. She tried not to laugh at first, but he got her right beneath the rib cage. She began to laugh and flail her arms. She actually did hit Kevin with the remote control. Kevin feigned anger and began to walk away from Regina. Then he turned around suddenly, grabbed her knees, and took her to the floor like a wrestler. Shocked initially, Regina tried to break free from Kevin's hold, but he started tickling her again. Just as suddenly as he picked her up off her feet, Kevin pinned Regina's arms on either side of her head as he sat on top of her and looked into her eyes. "I'm serious, baby," Kevin continued. "I apologize about dinner. Will you let me make it up to you? Turn this TV off, go get showered, and I'll make you an egg-white omelet with all of your favorite veggies. I will cut you up some fresh fruit and make you my famous orange juice. But I'm still having some pancakes."

"And bacon," they both said in unison.

Regina lifted her head and kissed Kevin. "Apology accepted."

Kevin stood up and then held out his hand to help Regina. As she reached for his hand, he yanked it back. "Psych."

"Ha ha, very funny. Just go make my breakfast Duh-JANE-Go."

Kevin roared in laughter as he headed toward the kitchen and yelled back at his wife, "The 'D' is silent."

The rest of the weekend was not only peaceful between Kevin and Regina, it was actually enjoyable for each of them. Although they did not have sex, it was clear that both Kevin and Regina wanted to regain their intimacy. All weekend, they gave each other kisses and love pats whenever they crossed paths. On both Saturday and Sunday, Kevin and Regina played cards together and cooked together, and each night Regina fell asleep curled up in Kevin's arms. The way they teased and played with each other reminded Regina of old times between them. She remembered the good times in their relationship, until the recent past. Regina also had a fleeting thought, wondering how it would have felt to be falling asleep in Mike's arms.

*****

"What's going on, man? You okay?" Kevin had just finished playing Call of Duty with a young man at the Golden Choices Center when he received a text message from DeShawn to call him as soon as he could.

"Yeah, I'm cool," DeShawn answered. "Just have some important stuff to get off my chest."

"Did something happen over the weekend, DeShawn?" Kevin was a little worried. He knew that DeShawn's emotional health was fragile right now. He wanted to be available to help this kid. Most importantly, he wanted to ensure that DeShawn did not feel abandoned by him.

"No, no. Nothing like that, Mr. Kevin. Hey, I know it's the beginning of the week and probably busy at the center. I was wondering if me and Moms could come down there after hours tonight? I mean, if you have the time. I don't want to cause any problems for you, sir."

Kevin was actually touched by DeShawn's concern. "No problem at all, DeShawn. You and Ms. Martin are more than welcome to come down this evening. For right now, though, you sure you straight? I can move some things around and get you guys in here in a few hours."

"Good looking, Mr. Kevin, but I ain't trippin'. We'll just be down at, like, seven o'clock. That will give Moms time to get in and do whatever she do. Cool?"

Kevin couldn't help but smile to himself. No matter how long he'd been out of the high school setting, he knew he could count on his youngsters to communicate with him using the latest lingo. "Okay, man, I'll see you and Ms. Martin at seven."

Since Kevin knew he was going to have a late night, he called his wife so there would not be any issues or arguments.

No answer.

Kevin left a voice message informing Regina that he would be working late.

$$***** $$

"Okay, so are there any questions? Anybody? Nothing from you, Melissa? You are the newest to this position, and I'm sure you are lost. It's a mystery to me why they gave the position to you anyway. As I recall, you weren't a standout as a coordinator. But that's another story. So anyway, I figured you would probably have a lot of questions. Do you understand the rollout of the new program?"

Alicia had given a presentation to the group of six supervisors. The other supervisors detested Alicia, but nobody ever confronted her. They had learned the hard way that it was an exercise in futility to try to get a sympathetic ear from their superiors regarding Alicia. Her grandfather was a previous Bright Star CEO, and her father was currently one of the vice presidents. Alicia's peers and subordinates alike had complained about her being rude and abrasive, unapproachable, and insulting to customers and account holders. The last supervisor who tried to report Alicia to upper management was accused of not being a team player. One week later, he was demoted to a coordinator position. Two weeks after that, he left Bright Star, rather than be demoted to an account specialist, working with the very group he used to supervise and taking a pay cut of over $10,000. So even though Alicia was being her usual belittling self and Melissa would have enjoyed nothing more than shoving her ink pen through Alicia's eardrum, she took the higher road and decided to try to kill her with kindness.

"Thanks, Alicia. You did such a great job with your presentation that I can't think of a single question. And while I am indeed the newest member of the supervisor team, I look forward to learning as much as possible from you."

Mike slowly shook his head and cleared his throat. He knew that Melissa felt the same way everyone else did about Alicia. But she played her hand very well. She should do just fine. He took out his phone and shot off a quick text.

ur buddy is gonna b a good fit. she plays the game well of pretending to get along with alicia.

lol. yeah I knew melissa would be fine. she is professional enough to play the game. people think she is passive or weak because of her quiet and non-confrontational demeanor...that is her strength tho

wut r ur strengths ms. golden?????

i have a lot of strengths

name two

left thigh and right thigh

o. i c...and wut do u use those strengths 4

riding

saddle up ms golden. i wont buck if u wanna fuget that…hey have u heard that song that goes 'if u wanna ride, ride the white pony'

no honey i don't think so. i ride black stallions not little white ponies

i have a magic pony - -yea he starts off little but he grows when u suck him. u like magic don't u? i can show u a few tricks

tricks r 4 kids mike. im a grown woman with grown woman needs wants and desires. when im hungry i want a real meal not a happy meal…on the other hand if i allow u to eat at this Y then YOU would be enjoying the happy meal

eat at the Y? I don't follow you

LOL. believe me, after u eat at this Y all you would want to do is follow me. let me break it down mike. next time you see a female wearing pants standing with her legs together, glance at her private area. see what letter is formed. u gotta be careful which Ys u join mike. hey how are doing all this texting in one of alicias meetings? u better watch it

im not worried about her. she knows i don't put up with her crap.

whatever u say mike. ill catch up with u soon count on it cuz we need to finish this convo k. ttyl.

how about later today. can we meet for a bite to eat after work and finish this discussion

name the place and I'll see ya there

Regina's heart ran like a rabbit. She had never done anything like this, never been so bold and forward with another man while she was married to Kevin. She really did love Kevin, and she did not want to hurt him or risk destroying their relationship. On the other hand, this was not about Kevin; it was about Regina. She had needs, and they were not being met, so she excused her inappropriate behavior as being the harmless result of Kevin's inattention. *Shoot, if Kevin focused on me as much as he did that thug and his sad-sack momma, there wouldn't be a gaping hole for someone else to walk into,* Regina justified to herself.

i love those burgers from Flemings. wanna meet there after work?

hell yeah…its a d8...and i will NOT b 18…n i hope when we done, food wont b all i 8

no no no. it is not a date and the ONLY thing you will be eating is what they serve on your plate

The rest of the work day was a blur. Regina honestly could not remember anything beyond the staff meeting, during which Melissa's promotion was announced. Although Kim sat next to Regina at the meeting, she did not hear anything Kim said to her. Rather, Regina was too busy trying to avoid looking at Mike's sexy self. She was failing miserably, and to make things worse, every time she glanced Mike's way, he was looking at her like he wanted to devour her. After two unanswered questions, Kim stopped trying to get Regina's attention. Instead, she, too, became distracted. *Regina is not all that she tries to get people to believe,* Kim thought to herself. *And the bitch is too stupid to keep her dirt under the carpet.* Kim silently took note of the gestures and looks between Regina and Mike. *I don't like the fact that Regina comes off like a Goody Two-shoes. She's as bad as that damn Melissa's Pollyanna ass.* Kim decided she was going to have to pull the carpet from under Regina's feet. *Not that I'm opposed to the girl getting her some on the side. Shit, who am I to judge? Kevin is fine and all, but he's kinda corny, too. Regina is entitled to add a little vanilla flavor to her coffee if she wants to. The problem is that Mike totally overlooked me and tried to get with Regina instead. That is some bull!* Kim sent a quick text to Regina, Melissa, and Regan saying that she was very excited about this week's girls' night.

Kevin did not want to piss off his wife so he'd sent her a text letting her know that he would be late getting home because DeShawn and his mother were coming to the center for a meeting. Not only did Regina reply that it was okay that Kevin have a meeting after work, but she told him to take all the time he needed with them because she was going to do some running around after work. It made Kevin feel good that he did not have to choose between keeping Regina pacified and providing service to the young men and their families at the center. He was glad she had other things to do. That would take some of the focus off of her desire to have Kevin in her face all of the time.

DeShawn and Ms. Martin arrived promptly at 7:00 p.m.

"Ms. Martin, good to see you." Kevin greeted DeShawn's mom by shaking her hand and giving her a respectful kiss on the cheek. "DeShawn, what's going on, brother?" They exchanged a brief man-hug before everyone sat down.

"Yes, son, what *is* going on? I barely had time to come in and cook. You know good and well I watch my recorded shows while I'm eating, and I was ready to see what happened on *Grey's.* Oh no, did something happen at school?" Ms. Martin wanted to be supportive of her son. What she lacked in money and material possessions, she more than made up for in love, time, and attention with DeShawn. After the deaths of her other two children, Ms. Martin vowed that no matter what day she or her son died, he would know beyond a shadow of a doubt that his mother loved him with all of her heart. Even so, Ms. Martin was weary. She worked tirelessly both in and outside of the home. And since DeShawn's trouble with the rape situation, she was as drained emotionally as she was physically. There were just a few things that gave Ms. Martin the peace and relaxation that she so desperately needed. Among them were her prayer time, her hair salon appointments, and her TV shows – *Grey's Anatomy*, *The Good Wife*, and just about anything on Lifetime Movie Network. Sure, a lot of her coworkers teased her for not keeping up with the latest reality shows, but Ms. Martin reminded them that those shows were so scripted and edited that cartoons were darn near more realistic. Besides, where would she find time to get caught up in someone else's life issues when her hands were full trying to make the best life possible for herself and her son?

DeShawn leaned forward and rested his elbows on his knees as he sighed deeply. "I'm ready to talk." Kevin and Ms. Martin exchanged surprised glances and remained silent so that DeShawn could continue. "Momma, since my arrest you have been asking me to tell you what happened that night, and I never wanted to talk about it. Honestly, I didn't think you would believe me."

"Well, son, if that were true, I wouldn't have put up my house to get you out of jail. I told you the day you were arrested that I just needed you to tell me if you really raped that girl. I know you, DeShawn, but I don't know everything you do. I am not with you when you are hanging out with your friends, and I'm not that parent who thinks her child would never do anything wrong. But like I said, baby, I know you. When I look into your eyes, I know when you are scared, when you are mad, when you feel insecure, and when you are lying. So after I got you home, of course I wanted to know the details about that night. It seemed like I was entitled to that."

"I know, Momma; you're right. You and Mr. Kevin have been the only people in the world to stick by me and have my back. My so-called homeboys all scattered like roaches when I got arrested. The only people who *really* know what I'm going through are Josh and Brian. But our lawyers really don't want us kicking it all like that anymore. It's been hard holding all this shi…I mean, all this stuff in."

"Man you did not have to keep anything held in," Kevin chimed in. You know I'm always here for you, and you know that my support comes without any judgments or strings attached. Why didn't you talk to me when I asked you about the events of that night?"

"I don't know, Mr. Kevin. Keepin' it one hundred, I didn't really know how to talk to you, 'cause I didn't want you to be disappointed in me."

"So you are ready to talk now?" Kevin asked.

"After I bonded out of jail, that lawyer was saying the next step is to see if a grand jury will indict me. Dude was talking above my head, but I guess that means—"

Kevin cut DeShawn off without thinking. "That means that the police believed there was enough suspicion against you to arrest you. However, the police do not decide if you will be charged with a crime. The prosecutor will present the evidence to a grand jury, and they will either decide that charges will be brought against you, which is an indictment, or that no charges should be brought against you, which is a no bill. Meanwhile, since your mom hired a bail bondsman, you are allowed to be at your mom's house instead of in jail."

"Oh, ok, cool. That's kinda what I thought. It just seemed like most people had their minds made up, so I was just like, whatever. But the more I thought about it, the more I just wanted somebody to know the full truth. So that's why I wanted you and Moms here now, to tell you both at the same time."

Ms. Martin was a statue, except for the tears quietly rolling down her face. Her lips barely moved, and her voice was barely audible. "Go on, son."

"Well the night started just like every other Friday night. We beat the Stallions that night, more like slaughtered them since we didn't let them score a single point to our forty-two. So anyway, we rode the bus back to the school, and we all got showered after the team meeting. Then me, Brian, and Josh wanted to go hang out. Remember, Moms? I called you and asked if it was cool for me to chill at Josh's and you said fine so long as his parents were home, and we didn't go anywhere else. Keeping it real, Moms, if you remember, the only thing I said to that was 'quit worrying, I love you'."

Ms. Martin never took her eyes off of DeShawn. She was not sure she wanted to hear the rest of this story, and she feared that she already knew the rest. "You were being purposely evasive, son? Why? Were you boys drinking or…oh my God! DeShawn Nathaniel Martin! Were you doing drugs?" Catching both Kevin and DeShawn by surprise, in the quickest flash, Ms. Martin was on her knees in front of her son. She had clasped his hands in hers and kissed his knuckles through her tears. She kept mumbling about being stupid for not seeing the warning signs that DeShawn was on drugs. "You should have come to me, son. How could you—"

"Moms!" DeShawn leaped to his feet and dropped his hands from his mother's clasp. "Gone wit' that. For real? You know I don't do no drugs. See, this is part of the reason I didn't wanna even say nothin' to you. You bring all this drama and stuff, and it's just too hard to talk to you. Maybe this wasn't a good idea."

Kevin knew this was a crucial moment, and he did not want to let it escape. DeShawn had finally worked up the nerve to discuss the events of the fateful night, and although he could understand Ms. Martin's fears and concerns, this was about DeShawn, not her. Ms. Martin needed to chill out. Kevin gave Ms. Martin a look that was intended to speak volumes. Apparently, the message was properly received because Ms. Martin quickly took her seat, apologized to DeShawn, and asked him to please continue. She promised not to interrupt again.

DeShawn hesitated. Then, with an approving nod from Kevin, he sat down and resumed his story. "So like I was tryna say, I did not answer you 'cause I didn't wanna tell you a lie. The truth is, that—"

"Joshua's parents were not home, were they?" Ms. Martin blurted out before she could stop herself. She slapped her palm over her mouth and sheepishly looked between Kevin and DeShawn as she sank back into her seat and nodded for her son to continue.

"No, his parents weren't home. My bad, Moms. We weren't even try-na do anything bad, though. We were just gonna chill, alright? So we invited a few of the guys over from the team and were just playing Xbox Live and stuff. Then one of the guys told us that his brother was home from college and could get us some beer. We were bored and knew we wouldn't be driving or anything, so we didn't really see the harm. Dude's brother dropped off some beer and kept it moving. We just chilled for maybe another forty-five minutes or an hour, and somebody said we should invite some pams over."

"*Pams*?" Kevin could usually figure out what the kids meant, and he assumed 'pams' meant girls, but he wanted to be sure.

"Yeah. You know, Mr. Kevin. Pams. Girls that are easy. They let you slide in, cook a lil bit, then you slide out. Ain't nobody tryna fall in love and be booed up, so we just kick it with the pams. Usually they are just desperate girls with low self-esteem…or either hoes with too much self-esteem."

"Come on, man, you know the rules. You can't talk disrespectfully about the females." Kevin knew it was popular for females to be referred to as bitches and hoes. It was in the music, in the videos, and certainly in the hallways of schools across America. But it was not allowed at Golden Choices.

"No disrespect, Mr. Kevin. I didn't mean any harm. It's just that there are certain girls who are easy to have sex with. Sorry Moms. I don't know how else to refer to a girl who is so willing to give it up like that. My bad; I'll just say *pams*. So anyway, Brian called up these girls from uh…aww shoot, it's Saint something or another over on the northwest side of town. These pams had partied with us plenty of times before, like four or five of 'em. They usually came thirsty and just basically were al-ways down for whatever. That night was no different. They brought their own drink, just like they always did. And one of 'em even had some pills she scored from her mother's purse. Josh and them fools be into that; I'm cool though 'cause at the end of the day, I need to be in control of my thoughts. Anyway, we just kicked it like usual. You know, turned on some music, started playing strip poker, just chillin'. Some of the guys and those pams were trippin' because they were drinking and taking those pills. We were laughing and stuff 'cause they were acting like they were exotic dancers. They were trippin' for real. One of the pams even wanted somebody to videotape them. The one girl that always acts like she is feelin' me, her name is Hilary. She is actually the one who always be gettin' pills from her Moms. It's funny, too, 'cause she always get the pills, but she don't never take any. She ain't no lame though, because she definitely gets her drink on. When the pams come over, it's usually me and Hilary that hang out. She just kinda lays back and chills with me while everybody else cuts loose.

"So anyway, after watching everybody clown for a while, me and Hilary went to another room so we could have some privacy and just chill and whatnot. Keeping it one hundred, I turned on the TV to try and catch the highlights on NFL Network. Baby girl had something else in mind, though. Now picture this setup. I'm sitting on the floor on this pillow-like chair, facing the TV that's mounted on the wall. Hilary comes at me from behind, and she starts kissing my neck and rubbing my chest. I give her a peck or two, but basically I'm still watching TV. She slides around to my right and is kinda laying on her right hip. So she takes her hands and starts rubbing my di…starts rubbing me down there. Know what I'm saying? At this point, I'm thinking, 'Shit, I can catch those NFL highlights anytime.' No dude is gonna just sit there, so I let her do her thing, you feel me. She took my zipper down and…wait. I don't wanna seem like I'm being disrespectful or giving too much detail or information. I don't know what you wanna hear or what's too much."

Kevin wanted to know everything that DeShawn had to report about that night. It could prove very helpful later on, especially to DeShawn's attorney. "DeShawn, your mom and I are adults and neither of us blush or scare very easily. Even if you think something may be hard for us to hear, don't hold back. Nothing is too big, too small, too shocking or too graphic. Deal?"

"Yes, sir, deal." So DeShawn continued. "So she takes my zipper down and puts her hand down the front of my pants. I start undoing her shirt, and we are getting ready to turn up, so I lift up my hips and slide my pants down a little bit. At first she rubbing on my joint, which is cool for a minute. Then I told her she need to get busy, 'cause that D wasn't gonna suck itself."

For DeShawn, it was easier looking at Kevin rather than at Ms. Martin, as he could see the disappointment on his mother's face from the moment he started talking. He'd taken Kevin and his mother at their word when they said they wanted to hear everything. He was not trying to be shocking or disrespectful, just honest. He took a deep breath and continued.

"Okay, so the pam...Hilary...put her head in my lap and got busy. Baby girl got mad skills. She told me before that she been suckin' di... 'cuse me, Moms...she said she been having oral sex since she was an elementary student, in like fifth or sixth grade. That night she was in grad school, know what I'm saying, Mr. Kevin?"

Kevin just looked at DeShawn with a 'hey man, cut that out' kind of expression.

DeShawn got the message, nervously cleared his throat, and resumed. "I just mean she was an expert. Just when I'm about to get to the happy ending, I hear giggling and stuff. I look up, and Hilary is waving one of her friends in from the door. The pam that was in the hall comes in with her phone in her hand like she is about to take a picture or something. So I asked her what the heck she was doing, and Hilary says she wants her friend to videotape us. I was like, 'Hell naw!' No way was that going down. The pam leaves the room, and I ask Hilary what was up with that. She said she wanted to have me and her videotaped, that she did that all the time with guys and nobody ever seemed to mind so she didn't understand the big deal. I let her know that I didn't get down like that. And then I told her, 'Speaking of getting down, you need to get this joint on swole again.' We laughed it off, and she went on and finished what she started. After that, she started undoing her shirt, and I was kissing on her and stuff. And she kept saying, 'Now...now...now.' I didn't know what she was talking about, so I just do my thing...you know, kissing her neck and breasts and stuff. She gets on her knees like she wants me to hit from behind. Then she turns over all of a sudden and says she wants me to take her to homecoming. I told her to quit playing, that she knew what this was. Keep in mind, we are not even kissing or anything at this time, just laying there talking. Her shirt is off and my pants are unzipped and part of the way down, but we had not had relations yet. Out of the blue, she yells at me to stop, and she is yelling that I'm hurting her. I told her she was trippin'. I got up and pulled up my pants and told her I was out. Hilary just got weird. She was crying…well, it sounded like she was crying. But it looked like she was just acting crazy, and she yelled that she could not believe I was gonna leave her like that after I'd gotten what I wanted. I told her that I didn't even know her last name and that I certainly wasn't taking her to homecoming, so she could gone somewhere with that noise. She said I had until Sunday night to agree to homecoming, or I would really know what kind of noise she could make. Moms… Mr. Kevin, I'm not proud, but you wanted to hear the truth, so keeping it one hundred, I called her a bitch and told her maybe she needed to take some of those pills she was always stealing from her crazy-ass momma. Then I walked out of the room. For the rest of the night, me and Hilary never spoke. Her girls were all huddled around her, but I really didn't pay them any attention. They left sometime after I'd fallen asleep, so I don't really know what they did for the rest of the night, or exactly when they took off.

"All of that was on Friday night after the football game. I went home on Saturday afternoon, and the rest of the weekend was normal. Just chores, homework, and chilling with Brian and Josh. Then, Monday at school, the shit…I'm sorry, Moms…the crap hit the fan. Every time I walked by people, it seemed like they would stop talking or something. You know how they show that stuff in the movies, like all eyes are on someone as they walk by, and then people start whispering after they pass? Well, that's exactly what it felt like. It was strange. After fourth period, Josh and Brian met me at my locker and asked me all these strange questions about Friday, like what I did to Hilary and stuff. I had barely even opened my mouth when the principal came up behind me and told me he needed to see me in his office right away. That's pretty much where you two came into the picture. The school called you, Moms, and once you got there, they started grilling me about Friday night, asking if I had anything I needed to come clean about. As you know, I told them that me and some of the fellas were just chillin' at Josh's house. I had no idea what they were tryin' to get at so I didn't say anything. That's when they played that recording of Hilary screaming at me and asking how I could do her like that. Of course Principal Sterling didn't believe me when I told him that it didn't go down like that. To be honest, you were giving me the stank-eye too, Moms. Like I told you then, Hilary did scream and say those things to me, but it wasn't like it sounded. She initiated all the touching and everything. She got mad when I said I wasn't taking her to homecoming."

Nobody said anything for a few minutes, though it seemed like an hour. Kevin and Ms. Martin looked at each other, and he gave her a slight nod, indicating that it was okay for her to speak, as she'd looked like she was itching to say something.

Ms. Martin cleared her throat and began, "Baby, do you mind if I tell you something…just to clarify?"

"What's up, Moms?"

"I just want you to know that I never wanted you to feel abandoned or like I did not trust you. DeShawn, you may not understand this until you become a parent, but I was hoping against all hope that you had not violated that girl like she accused you of doing. No parent wants to believe that their child has done something horrible, especially when it goes against their character and past behavior. But I was caught in the middle of a terrible tug-of-war between what my heart wanted to be true and what the evidence seemed to present. During that time, son, you lied to me about Josh's parents being home. You were deceptive with me and Principal Sterling about the underage drinking. You were not forthcoming about that girl and any interaction that you may have had with her. And there was…they had—" Ms. Martin burst into tears. "The police had her shirt with DNA from your semen on it," she continued between sobs. "Even with all of that, DeShawn, you still would not tell me what happened. Today, all these months later, after I got you out of jail, after I drove myself sick with worry and grief, after your own emotional roller coaster…now you bare all and look at me like I did something wrong. Like I said before, if I did not believe you, or at least want to believe you, trust and believe that you would still be sitting in the detention center. You are seventeen years old, DeShawn, but if they decide to indict you, they can charge you as an adult. This is serious. So I ask you, is there anything else? Are you sure that you were watching television, she started rubbing and kissing you – everywhere, you turned her over, she stopped and asked you to take her to homecoming, and when you said no, she staged that whole victim scene? Is that what you are saying happened, son?"

"Moms, yes! That is *exactly* what I'm saying. I mean, you made it sound simpler, but that's what happened. And now that I think about it, I should have known something was up when she was trying to get that other pam to record us. Most girls would shy away from something like that, but this girl was inviting it. It's like she was proud of what she was doing. She was setting me up from the beginning."

Kevin moved from his seat. He pulled up a chair next to DeShawn and began, "First things first, bro. It took a lot of guts for you to sit here and tell us all of that. I already had mad respect for you, but you can be sure that has doubled tonight. I have told you and all of the young brothers here that me and the rest of the staff are here to encourage, support, help, and motivate all of you in any way that we can. You already know that we have a keep-it-real policy around here. Nobody is going to beat you up, but rather our goal is to lift you up. That being said, we can't sugarcoat the truth or not call a spade a spade, you know what I'm saying?"

"Uh, no, sir. Not really."

Kevin pointed to a sign painted on wall. "What does that say, son?"

"It says 'Golden Choices'," DeShawn answered.

"Exactly. And what does that mean to you?"

"Well, it means that we have the right to make whatever choices we decide and also the responsibility to accept or deal with the results of those choices. So if we make golden choices, then usually, sooner or later, we reap golden rewards. By the same token, if we make tarnished or warped choices, then sooner or later, we have to deal with the consequences of those choices."

"Very well said, DeShawn. That is actually a very mature outlook for a seventeen-year-old. In fact, a lot of adults would do well to adopt such an attitude of personal accountability. So let me ask you something: Given what you just told me, do you think you were making the best choices that night at Josh's house?"

"I mean, for real, for real Mr. Kevin, I didn't really do anything wrong. Yes, that girl has my DNA on her shirt, but I just explained that. She performed oral sex and that's how that got there. I did not rape that girl, did not have sex with her, and didn't even initiate the contact that we did have. It's not my fault that she wouldn't take *no* for an answer about homecoming. I don't know her all like that, and I didn't feel like I owed her anything."

Kevin looked at Ms. Martin. This time she nodded to him. She knew that DeShawn was missing the point here, and she wanted to see if Kevin could get him to see what he was missing.

Kevin continued, "Okay, I see what you are saying. She initiated everything and then she flipped out. I get that. Do you think you played *any* role in the events of that night and the resulting situation that you now find yourself in?"

DeShawn stood up. He was starting to feel crowded and pressured. He didn't know what Mr. Kevin wanted from him. Was he missing something? Did Mr. Kevin want him to admit to raping that girl? Hell no, that wasn't going to happen.

"I don't get it, Mr. Kevin. I don't know what you want me to say. I don't see what I did wrong. I mean, I could've told my mom that Josh's parents weren't going to be home, but then she would've been trippin' about me being over there. You could look at it like I was wrong for drinking or whatever, but it was only beer, and I didn't buy it, someone else did. Am I perfect? No. But I could be a lot worse. I'm not in a gang, I have never got any of these pams pregnant, I am about to graduate, on the Merit Roll mind you, and I've never been in trouble."

"Until now," Kevin reminded DeShawn. "You just did what a lot of us often do when we are faced with the consequences of our actions.

We compare down instead of comparing up. It's like the bank robber in prison bragging that at least he didn't rape anyone. And the rapist brags that at least he is not a child molester. And the child molester brags that he is not a murderer. And so it goes. When we look to how we should behave, we actually belittle ourselves when we argue how much worse we could be. Anyone can be worse. That is no great feat or accomplishment, DeShawn. Instead, compare up. And I'm not saying compare yourself to another person. I'm saying compare yourself to your best potential. Although someone else brought beer, did you have to drink it? Even though Hilary offered and initiated sexual acts, did you have to participate?"

"I hear you, Mr. Kevin, but that's just not realistic. You're a grown man, so it's easy for

you to sit there now and say what I should have done. But what about when you were my age? I don't know any seventeen-year-old dude who would have turned down what Hilary was offering. And the beer thing, even that's not bad. I guess I could have drunk water, but you're not looking at the point that we were not being irresponsible. We were not driving while we were drinking. That's what makes it so hard for people my age to talk to older people. It's like you can't see what we are really going through or like you never had fun in your past or made choices that your parents or teachers would not have liked. I'm an above-average teen if you ask me."

"I respect what you are saying. It can come off that adults act like we can't relate. I don't think it's intentional. I believe that we are just trying to prevent the young people that we care about from making some of the same mistakes that we made. It's a tough balance sometimes. You're right, DeShawn. I've been down the road you are now traveling. I'd be less than responsible if I did not warn you about the potholes, road blocks, and other hazards that lay ahead of you if you continue on that road."

Ms. Martin rose to her feet. "Get up, son, and give me a hug. I'm very proud of you for telling us what happened that night. You didn't do everything perfect, but I'm glad it was not any worse. I am more convinced than ever that you did not rape or take advantage of that girl. I will be right by your side throughout this entire process. No matter what it takes, we will fight this thing and clear your name."

"I agree," Kevin said as he stood up. "I have a close friend who is an attorney. If you two don't mind, I'd like to run all of this by him tomorrow and get his opinion. Meanwhile, I will stand firmly with you two during this process. Social media has made such a scandal of the entire situation. It's ridiculous."

"Now you said the magic word, Mr. Kevin...*Scandal*," Ms. Martin chimed in. "We are going to head on out so I can tune in to Olivia and the Gladiators."

DeShawn and Kevin both shrugged their shoulders and looked at Ms. Martin like she had two heads.

"Never mind. Come on, DeShawn. Let's go so we can stop and get some dinner, and I can watch my show before bed. We appreciate you taking so much time with us, Mr. Kevin. I hope it doesn't cause any trouble for you. You have a good night."

Kevin walked DeShawn and his mother to the door. "It was my pleasure, Ms. Martin, no trouble at all. In fact I bet my wife is in bed as we speak."

*****

"So you have a problem with my bed?" Mike was talking to Regina, but she was staring off into space. "Hello...earth to Regina! You okay over there?"

"I'm sorry, Mike. I'm just trying to take this all in. Let me get this straight: you have a *water* bed? You do know what year...heck, what decade we're in, don't you? I haven't known anyone with a waterbed since the 1980s."

Mike sat back in his chair at Flemings, took another bite of his burger, and feigned anger with Regina. "Now wait a minute. I'm not going to sit here and have you making fun of my bed when you haven't even experienced it yet."

"*Yet?*" Regina raised her eyebrows, as she thought about the nerve of this man sitting across from her.

"We're both adults here. Let's not pretend that we're not attracted to each other. As good as this burger is, the experience is enhanced just because I'm able to sit here and enjoy it with you. I've told you before; it's not just your perfect skin, smile, and tight body that make you attractive. It's that great personality as well. I'd be interested to see what can develop between us. I know that you are married, so I know that things will not get too serious between us. But still, we can take this thing as far as you feel comfortable. I'm not big on playing games or misleading people, so excuse me if I sound too forward. I just think it's best that everything be laid out. Speaking of *laid*."

"Mike, you are too much. Thank you for being upfront; I appreciate that. Let me be just as forward. Try as I might, I can't deny that I am attracted to you as well. We've worked together for a number of years, and I've never felt this way. To my knowledge, you haven't either. So I'm really puzzled. Maybe I'm more vulnerable because things aren't exactly great at home. Still, I don't want to do something that I'll regret. In my heart and head, I know I've already gone too far with you. But still, I have never had so many senses awakened as when we are around each other. You are one smooth operator, Mike, and you know it, too. I don't know why you've taken a sudden interest in me. And frankly, I don't even care at this point. I know that I'm being selfish by dealing with you, and I'm cool with that. I don't know how far things will go with us, Mike. One thing I must insist on, though, is that we never discuss my husband or my marriage. This thing – whatever it is or is gonna be with me and you – is to the exclusion of anything else going on in my life. Deal?"

"Deal."

"Now, let's wrap up dinner so you can show me this water bed of yours."

Mike leaned forward and gave Regina a long, hard kiss. "That's what I'm talking about. Let's go get wet!"

*****

A few nights later, the girls were meeting for an impromptu night out. Kim had told the other ladies she needed to get together immediately, or she was going to explode. Once everyone was seated and had given their drink orders, Regan asked Kim what was going on. Kim shared how she was frustrated because a person who worked out at the same gym was "living foul," and it just burned Kim up. She said she felt like she should do something, but she didn't know what.

Melissa had no idea what Kim was talking about, but was shocked to see that Kim was actually upset about someone else's misbehavior.

"Kim, what are you talking about? What happened?" Melissa asked.

"It's this trick that goes to the same gym where I work out. We have become pretty cool over the last few years. I'm not saying we are friends or anything like that, but we talk and socialize and whatnot while we are working out. I've even met her husband and kids. To listen to her talk about her relationship and her family, you'd think she was damn near perfect. Gorgeous husband, smart and well-behaved kids, lives in a gated community, blah, blah, blah..."

Regan, like the other ladies, didn't get it. "Okay, so she has a great life, Kim? That's not a crime is it?" she asked.

"No, having a great life is not a crime. But *pretending* to have a great life, when you are really living foul *is* a crime. Okay, listen to this: a few weeks ago, I noticed that instead of wearing her typical sweatpants and t-shirts to the gym, this bitch started wearing tight little shorts with matching sports bras."

Regan rolled her eyes. "So what, Kim? You dress like that all the time when you go to the gym."

"Exactly! I dress like that *all* the time. I'm consistent. But this broad is getting brand new. So I just sat back in the cut and observed. I saw her making goo-goo eyes at this one trainer that works there. Now, all of a sudden, she can't turn on the freaking elliptical without him running over to provide assistance. Then earlier this week, I saw them come out of the men's locker room one after the other, looking around all suspicious and shit like Secret Squirrel."

Melissa couldn't believe that Kim was so upset about this. Normally,

Kim would be the main one telling someone to "go on and get yours" and to "just do you." But she was hot about this lady at the gym, whom she barely knew. It just didn't make sense.

Kim continued, "So I got to thinking, *Am I trippin'?* Because to me, this lady is being a fake, fraud, and phony, and I don't like it. I hate smiling and waving at her husband and kids when I see them, knowing good and well that cow is foul like bowel. I just have a problem with people pretending to be one way, and they are really something the complete opposite. Don't you agree, Regina?"

Regina almost choked on her Moscasto. Suddenly, her cheeks felt warm and her armpits felt like they had little pins in them. "Girl…look, what do you want? You want her to broadcast that she is stepping out on her husband? And you don't even know if that is the case. You are letting your imagination run wild. And even if she is fooling around on her husband, what is that to you? Why are you so angry?"

"Because, it's the phoniness of it all. If you gon' be a thief, don't steal packs of gum from the gas station. Get some jewels and shit. If you gon' be a racist, don't sabotage me behind my back by denying me educational and employment opportunities. I'd just as soon have you wear your white hood and display your Confederate bumper stickers from your 1999 pickup truck. Go on and announce that you don't want black people coming to your basketball games. That way, everyone knows where everyone stands." Kim took a breath and paused for a moment. "Well, even that's not entirely true because we know how Massuh snuck into the female slaves' beds. And even now, how the biggest proponents of racial "purity" sneak around with their brown-skinned side pieces. My grandmother used to say 'Don't sneak into hell, bust it wide open.'"

"No disrespect to your grandmother, Kim, but that is just stupid," said Regan. "That's one of those untrue sayings that we all heard that may have rhymed or sounded good, but it makes no sense. For example, I remember our mom used to tell me and Regina that sticks and stones would break our bones, but words would not hurt us! Huh? Since when? I've been more hurt with words than with any boulder or baseball bat."

At first Kim wanted to slap Regan for talking about her grandmother, but as she thought about it, she knew there was some truth to what she had said. "Yeah, I guess. 'Cause my grandmother also said cheaters never win, and I'm living proof that shit ain't true. I know good and well I barely picked up a book in high school or in college. I just faked the funk, played my cards right, and look at me now. How does that song go? *Started from the bottom—*"

"And you're still right there," Melissa cut Kim off. "Listen to yourself, Kim. You are all mad about some lady you barely know because she may or may not be messing around on her husband, yet you brag about cheating your way through school. You actually sound happy that you have not worked for the blessings that you enjoy."

"Ugh, don't hate me 'cause you ain't me. You damn skippy I'm happy that I know how to work smarter instead of working harder. My grandmother did have some wisdom with her sayings because she said there is a sucker born every minute. I just lucked out and ran into more than a few of them."

Regina was getting tired of Kim, and she certainly had better things to think about. "As far as that lady at the gym, if she is doing something wrong, she is handling it like anyone would…privately. Do you expect her to hold up a sign to announce that she is messing around? Just because people don't broadcast their business doesn't mean they are being phony. It just means they are being discreet and minding their own business. We would all do well to learn that lesson."

"I'm not Johnny Gill, but my, my, my! Aren't we touchy? Did I strike a nerve, Regina? One thing my grandmother did mention was that stuff done in the darkness does come to the light. Have you heard that one?"

Regan had a look of terror on her face. Had Kim somehow come to know about her sister and that guy from work? Surely Regina would never have said anything, but Kim was attracted to messy drama like a bee to honey. Regan was getting upset because she did not want her sister to be put on the spot or feel attacked by Kim. Regan knew she had to get the focus off of her sister before things got really ugly, really fast. "Well, I've heard that it is better to be silent and considered a fool than to open your mouth and release all doubt."

"Oop, no you didn't, little Ms. Regan! Well, I heard that closed mouths don't get fed," Kim retorted. "So now what?"

"Huh?" the other ladies all asked in unison. Nobody understood where that came from or why Kim had said it.

Regina knew and appreciated what her little sister was trying to do. She had to smile at Regan trying to come to her rescue. But she didn't need to be saved from Kim.

Melissa stood to leave. "It's been real, ladies, really…something. I have to get my niece and nephew in the morning, so I'm out of here. And Kim, while you are talking about closed mouths, just remember that sometimes there is wisdom in silence."

The rest of the ladies stood to leave as well. Everyone hugged and said their goodbyes, and as Regina was heading out of the door, she couldn't resist getting a last word in on Kim. "Maybe you should not worry about that other woman and what she is doing. You don't want to open your mouth inappropriately and unleash a dragon. You know what they say, girl, about silence being *Golden*."

As Kim and Regina each got into their cars, which were parked next to each other, Regina could have sworn she heard Kim mumble something about all that glitters not being gold. Regina didn't know what that was all about, but she knew that she was going to keep an eye on that heffa.

5 WEEKS AGO

how do i know thats not water????

*WHAT? boy don't even TRY it! u know cuz i told
u. if thats not good enough then its just 2 bad.
Im not getting up from this desk anymore until I
go home 4 the day*

touchy r we? no pun intended LOL

*ha ha. very funny mike. im touchy alright. no
thanks to u ive been touching myself all day...run-
ning back and forth to that bathroom*

*dont act like u didnt like it...admit it, that
was sum freakin hot shit wasnt it*

Regina hated admitting that Mike was right. She had never done anything like this in her life. All day at work, she and Mike had been exchanging X-rated text messages. They both lamented how they would
have loved to have been able to have stolen a kiss or a touch. While
they knew that would not have been wise or practical, Mike instead convinced Regina to try something. He'd told her to go into the bathroom
and pleasure herself. Regina was at the same time shocked and intrigued.
She considered that it might be fun to try, though, awkward as she felt.
At first, Regina sent a text saying she had touched herself sexually, although she really had not. Mike knew better. He told her that if she didn't
want to go along with what he asked, she just needed to say so, but she
did not need to lie or be childish. Just as Mike figured, that did the trick.
His comment made Regina angry enough to take action. She would show

him that she was far from childish.

Determined to prove to Mike, as well as herself, that she could be as savvy and adventurous as the next person, Regina stormed into the bathroom, locked herself in the farthest stall, and began to fumble her clitoris between her thumb and index finger. The fact that she was at work doing this should have prohibited her from enjoying the sensation. In reality, the fact that she was doing this at Mike's urging ensured that she enjoyed it more than she thought possible. That tweedle-dee-tweedle-thumb routine was not working, so Regina began to massage herself with her index and middle fingers. There, that's more like it! Regina thought to herself. She could feel her bud growing as she began to ascend that climatic ladder. She squeezed her thighs together so tight during her orgasm that she thought she was going to get a leg cramp. Someone coming into the bathroom made Regina snap out of it. She almost laughed at herself as she realized she was holding her breath. Regina rolled her eyes as the person entered the stall next to hers. I hate when people do this. There are over eighteen stalls in this bathroom. Seventeen of them are empty, but someone has to hunt down and occupy the one right next to mine. That was so rude! Thankfully, they only have to do Number One. Regina decided to wait until she heard the person wash her hands and leave before she exited. Did they just leave without even a splash of water? Dang, somebody is rude and nasty! Regina took several pictures of her glazed fingers with her cell phone. On one, she posed like she was licking her fingers. She figured Mike would be sure to enjoy that one.

It had taken her at least three trips to the bathroom to complete that mission. The first time she was simply too nervous. The other times, there were people in the other stalls, and there was no way in the world Regina was going to attempt that little stunt with other people in the vicinity. Finally, with just under an hour left in the work day, Regina had finally completed her mission. She sent Mike the pictures of her hands as proof of her deed, and he had the audacity to suggest that she'd simply put water on her hands. Regina almost sent him another finger picture, one solitary middle finger this time.

it was alright. i bet your fingers would've

felt better than my own though. we will have to make that happen someday

make a fist

what?

make a fist

you are so weird. okay...made a fist...now what

thats about the size of wut i'll b puttin n u

is that a fact?

yes ms golden...that is a very long detailed pleasurable life changing fact

goodbye mike...its time to go

Regina tried to rush out of the door as she saw Cassie begin to trot, trying to catch up to her.

"Oh boy! Whew, I gotta catch my breath," Cassie huffed. "I almost broke into a sweat trying to catch up, Regina. Hey, did you have the runs or something today?"

"Excuse me?" Regina snapped. That came out a bit more biting than Regina intended. She was used to how irritating Cassie could be, so Regina hardly got angry or offended by her nosiness anymore. But her question meant that she'd noticed that Regina was up and down from her seat today more than she normally was.

"I figured you musta had the runs because you were gone from your seat an awful lot today. Don't be embarrassed, Regina, I get that way when I eat too much grease or dairy. Does your tummy get all hard and bloated, too? I hate that. I remember this one time I had to—"

"Thanks, Cassie, but I'm fine. Why would you assume that I was going into the bathroom, though? I could have been going to talk to someone, to the break room, or any number of other places."

"Well, you just had that funny look on your face, like something wasn't sitting quite right. When you first got up, I told our other neighbor that you must've gotten your friendly monthly visitor. I sure remember those days, too. But when you kept getting up looking uncomfortable, I knew what it was. It was the runs, wasn't it? C'mere." Cassie leaned in to give Regina a hug. "It's okay, Regina. We all get sick at work from time to time. Heck, I had a touch of something this afternoon. I'll tell ya, I had a customer on the phone who wouldn't shut up so I just pushed the mute button, ran and did my business, and ran back to the phone. Since I'm so courteous, I just hurried right back to the phone before I could rinse my hands. It's not like I'd done Number Two or anything, you know what I mean? Plus that foam soap can really dry my hands out. Would you believe that when I got back on the phone, that customer was still yapping away as if I'd never left. Can you believe that? Some people just don't know when to—"

Regina jumped a foot back away from Cassie. "Yes, yes I know, Cassie. Some people are so rude *and* nasty. Hey, I really have to go. Guess it's those runs, as you say. See you tomorrow."

*****

"Are you sure you don't want me to come in there and help?" Regina asked. "It smells wonderful, and I feel guilty just sitting in here while you're slaving in the kitchen."

"No worries. I told you, I am a master in just about every room in my house. You just sit in there and keep looking sexy. You can get out another bottle of wine if you want," Mike yelled from the kitchen. Regina was sitting in the living room, waiting while he cooked dinner. This was the second time in as many weeks that she had been to his house.

Regina couldn't believe how beautiful Mike's home was. It was exquisitely decorated and smelled aromatic and inviting instead of like a gym. Even the bathrooms were immaculate. It was hard to believe that there was no woman living there, or at least a maid who came in and cleaned. To top it all off, the man could cook his butt off. Well, Regina assumed he could. Mike had been in the kitchen for over forty-five minutes chopping and mixing and whipping up something that smelled heavenly. She had been given the remotes to the Bose stereo and to the television, along with instructions to turn on music or TV and make herself comfortable. Although she didn't have anything in particular that she wanted to watch on television, Regina turned the unit on. "What the—"

"She must've awakened the dragon," Mike chuckled to himself in the kitchen. He was used to that reaction from the ladies. Guys tried to act unimpressed, but he knew they were equally as blown away.

"Oh my goodness! Mike, this thing is crazy. The sound alone darn near blew the curls out of my hair. What is that thing, like seventy-five or eighty inches?"

Mike had walked around the half wall that separated the kitchen and the living room. "84.6 inches, 4K Ultra HD, to be exact. I don't ever have to go to the theater, 'cause it's right here."

"You are right about that. It takes up the entire wall. And the picture. I mean…wow! I don't even know what to say. It's beautiful. Shoot, I like my job and all, but maybe I need to become a supervisor if that's how y'all get down. Dang, I'm living the struggle with my little fifty inches."

"Naw, Mrs. Golden, you are gonna be living the struggle with these eleven inches."

Despite her best effort, Regina immediately got aroused. Her nipples were as hard as her box was moist. "Whatever, boy. You keep trying to impress people with these sizable objects, but you seem to forget that bigger doesn't always mean better."

As Mike headed back to the kitchen, he announced over his shoulder that dinner would be served in five minutes and that he expected dessert immediately thereafter. Regina couldn't help but blush.

MEANWHILE…

"Un-uh! What you mean, 'she ain't here'?" Kim asked. She was standing in the foyer of Kevin and Regina's house, having just bogarted her way in after Kevin answered the door.

"Please, Kim, won't you come in? I wouldn't want you standing out on the porch waiting for an invitation like everyone else does." Kevin knew his words were dripping with sarcasm, and that was fine with him. Of all of Regina's friends, Kim was the one he least trusted. She had never really done anything harmful to speak of, but Kevin just got the sense that Kim was always plotting or scheming. He couldn't look at her for too long, though, because she was fine as hell. Regina would kick his ass if she ever found out that Kevin had actually imagined himself making love to Kim while he and Regina were getting it on. He remembered those times vividly because he'd tried to murder that pussy.

"Well, why are you up in here all half-dressed? You expecting company?"

Kevin moved toward the front door to get this beautiful demon out of his house. *This is how people get caught up. Not recognizing a trick because it's dressed up to look like a treat*, thought Kevin. *Nobody dangles a brown apple or banana in front of you if they want you to take a bite. They dangle a nice, firm, beautifully colored piece of fruit in front of you...one that looks too irresistible to pass up. It looks good, it feels good, heck it even smells good. Then BAM! One bite and the rotten flesh is in your mouth, down your throat, and coursing through your system.* "No, Kimberly. If you must know, I just got finished working out and was about to jump in the shower. I'll be sure and tell Gina you stopped by."

"Damn, a sistah can't get offered a drink of water or something? And you know good and well I don't go by *Kimberly*. My teachers and my doctors are the only ones who use that name. Are you trying to teach me something, Kevin? Or give me an exam?" Kim knew she was being risky, but she didn't care. Taking risks was what she did. *Shit, if Regina is too stupid to appreciate this fine-ass husband of hers, I don't mind doing the job.* Something was going on with Regina. She was distracted with Mike and had been for the last few weeks. Just like she'd done with their house a few moments ago, Kim would burst right on through the open door of Kevin and Regina's marriage. *And just like Kevin had opened the door to their home, dumb-ass Regina had opened the door to their relationship.*

"Only thing need to be examined around here is your head. Now like I said, I'll tell my *wife* – your *friend* – that you stopped by. If you'll excuse me, I've had a long day, and I have an early one tomorrow, so—"

"Yeah, Regina mentioned something about you working a lot of hours at the center. In fact, that's all she seems to do is complain about how you are never home. That's why I came by. I wanted to surprise my girl and keep her company, since I figured you wouldn't be here." Kim waited a beat before continuing. "Dang, that's weird, huh?"

Knowing he would regret it, Kevin asked the question anyway. "What's weird, Kimberly?" Maybe if he kept calling her that, she would get pissed enough to leave.

"It's just weird that Regina isn't here, and it's almost bedtime. Well, bedtime for corny people like y'all. Oh well, maybe she just went for a walk or something…to Alaska. But hey, who am I to be asking questions about y'all's happy home? Your *wife*…since you want to emphasize shit…could be at the mall buying you a gift or something. Or maybe not, since the mall closed hours ago. Who knows? Anyway, yeah…just tell her I stopped by."

Kevin noticed that Kim made a statement like she was about to leave, yet she hadn't moved a muscle. He cleared his throat. Still, no movement from Kim. He put his hand on the doorknob. She didn't even flinch. *Damn*, he thought. *What is up with this girl? And why did she come over here with that short, tight skirt on? Making her ass look good enough to wax. And that so-called shirt, which is nothing more than a piece of lace material that stops above her navel, barely covers the nipples on her braless titties.* Kevin didn't know if he was angrier at Kim for being a dirty-ass broad, Regina for not being home, or himself for not being able to stop his erection.

Kim was elated. She could almost hear what Kevin was thinking by the way his eyes slowly took in every centimeter of her body. *Team Kim, one; Team Kevin, zero!* "Dang, boy, what are you trying to do…stare my panties off? Never mind, I'm trippin'."

"Yes, you *are* trippin' because if you think for one minute—"

"I know, I'm trippin' because I know good and well I ain't got on no damn panties. See?" With that, Kim took a pink thong out of...well, Kevin had no idea where she'd taken it from. It seemed to him that it came out of thin air. He had not seen her reach into a purse, pocket, or anything else. "Boy, let me go. I got you up here all nervous and shit." Kim lightly glided her fingernails across Kevin's chest and down his arm as she slid out the door and transferred the pretty pink thong from her hand to Kevin's.

Before she made it down the walkway, Kim glanced back to see if her suspicion was right about Kevin. She almost high-fived herself when she saw that it was. He was still standing in the doorway with a hard dick, smelling her panties. She was so glad she followed her mind. As soon as she had left Fredericks, she removed the price tag from the thongs and sprayed it with Ralph Lauren Romance perfume. Operation Takedown was in full effect.

*****

"What do you mean, I can't say that? My answer is my answer. *The Godfather I, II,* and *III.*" Regan stubbornly folded her arms across her chest and looked to her sister for support. Regina wondered how their girls' night sessions often turned from lively debates, into matches that had to be refereed. And why was it always Kim getting into it with someone? This time, though, Regina could see Kim's point.

"Well, Regan, I do see what Kim is saying," Regina countered. We were playing Top Three, and for your movies you picked the same movie."

"But I didn't pick the same movie. There are three separate and distinct *Godfather* movies. Those three movies happen to be my top three faves of all time. I can do that. That's like saying all of the *Saw* or *Friday the 13th* movies are the same."

"*They ARE!*" Kim, Melissa, and Regina yelled in unison. Then all of the ladies, Regan included, shared a good, long laugh.

Kim gave Regan a light push on her arm. "Fine then, Regan, if you can't be any more creative than that, then we will accept your answer.

Okay, what about cars?"

Melissa spoke up first. "Nissan Maxima, Toyota Avalon, and the new Ford Taurus is nice. They are all cars known for dependability and resale value. Plus, all of them are stylish."

"Bore-ring!" Regina teased her friend. "Mine would be that Audi A7, the Infinity SUV, I think it is the QX80...and for my sporty moods, that SL Convertible Benz. All of them in either black or pearl white."

Kim was surprised. She didn't think Regina had even heard of those cars, much less liked them. "Okay, Regina, I see you. I'm going with the F Type S Jaguar, that Ferrari 430 Scuderia, and for my bummy days I can slouch around in that Mercedes truck, that G550. What about you, Regan? And you better not say a mountain bike, a tricycle and a unicycle."

"Ha, ha, very funny, Ms. Name-the-stuff-I'll-never-own. My three favorite cars – being realistic, unlike *some* people – would have to be the new Ford Mustang, because it is sporty and fun and an updated version of the classic, the BMW 5 series hybrid, because it is nice and comfortable, stylish, and eco-friendly, and the Cadillac Escalade, just because everyone needs an SUV. Okay, I went last, so my turn now since Kim took my turn. What about game shows?"

Melissa jumped up and down like she was actually a contestant. The girls, people at work, and even her family members often teased her about her love of games shows. She had actually been late to work on several occasions, trying to catch the last few minutes of some of her favorite game shows. Melissa almost thought she had died and gone to heaven when her local cable provider finally aired the GSN, the Game Show Network. "Okay, I'll do my best to narrow it down to three because there are the classics, and there are also the new ones. So if you want, I'll break it into two categories and name six shows."

"No!" everyone yelled at once.

"Because *Are You Smarter Than a 5ᵗʰ Grader* is good, but *1 vs. 100* is good, too. I really like that one because so many people have a chance to participate and win. Oh yeah, remember *Deal or No Deal*? Kim, didn't you go audition for that show? What ever happened with that?"

Kim and a few of her cousins had actually gone to an audition for *Deal or No Deal* several years ago. She even concocted a story about being an orphan and sleeping in her car as she worked her way through her last year of high school and then college. Kim thought about it briefly. *Those lames still didn't pick me even though I was energetic and everything! Oh well, their loss. They didn't pick me, and look what happened...the corny-ass show got cancelled.* "Girl, I don't recall that. I generally don't have time for games. And never mind me, you're supposed to be naming your top three favorite game shows of all time. Was that your list, or was that your slick way of naming extra shows?"

"Okay, okay, I have to say that my all, all, ALL-time faves would have to include *Family Feud*. I mean, I've watched that show from the original host, Richard Dawson, to the current host, the handsome Steve Harvey. Let's see, I would have to say *The Price Is Right*, and my third all-time favorite game show would have to be *Jeopardy*."

"You are too old for your age, Melissa," Regina teased. "Okay, I'll go next. My favorite game shows would be *Love Connection*, *The Newly-wed Game*, and *Whose Line Is It Anyway*. Watching that show made me realize how talented Wayne Brady is. I love him. I even bought his CD."

"Who is Wayne Brady?" Kim asked. And his CD must not go too hard because I've never heard it on the radio."

Regina didn't know how she still managed to be amazed by Kim's ignorance. "Kim, saying a musician or their music is not hot because it isn't on the radio is as silly as saying something is true because you read it on the internet. That's silly."

Regan, never straying far from teacher mode, had to step in. "I know what you are trying to say, Reggie, but that is not a good example. Kim, what you said is like saying a certain type of food must not be good because they don't sell it at McDonalds or Burger King...and those are the only places you eat. You would be making a judgment based upon your limited experience. You usually just listen to hip-hop. They would not play Wayne Brady's music on the station you listen to. I'm sorry, Regina, I just wanted to clarify."

Kim gave Regan a dismissive wave, as if to say "child, please" and took another sip of her Nuvo. "I don't really play games or watch games.

If I had to pick, though, I would say *The Joker's Wild* because I remember my grandmother watching that show, *Wheel of Fortune* because that chick that turns the letters wears some nice dresses sometimes, and *Lingo* just 'cause my word game be on point, so I'm good at that. Your turn, Ms. Regan."

"That's easy. My all-time favorite game shows would be *Pyramid*, *The Price Is Right*, and *Who Wants to Be a Millionaire*. Let's do candy bars," Regan suggested.

Kim was bored. "Wasn't there a candy bar called Zero? Well then, that's it. This game is corny, and plus, Regan, you are the one who picked game shows. It's someone else's turn."

"Fine," Regan pouted. "What top three do you want to list, Kim?"

"The top three reasons this game is over," Kim said as she rolled her eyes.

Melissa chimed in, "How about actors or actresses?"

"Boo! Whack! Ho Hum! That's too close to movies," Kim retorted. "And we had a hard enough time doing movies."

Melissa couldn't resist the opportunity to jump back on the movie bandwagon. "I forgot some of the best tearjerkers ever. Remember *Beaches*? And what about *Joy Luck Club* and *My Sister's Keeper*? Oh my goodness, did you guys see *American Crime*? That was based on a true story. That was a good movie, but I don't think I could watch it again."

"Yes, Melissa, we all saw that," an agitated Kim answered. "Denzel portrayed Frank Lucas. But how did you manage to get us back on movies again? You had your turn. Dang, you always overdoing stuff. Get it together." Kim was getting irritated with Melissa.

"Nooo, *you* get it together, Kim. The movie you are referring to is *American GANGSTER*. *American Crime* was about this sadistic witch who had like five or six kids. Well, this couple ended up leaving their two daughters with her for a few months, while they traveled with this carnival that the dad worked for. This lady and her kids, even kids from the neighborhood, were abusive in every way to the one sister. When I say unspeakable horrors...I won't spoil the end in case any of you want to watch it, but—"

"Girl, ain't nobody tryna watch no sad shit like that," Kim cut in. "Why would you think that would be a good idea? To sit up and watch something you *know* is gonna make you cry or mad is just dumb. You supposed to be the happy, positive, perky one. I'm surprised you don't watch cartoons."

As usual, Kim and Melissa were about to have their own personal war. "How about top three world inspirators or influencers?" Regina offered.

Kim expelled a deep sigh as she shifted in her seat. "Fine, but after this, I'm done for real. First, I'm going to say Barack Obama, for obvious reasons. My second would be Malcolm X because he was smart, proud, and he didn't take any shit. My third most influential person would have to be Jesus."

Melissa wiped her mouth, as she spit out some of her tea. "Jesus *WHO*? Not that one kid who graduated from high school when he was just sixteen? Sure, he was smart, but I didn't realize he had that much of an impact on you, Kim. And you poor thing, his name is *spelled* J-E-S-U-S, but it's *pronounced* hey-SOOS!"

"Uhhh...I'm talking about God's son, Jesus Christ, you idiot!" Everyone sat up straight and stared at Kim like they were seeing her for the very first time. Kim decided to elaborate so these broads would stop looking at her like she had two heads. "I just don't know of anyone who has been more studied, debated, and followed than Jesus. No matter what a person's religious beliefs are, it is hard to deny the influence and impact of Jesus on the world. Now can we move on? Please?"

Melissa decided to go next. "This is actually a tough one for me. There are so many people I admire who have impacted this world. I mean, when I look at it from the standpoint of people who have changed all of our lives, I think of people like Thomas Edison, obviously for inventions like the electric light bulb and sound motion picture. Then there is Benjamin Banneker, who invented the first clock in the United States. How life changing was *that*? Oh yes, Alexander Graham Bell... he invented the telephone. Imagine the world without telephones. The automobile was obviously an immeasurable invention. Although we don't know who invented the first car, we know that the first car to use gasoline was invented in 1885 by Karl Benz. That must've been a good year, because Gottlieb Daimler and Wilhelm Maybach put their engine into a stagecoach that year. Then in 1889, they invented a vehicle with a four-speed transmission." Melissa had been talking so much, she had not even noticed the other ladies looking at her in amazement.

"I'm the teacher, and yet I feel pretty darn uneducated right about now," Regan said as she sat up in her seat.

"Yeah, Melissa," Kim chimed in. "How do you know all that stuff? You have actually inspired me to respect history more than ever. I think my next car will be a Maybach."

Regina laughed and couldn't resist making a comment, as Melissa and Regan looked at Kim and shook their heads. "Girl, please, you *might* get a May*TAG*, but that's about it."

"Okay, Regina, you got jokes. Laugh now, girl, but we will see who has the last laugh." Kim hoped that she sounded just like she intended to sound, as if she was only half-joking. "All of you heffas are on a roll today. Hurry up, whoever is next, so we can get this stupid mess over with. So that was your list, Melissa?"

"Well, no, I'm just saying, all of those people influenced…heck, they actually revolutionized the way of life for the entire world. But that was on the invention side of things. So my top three, for purposes of this discussion, would be Oprah Winfrey, John F. Kennedy, and of course, Robert. How about you, Regan?"

Regina spoke up before Regan could start her list. "Melissa, you list both Kennedy brothers as being in your list of top three most influential people?"

"Huh? No! Not Robert Kennedy, silly…Robert Kelly!"

Now it was Kim's turn to be stunned. "Bitch, I know good and well you don't think R. Kelly's pedophile-ish ass is a major influence. The only thing that nigga be doing is trying to influence middle school girls to come to his hotel room. That fool be sitting across the street from playgrounds offering candy to little girls. To be honest, I'm surprised at you, Melissa. As goody-two-shoes as you act, I can't understand your obsession with R. Kelly."

"Oh my goodness, are you serious right now?" Melissa stood up. "First of all, Rob has not been convicted of any crime against children… *ever*."

"Oh, he's *Rob* now, huh?" Kim shook her head.

"Well no matter what you think you know, or whatever rumors you have heard, no real music lover can deny the genius of R. Kelly. He is a writer, a singer, a producer and more. That whole *Trapped in the Closet* series was masterful and supremely creative. I consider him influential because of the impact that he has had on the music world. You love Michael Jackson, right? And one of your favorite songs is "You Are Not Alone", correct?"

"Yes…so?"

"I bet you don't know who wrote that song?" Melissa challenged.

"Betcha I do," Kim defiantly responded. "The King of Pop wrote and sang the mess out of that song."

"I hate to burst your bubbles – no pun intended on the monkey – but Rob wrote that song." Melissa proudly made that announcement as if she had written the song herself.

"Whatever, Melissa. You can sweat that nigga all you want. You are about twenty years too old for his liking, so you might as well keep it moving," Kim declared.

Regan folded her arms across her chest and tapped her foot up and down, pretending to be anxiously awaiting her turn. "Well, ladies, if I can interrupt, this is a tough category. Let's see, Nelson Mandela for sure. He was so influential because he was so patient, wise, and forgiving. He is known by and relatable to our generation as well as our parents' generation, and also kids today. A very inspirational man. I think Oprah is very influential. And for my third person, I'd have to say Michael Jackson. Love him or hate him, there is no denying his influence. While Michael Jackson was all the rave like Elvis and The Beatles before him, he was something more. He actually changed and elevated music, videos, and live performance. Now you talk about a musical genius, Melissa. It would have to be Michael Jackson. And one could make a valid argument that he impacted and influenced far more people than R. Kelly. Michael was more universal."

Regina couldn't let this conversation end just yet. "Well, if you wanna talk about a musical genius, you have to name Prince. He plays several instruments, sings like nobody else, and has a swag that can never be imitated. Prince is cold!"

Never one to miss an opportunity to chime in, Kim spoke up again. "Well, we weren't listing the top three musical geniuses. That list would include Kanye West, Stevie Wonder, Carlos Santana, Prince, Eminem, Elton John, Jimi Hendrix and on and on. Lots of people have great musical talent, but that doesn't mean they are inspirational or that they've necessarily influenced society. So do you want to make any changes to your top three?"

"My list is fine." Regan rolled her eyes, adding, "And it's staying just the way it is. I'm just tripping that you guys don't get how Michael Jackson influenced so many aspects of millions of people's lives. And don't forget all the artists and musicians he has influenced, everyone from Usher to Chris Brown."

Regina had to jump in again. "Well if that's the case, you would have to list James Brown because that is who Michael Jackson was influenced by."

"Okay, we get it guys. Can we move on?" Kim was growing more impatient by the second. "Regina, how about wrapping this up for us. Who are your top three?"

"Princess Diana would be one. I am not sure about her political power, if she even had any. But she was extremely influential. She had so many people trying to copy everything from her haircut, to her clothing, and even her engagement ring. People could not get enough of her, and it seems like the world took a collective gasp at the news of her tragic and sudden death. I'm surprised nobody listed him already, so my second person would have to be Abraham Lincoln. Clearly, the Emancipation Proclamation changed the course of American life forever. Maya Angelou would probably be my third pick. She seemed to be loved and admired by everyone who met her. And to read her work made almost everyone feel like they really did know her. Having been violated as a child, Ms. Angelou didn't speak for five or six years. Then, once she did, what beauty, dressed in love, wisdom, and forgiveness, poured out. I get chills just thinking about her."

Kim was impatient as ever. "Well I may not know why the caged bird sang, but I know this eagle is tired of playing with y'all turkeys. Are we done now?"

Regan remembered something as everyone was preparing to leave. "Oh, really quick, I just thought of someone who really influenced and changed society. Dick Clark. He provided such a platform for all kinds of artists to be exposed to the masses. But I actually agree with Kim that we need to wrap things up. Although it was different getting together for brunch for our 'girls' night', it was kind of fun. It's kind of cool that we have the rest of our Saturday to run errands or do whatever."

"Dick Clark is cool, but if you are gonna say him, then you have to say Don Cornelius, too. Don was the first black person to create, produce, and host his own television show. That's huge! Plus, he gave us the Soul Train Line. That is universal." Kim wanted to be the one who ended the gathering, so she had to add her commentary.

Melissa agreed that getting together for brunch was a good idea, although she was annoyed with Kim for being the only one who had any alcohol while they were together. "Some people might have to go take a nap since they were drinking Nuvo, and it's barely noon." Everyone knew that Melissa was referring to Kim, just like they knew that Kim couldn't care less what Melissa said or thought about her.

Regina was also glad that the ladies had gotten together early this Saturday because Kevin had been gone since early that morning, and she didn't expect him home until later in the evening. That gave her plenty of time to enjoy a matinee at her favorite new movie theater... Casa de Mike!

✶✶✶✶✶

"This has been a long, exhausting, fun, much-needed day," Regina said. She gave Melissa a side-hug as they walked through the mall.

"Oh my goodness, yes; I totally agree. It has been ages since just the two of us hung out together. I really appreciate you coming to help me find a dress for the funeral. It is still hard to believe that my aunt is gone. She was not sick at all. In fact, she was the picture of health. My Aunt Ginny had never picked up a cigarette or a drink in her entire life. She exercised regularly and ate healthy, organic foods. And she was only fifty-eight years old! That is so scary, Regina, and what's worse is that Ginny was my dad's only sister. It's hard for me because she showered me with the love and warmth that my mom never gave me. And it's hard for my dad as well. He has nobody now because both of his parents are gone, and now so is his only sibling."

Regina stopped and faced Melissa. "No thanks needed, girl. I know that you would be there for me in a heartbeat. It's just how friends do." Regina then posed the question to Melissa, "Do you know what else friends do?"

Melissa looked puzzled. "No, what?"

"They treat their friends to dinner after dragging them around the mall all day," Regina joked to her friend.

"What time is it?" Melissa asked as she checked her watch. "You are *right*. I've had you out all day. Come on, let's go eat right now…my treat. What do you have a taste for?"

"What do I have a taste for? Let me see…this bench right here, that door over there, that big fountain over there in the middle of the mall. I could eat a horse right about now." Regina knew she was exaggerating, but she was really hungry.

"Well, let's go to the food court. I'm sure we can find some horse, cat, dog, and some of everything else there. Sound good?"

Melissa and Regina headed off to the food court and then decided from where they wanted to order. Regina offered to get the food while Melissa took their bags and purses and found a seat. Not only did she want to be supportive of Melissa and not allow her to pay, but it was a perfect opportunity to check her phone. All day while they were shopping, her phone kept blowing up. She knew it was Mike because they had been sexting all last night and earlier this morning. Kevin had even asked Regina last night if everything was okay and Regina had told him that Melissa was just texting to vent about her Aunt Ginny's unexpected death.

its nice u r hanging with melissa. shes a cool chick. but would u rather look 4 dresses wit her or get undressed wit me…

Regina just shook her head. She would respond to Mike later. She could not get distracted by him right now. She needed to focus on Melissa. When she got back to the table, Regina gently stroked and patted her friend's hand as Melissa relayed various stories about Aunt Ginny. Before they knew it, the ladies had sat at the table for over two hours, resting, talking, and reflecting. Since Melissa seemed to have more to get off of her chest, Regina offered to get them something sweet from the pastry eatery. Melissa yelled after Regina that her phone was yet again vibrating, but Regina had walked away too quickly. She hadn't heard Melissa any more than she heard her phone notifying her that she was receiving a text.

Melissa glanced at the cell phone buzzing on the table. She had never known Regina to have so much activity on her cell phone. Knowing it was none of her concern, Melissa pushed Regina's phone back to her side of the table. A few seconds later, the phone buzzed again, and Melissa couldn't believe her eyes when she looked down and saw Mike's name. Why in the world would Mike be texting Regina?

Regina returned to the table. "Here you go. A mocha-caramel-choco-something for you, a lemon tea for me, and a cinnamon bun for us to share." Regina placed everything on the table and sat down.

"Thanks, girl. I need to call my sister and tell her I'll get the kids in the morning instead of tonight. Can I please use your phone since my stupid battery is dead?"

"Of course! Here, sweetie." Regina slid her phone across the table to Melissa, not giving a second thought to the fact that Mike had been sending her explicit text messages all day. Melissa let out a gasp as she slid the lock off of Regina's phone to make her call. There was a picture of a penis with a text that read:

u can ignore ME but I bet u cant ignore HIM

In an instant, Regina knew that she'd made a terrible mistake. She'd been too caught up in the moment and allowed Melissa to use her phone without thinking. In a millisecond, Regina snatched her phone from Melissa's hand, but it was too late. The text and picture had been seen. The cat was out of the bag, the fat lady had sung, the curtain was pulled away from the wizard, the gig was up!

"Regina?!"

"Melissa, I already know. You can't say anything that I haven't already thought about. I know I'm wrong. I know I have a good husband, and I know that there can't be a serious future for Mike and me. It's just that…"

"Shhh," Melissa said as she came around the table and sat next to Regina. She faced her friend and took both of Regina's hands and clasped them in her own. "You don't ever have to defend or justify your actions to me. I love you, Regina, and there is nothing you can do about it. Now tell me, why is there a picture of Mike's penis on your phone? What's going on, honey?"

Over the next forty-five minutes, Regina told Melissa about her dealings with Mike, from their elevator kiss up to the current texts and picture.

Melissa hugged her friend tightly. "I understand. Regina, you are just caught up right now. As your friend who genuinely loves you, I would be remiss if I didn't tell you that you were skating on thin ice. I don't want to see you fall and drown. Listen, I'm very aware of the names people call me, like 'Mother Melissa' and 'goody-two-shoes.' Believe me when I tell you that I'm not a saint by any stretch of the imagination. Even if I was, I'm fully aware that every saint has a past, and every sinner has a future. Yes, I pray and offer praise and thanks to my Lord and Savior Jesus Christ. I will never apologize for that. But that does not make me feel like I'm better than anyone. I'm not a follower of Christ because of how good I am; I'm a follower of Christ because of how needy I am. I'm a follower of Christ because I'm living proof of His redemptive power. You've met my parents. Most people think that my dad is really laid back and that my mom is a strong woman. The truth is that my dad is weak and cowardly, while my mom is mean, domineering, and judgmental. My earliest memories…heck, my *only* memories of my mom are those in which she is being critical and overbearing. I remember once when I was maybe five or six years old, I was so excited to give my mom the card I made for her in school. Instead of hugging me and putting the drawing on the refrigerator like most mothers would do, mine showed me all the places where I colored outside of the lines. I was devastated. I went crying to my dad, and he told me then – just what he still tells me to this day – that 'that's just your mother's way.' I learned very quickly to be a straight-A student. Early on, when I got a B, my mother let me know how stupid I was. She let me know that I was a disappointment when I was born a female instead of a male, and I am still a disappointment now. It's funny because even when I started getting all As my mom was not impressed or satisfied. She would tell me those are the grades I should have been getting anyway, so I wasn't doing anything special. My hair was never styled right. My butt has always been too big. My skin was never smooth enough. And I certainly was never as pretty, smart, or talented as any of her friends' children. I really can't tell you which was worse, being criticized and oppressed by my mother, or not being defended or protected by my father! Growing up, I felt that I was never good enough and that I was not important enough for anyone to care about me. I carried those messages into my teenage years, and it cost me dearly. I was depressed and withdrawn. I was a perfect shell on the outside and an empty void on the inside. I just performed like a programmed robot because I'd learned that feelings and expectations would result in great disappointment. By the time I got to college, I had decided that I would live life on my terms. My mom was no longer there to critique my every move. I was free from the sphere of her influence…or so I thought. I dressed like I wanted, did any and every thing to my hair, shopped and bought like I wanted, and lived by my own rules—which was to have no rules at all. Although I did not live with my mother while I was at school, she lived in my head. I was so busy changing my outward behavior that I neglected to change the taped messages in my head. Those messages told me that I was without value, not worthy of respect or protection, and would never be good enough. If my own mother did not think I could amount to anything, then why would anyone else? I allowed myself to be used by men, I abused my body, and I even tried to kill myself. That was my lowest point. One of my roommates found me, and I spent almost three weeks in the hospital for psychiatric care. It was helpful to be sure, but the turning point in my life came after a visit from one of the ministers who came to the hospital a few times a week. I began to read and eventually study the Bible. That gave me a sense of hope. It gave me a message that I was wonderfully made and that even though I did not know Him, Someone loved me enough to die for me. So that newfound hope, coupled with my medication and counseling, were the beginning of my road to recovery. Before that, I had said and done some terrible things. I'd been as uncaring as my mother. I asked my parents to seek counseling, and they have refused. That's fine; it's their choice. So for me to remain healthy, I can only take my parents in small doses. I can't change them, and I don't try. I just look at them as people who give all that they are equipped to give. They can't do any better than they know. I don't blame them for not showing me love and protection any more than I blame a first grader for not knowing geometry. A person cannot be expected to demonstrate lessons they have not learned, or have no capacity to retain. Why am I telling you this? Well, I was seeking something, Regina. I was insecure and was trying to meet a legitimate need in an illegitimate manner. That is what you seem to be doing now. You are justified to want time with and attention from your husband. It's natural to feel flattered when a man compliments you and finds you beautiful and attractive. Your needs are legit, my friend. You just have to be careful to not worsen your situation with the manner in which you get your needs met."

Having listened to Melissa, a teary-eyed Regina finally spoke. "Wow, Mel, I had no idea you went through so much. Thank you for sharing all of that. I will be careful, I promise. Everything you are saying is correct. But to be honest, I just don't really care right now. I mean, I care about what you are saying; I just don't care about the consequences at this point. I know I should, but I don't. I seem to constantly be angry with Kevin, and at the same time, having the time of my life with Mike. That makes me horrible, I know. But right now, I just accept the fact that I'm a horrible person."

Melissa stood up. "Now that's where you are wrong, you're not a horrible person. You are a wonderful person who is not making the best decision right now. But hey, who among us, right? Okay now, get up, girl, and give me a hug so we can let these people close this mall. You're going to be alright. And please know that I'm here for you...better yet, I'm here *with* you, Regina."

"Thank you, Melissa, for not making me feel dirty or judging me. This trip was supposed to be so I could support and encourage you, and here *you* are supporting and encouraging *me*."

"No thanks needed. What did Dionne, Elton, Gladys and Stevie say? 'That's What Friends Are For.' I love you, Regina."

"I love you too, Melissa. Have a good night. And thanks again."

4 WEEKS AGO

"No, I completely understand… Brother, that goes without saying… Plan? Naw man, I don't have a plan. Truth be told, I'm shocked, although I'm not surprised—if that even makes sense…I just appreciate the risk you took by letting me know…Hey, I'm gonna jump off of here and go handle this business. Wish me luck…Yeah okay, you got jokes. I'll holla, and yes I will most definitely keep you posted." With that, Kevin slammed the cordless telephone on the counter before flinging it across the room. He didn't have time to worry about the broken pieces right now. Kevin made a call from his cell phone, as he dashed out of the front door and headed to Ms. Martin's house.

Although the Martin household was about a twenty-minute drive from the Golden household, Kevin had made it in thirteen minutes. DeShawn was almost afraid to answer the door because whoever was banging on it seemed like they had a mission, and it did not seem friendly in nature. DeShawn's anxiety was only minimally quelled when he looked out of the living room window and saw Kevin's car parked in front of the house. Although the visitor was benevolent, it did not appear – from the way he was knocking – that the message would be the same.

DeShawn yelled upstairs, "Moms, Mr. Kevin is here." DeShawn opened the door and began to greet their guest, "Hey, Mr. Kevin, how's it—"

The look on Kevin's face spoke volumes, and after one glance, DeShawn knew exactly how things were – terrible. Standing on the porch behind Kevin was DeShawn's attorney, Mr. Thomas.

"Well don't just stand there looking like y'all just saw the boogeyman. Come on in," said Ms. Martin, who had come down the stairs and was standing behind her son. DeShawn was so focused on Kevin that he had not seen or heard his mother. "Can I get you two a cold beverage? We have soda and bottled water?" Ms. Martin offered.

"Nothing for me, please," Mr. Thomas declined.

"Yes, please, for me," Kevin answered. "Do you have anything stronger than soda?" Kevin needed to calm his nerves.

Ms. Martin furrowed her eyebrows as she shook her head. "I don't know what kind of woman you think I am or what kind of house of ill repute this is, but I don't just keep liquor stockpiled in my home." Ms. Martin could see that her attempt to lighten Kevin's mood by playfully chastising him was not working. She figured things must be worse than she imagined. *Mr. Kevin and Mr. Thomas both showing up on my doorstep unannounced? Kevin might not be the only one in need of a drink stronger than soda.*

"I'm sorry, Ms. Martin. DeShawn did mention to me that you said you didn't like to drink. There is just a lot weighing on my mind right now." Kevin had not intended to be rude, but he was more focused on delivering this news about DeShawn instead of Ms. Martin's views about alcohol.

Ms. Martin softened her face, as she could clearly see that Kevin appeared to be more than a little agitated. "Have a seat, and I'll see if I can find something in one of these cabinets. Maybe there is something in there from back in the day." With that Ms. Martin disappeared through the doorway and into the kitchen. She yelled back toward the living room where the men were seated, "What's your pleasure, Mr. Kevin? I found a few things in here, although your guess is as good as mine as to how this stuff made its way in here. If you like tequila, we have some Jose Cuervo and some 1800. There is a little bit of Jack Daniels whiskey in here. Let's see, what else? Oh, here is some Absolut if you want vodka. If you prefer rum, then I can offer some Captain Morgan or Bacardi. Whew, I didn't realize there was so much stuff in here. Beats me how all these spirits got up in this house. See why you gotta stay prayed up? What's it gonna be?" Ms. Martin was concerned about the news she would receive when she walked back into the living room. She knew that she was talking more than necessary, maybe her way of prolonging the inevitable.

DeShawn had to almost bite his tongue to keep from bursting out laughing. He knew that his mother was stalling to avoid hearing whatever it was that the attorney and Mr. Kevin had to say. DeShawn had also long known about his mother's stash, but he never said anything since she wanted to pretend that she never drank alcohol.

Kevin called toward the kitchen, "Whatever you bring will be just fine, Ms. Martin." A few moments later, Ms. Martin returned to the living room with two medium-sized glasses containing brown liquid.

"Here you go, Mr. Kevin. You looked like you could use something to take the edge off, so I just poured you some brandy. There was some Courvoisier that was way back in the back. Now that stuff right there, that goes down your throat smooth as velvet." Mr. Thomas, DeShawn and Kevin all looked at Ms. Martin as if she had just sprouted horns. "From what I've been told," Ms. Martin cleared her throat and added. "I remember one night, back when I used to clean over at the country club, I tasted what had to have been liquid gold. It was an unfinished drink in the most exquisite tulip glass I'd ever seen. The bartender told me it was a brandy...well, Cognac if you're fancy, called Remy Martin Louis XIII. That little drink was $450! I was told the bottle cost $7,000." Ms. Martin slapped her forehead. She was doing it again, engaging in nervous idle chatter in an effort to avoid the matter at hand.

"The Cognac will be just fine, Ms. Martin, but I don't need two glasses, ma'am." Kevin reached for one of the two glasses in Ms. Martin's hand.

"Well if what you have to say is as upsetting as you look, I figured I'd better pour a little nip for myself...just in case."

Kevin downed his drink in one huge gulp. Kevin and Mr. Thomas had talked on the phone during the drive to the Martin's home. They had agreed that even though Mr. Thomas was DeShawn's attorney, Kevin would be better suited to do most of the talking. Although DeShawn was courteous toward his attorney, it was apparent that he didn't have the level of respect for him that he had for Kevin. Kevin believed Mr. Thomas was a fine enough attorney, but this was just another case for him. There was a professional bond, but not a personal relationship.

Kevin spoke up. "Ms. Martin and DeShawn, I have some bad news. DeShawn is going to be arrested, probably within the hour. I won't get into how I know that information, but I have it on good authority."

Ms. Martin burst into tears. DeShawn was stunned. He was both angry and scared.

"Mr. Kevin, that doesn't make any sense. I told you and Moms exactly what happened. I told you too, Mr. Thomas. How could you let this happen? I didn't do anything wrong. Okay yeah, I made some bad choices by drinking and lying about Josh's parents being home. But I didn't do anything that nobody else there wasn't doing. I really don't see why or how this is such a big deal. It's actually kinda ticking me off right about now."

Kevin scratched his head and then looked directly into DeShawn's eyes. "I know, man. It's a tough deal. She says you raped her, though, so—"

"That is some bullshit!" DeShawn yelled, cutting Kevin off. He stood up and began pacing back and forth across the living room, punching one of his fists into the opposite palm. "There is no way I raped that girl! Everybody knows that I didn't have sex with that pam. She is the one who started everything. Then she got mad when I said I was not taking her to a dance. I should have known her crazy ass was up to no good."

Mr. Thomas spoke up. "I know you're upset, DeShawn, and I believe you. But it is not about what I think or believe. At this point, there are enough people who believe there is enough evidence to support Hilary's allegation against you."

"He's right, man," Kevin chimed in. "And to keep it one hundred with you man, if I did not know you, I might think there was evidence to support what Hilary was saying. You have to remember that there is physical evidence that indicates that the two of you had sex. She has a shirt with your semen on it, and there is audio of her screaming at you. It looks pretty bad, DeShawn."

"Okay, Mr. Kevin, I hear what you saying. So what do we do now? She told her lies, so I need to be able to tell what really happened."

"Let me tell you all what is about to happen," Mr. Thomas said, looking back and forth between DeShawn and his mother. "Like Mr. Golden said, the police are coming here to arrest you. You will be taken to a juvenile facility, and you will remain there until the decision is made about whether to adjudicate your case or if you should be cleared and released. Based upon the seriousness of the charges, there will likely be adjudication. Unlike adult criminal cases which are typically heard in a Court of Common Pleas in front of a jury, your case will be heard in juvenile court in front of a judge. The judge will determine if you are responsible. That is akin to being guilty in Common Pleas."

Ms. Martin's silent tears turned into wailing sobs. In her mind, Mr. Thomas' words meant that she would be was losing her only living child. She knew that DeShawn was not a perfect kid, but he certainly was no rapist. If he said that girl was lying, then she was lying. No, this was not going to happen, Ms. Martin decided. She was not going to sit by and let her son be vilified in the local media, having his reputation and future tarnished. Ms. Martin decided at that moment that she had cried her last tear of despair over this situation. She would let Mr. Thomas and the juvenile justice system go through their processes, and meanwhile she would place this awful, heavy burden exactly where it belonged – in God's hands. An inexplicable peace came over Ms. Martin, and she began to wipe her tears. She stood up in the middle of the living room and stretched out both arms with her hands open wide. Mr. Thomas took her right hand, DeShawn took her left, and Kevin took DeShawn and Mr. Thomas' free hands.

"Alright, everyone," Ms. Martin said. "We need to look to the authority who is greater than any prosecutor, judge, or lie from the pits of hell." Everyone lowered their heads and tried to block out the knocking on the door as Ms. Martin began. "Dear Heavenly Father…"

*****

"I see why this is called a garden bathtub. It's so relaxing and inviting. And the way you have it set up in here, with the candles and the music piping through the walls…man, I could do this every single night." Regina was up to her neck in bubbles and surrounded by a least twenty-five candles as she luxuriated in Mike's expansive tub in his massive bathroom. She loved the way the tub sat on a huge platform in the middle of the bathroom. She had walked three steps up from the floor onto the platform which had some plants, tons of candles, and a remote control for the in-house stereo and the large television.

Initially, when Mike had sent a text to Regina asking if she could get out of the house, she'd told him she didn't think it would be a good idea. That was two days ago. Then, after having gone over forty-eight hours and not seeing her husband at all, she sent Mike a text asking if his offer was still good, as she could use some company. Mike was all too happy to oblige. He told Regina to come over directly from work, and he'd take care of the rest. Guessing her sizes, Mike left Bright Star early that day and went shopping. He purchased bra, panties, and an outfit for Regina. For good measure, he also purchased a pair of Ugg slippers. When she arrived at his house, their dinner was simmering and a hot, steamy bathtub filled with bubbles awaited her.

"Do you use this tub often, or is this reserved for all of your Bright Star conquests?" Regina asked.

Mike really didn't use that bathtub very often, but neither did anyone else. He actually had it built to impress people. "Neither, if you must know. I just liked the bathroom in the model home and told them to build the same exact one for this house."

"Well if this was my bathroom, I'd take a bath every single evening. This tub is just so deep. I love it."

"I like the deep, too," Mike smirked.

Regina stretched her arms above her head and let the warm water run over her face, neck, and breasts as she squeezed out the bath sponge. "Uhh, excuse me. What exactly are you doing?" Regina asked as she noticed Mike getting undressed. "I thought you said it was time to eat."

"Exactly!" With that, Mike finished undressing and joined Regina in the bathtub.

*****

Thankfully, everyone was in a light mood for this girls' night out.

Nobody discussed work, gossiped about anyone, or got into any heated debates. In fact, everyone was mostly on the same page, which was a rarity lately.

"Hey, did you guys hear those ladies on the radio the other day?" Melissa asked. "It was pretty disgusting. They were promoting their business, which is a consulting firm teaching women how to be appropriate mistresses, or sideline chicks as they called them."

Kim chimed in first. "I heard them, but I didn't think it was disgusting at all. I thought they were smart for capitalizing on something that is going to go on whether they are in business or not. Actually, they are doing a service to married couples because they are teaching the 'other woman' to not have false expectations and basically to just stay in her lane."

"Yeah," Regan offered. "But what they are doing is promoting and encouraging infidelity. I can't see how that is respectful at all. Why can't they promote self-worth and self-love, which will in turn promote respect for other people and their relationships?"

Regina spoke up. "Well, even if those ladies did not have their particular business or consulting firm, infidelity would still exist. So they are just turning a profit based on the decisions of other people. They aren't going out telling people to cheat, they are just saying since you have decided to do that, here is the best way to go about it." Regina did not want to sound like she was defending infidelity, but her views had changed about a great number of things over the past few weeks. And now more than ever, she could relate to the importance of the 'other person' not overstepping his or her boundaries and not having unrealistic expectations.

Melissa knew Regina's situation, but she was still shocked to hear her friend's cold outlook. "So according to that line of thinking, we should give demonstrations to people on how to shoot heroin? Because people do that anyway, so we may as well show them how to do it correctly, right?"

"No, that's not the same thing." Kim was actually speaking in an even, conversational tone, not her usual argumentative or loud tone. "Using heroin is illegal. Having an affair is usually a moral issue instead of a legal one. I just believe that it's not up to us to govern consenting people's behavior, especially when that behavior is not against the law. Shit, people have been cheating since the beginning of time, just like they have been getting drunk, lying, smoking, and everything else that appeals to the senses. As long as human beings exist, so will certain behaviors. Why not capitalize on it? These big-ass corporations do it all the time. You can't possibly think that they can't find a cure for AIDS or cancer? With all of the medical advances we've made in society! But if there were a cure for those terrible diseases, that would put a lot of these pharmaceutical companies in the red, wouldn't it? The point I'm trying to make is that everyone is always trying to benefit off of other people."

Regina agreed with Kim, "Yeah, just look at 9/11. As tragic as that was for this entire country, there were scam artists who had people sending them money that was supposedly going to be distributed to the victims' families. There was one idiot who pocketed over one million dollars! People just seem to want to profit from any situation, no matter how sad, immoral, or illegal the situation may be. It's sad, but it's a fact."

"Exactly, Regina," said Kim, supporting Regina's point. "People are going to do whatever they can to turn a profit, to make that money. If I'm doing me and not bothering anything else, my motto is I'm not a wrist, so quit watching me."

After a beat, everyone roared in laughter. Melissa was the first one to gain her composure. "Kim, that was corny, but I have a good one. I'm not Kidd, so don't try to play me." Melissa was practically giving herself high-fives, while the other ladies just shook their heads.

"I ain't no circus, so don't try to clown me." Regan was just as proud with her input as Melissa had been with hers.

Kim spoke up again. "I ain't no horse so quit riding my back."

"Okay, Kim, that was pretty good," Regina nodded.

"Well, thank you, Regina. But I ain't Keith, so quit sweatin' me." Kim said as she winked at Regina.

"You must be a travel agent, 'cause you trippin'," Regina retorted.

"Okay that's different than the type of sayings we are doing," Regan corrected.

Regina gave her little sister a look of warning. "How about this? I ain't no cigarette, so don't burn me."

Regan smacked her lips. "Ugh, 'Gina, I ain't slim so quit doing me shady."

"Ohhh…I got one, I got one." Melissa was in her game-show mode, as she was practically jumping up and down with excitement. "You must be a ship because you cuss like a sailor."

Kim playfully rolled her eyes at Melissa. "You must be lost, 'cause some village is missing its idiot. Did you not hear what Regan just said? You are supposed to say 'I ain't no *blank*, so don't *blank* me'."

"Okay, Kim, I ain't no stove so quit getting me heated." Melissa was thinking quick on her feet now.

"I ain't from Miami, but I bring the heat." Regina put up her hands in a boxing position.

"You sholl do bring the heat…with that hot-ass breath. And your teeth bring the yellow, too." Kim could not resist that one.

Regan lifted her glass, "Now I'll drink to that." Everyone touched glasses as they giggled and returned to their food.

Regina was the first one to break the silence of everyone focusing on their dinner. "Did you guys hear about that nut who did not brush his teeth for a week?"

"No!" everyone gasped in unison.

"That is foul," Regan said, scrunching up her nose. "What was the point, and why is that news?"

"Well, apparently his wealthy friend dared him to go to work and do all of his other normal activities for one week without brushing his teeth. At the end of one week, if he had not brushed his teeth, his friend would give him $7,000 - $1,000 for each day. People are so desperate and greedy. Some people will do anything for money." Regina shook her head as she continued working on her fettuccini alfredo.

Kim pondered Regina's words for a moment. "You know what I think? I think any of us would do almost anything for a price. In fact, most people would do almost anything for a price. Half of us at this table have been married, and all of us have been in committed relationships. I bet if someone offered us $50,000 cash money to cheat on our partners every last one of us would. Shit, some would cheat for free."

"I'm not so sure about that," Melissa disagreed with Kim. "Money does not solve every problem, and after the affair, there would still be the feelings to deal with. What is $50,000 going to do? No thanks."

"That's easy to say," Kim responded. "But think about this realistically. You have debts and obligations. And despite the way you dress, I'm sure you like to shop…obviously not for cute clothes but maybe for household goods or something. I got it! What about a vacation? You like to travel. Think about $50,000 cash money, free and clear, stacked up on your table. You could be compromised, Melissa. Don't act all high-and-mighty, because that is when you are really in jeopardy of falling."

Regan chimed in. "Shoot, my ex would've looked at me like I was crazy if I *didn't* take that $50,000. His crazy butt would have been offering to pick out my clothes, get my hair done, and everything else to get ready for that night. Heck that fool would probably have volunteered to chauffeur us for the night, just to make sure I was on my best behavior. One year's salary in just one night!? Girl, please! I consider myself a moral person, but I'd have to bend a little on that one."

"What about your mom?" Melissa asked.

"What *about* my momma?" Regan asked with more attitude than she'd intended.

"If you got paid $100,000 to slap your mom in the face so hard that her head turned, would you do that?"

"Hecks yeah!" Regina enthused. "In fact, if I didn't slap my momma for that kind of money, *she* would slap *me* and tell me how stupid, and still broke, I was."

"I'm with Regina. I love my mommy to pieces, but she'd have a red face that day," Kim added. "How about you, Melissa? Would you slap your mother?"

"I'd probably slap my mother for free, but that's another story."

Regina had one that she knew everyone would balk at. "Okay, how about for $500,000, if you had to go to a plantation in Mississippi and pick cotton for an eight-hour day. During that eight hours, you would get two breaks and a lunch. Nobody could touch you or be physical in any manner, but the owners of the plantation could call you the N-word and hurl any type of insults and obscenities at you that they wanted to. Would any of you do that?"

Melissa was the first to speak. "Absolutely not! That is so disrespectful. That would set our country back countless years. How absurd. Wow, I can't...I don't even know what to say to something like that. I'd slap the person who brought that offer to me. That is racist, and I can't imagine that any black person would ever agree to anything like that. Kim, I know you agree with me on this one. We all know how you are about being disrespected and stuff like that."

"Bitch, please! For half a million dollars? I'd be a cotton-picking, yessir-boss, Aunt-Jemimah-scarf-wearing, Kunta Kenta-looking, swing-low-sweet-chariot-singing nigga. Are you kidding me? I don't give a damn what he yells or calls me, just have that money in my account. Shiiiit! If he's looking for some entertainment, I'll dance a jig, play the fiddle, or shoot watermelon seeds out of my ass. I don't give a damn!"

"I'm with Kim," Regina agreed "In fact, depending on how hot it was, I might even ask for overtime." Regina and Kim high-fived each other.

"Right!" Kim said as she set her glass down. "I'd be like UPS in that piece – 'What can brown do for you?'"

"Yeah, me too," Regan agreed. "I mean, if our ancestors were forced to pick cotton for free in harsh and deplorable conditions, why wouldn't I do the same for a half million dollars? It wouldn't be forced, and if the plantation owners got their rocks off by reinventing slavery scenes, then so be it. I'd be laughing right with them...all the way to the bank. Sign me up. You know something we don't know? Is Donald Sterling hiring?"

Melissa was horrified. Who were these ladies, and what had they done with Kim, Regan, and Regina? Why was the only white person at the table offended at even the idea of something like that? It was not funny as far as she was concerned. "Wow, I'm sad to say, it does seem like almost anything has a price."

"Sure does," Kim announced as she stood up. "So since you so offended and whatnot, you can pay the price for this dinner." This time, there were high-fives and screeches of laughter all around.

Melissa thought she had a good one, and wanted to have the last word this time. "I ain't no homework so stop trying to do me."

*****

"Hello?" Regina raced to pick up the cordless phone before it stopped ringing. A few days ago, she came home and found the cordless phone from the kitchen smashed into a bazillion pieces. She had to run upstairs and get the phone in the bedroom. The telemarketer who was sure to be on the other end was about to get cussed out. Nobody called the home phone, except for telemarketers and Regina's mother. Since she didn't recognize the telephone number as her mother's, then somebody was about to get an earful.

"Hey, gorgeous."

"Drew, is that you? What are you doing calling the house phone? Kevin isn't here, so you can try his cell."

Andrew was worried about his friend. Earlier in the week, Andrew had gotten wind of DeShawn's pending arrest and had called Kevin to give him a heads-up. Since then, Andrew had only talked to Kevin for a few brief minutes on three different occasions, and Kevin sounded worse each time. The night that he told Kevin about the indictment, Kevin said he'd gone directly to the Martin home and met the attorney there. After DeShawn's arrest, Kevin had stayed at the house with Ms. Martin talking about everything, from DeShawn's defense to the first time he walked and his first date. Before Kevin realized it, it was far past midnight, and he knew Regina would either be highly pissed or sound asleep. Much to his relief, it was the latter. Kevin slept on the couch in his man cave that night, so as not to bother Regina. After a few hours of sleep, Kevin was at the center all day making calls and taking meetings on DeShawn's behalf. Before he knew it, another day had come and gone, and he had not eaten a single meal. Each time Andrew checked in with his friend, he could hear the exhaustion and despair in Kevin's voice. He just wanted to make sure his brother-from-another-mother was doing okay.

"I tried the cell, but it goes to voicemail on the first ring. I'm worried about him, Gina."

"Well if I ever see him, I'll let him know you called. That's a mighty big *if* though, considering that I have not seen or heard from Kevin in, like, two days. That's sweet of you to be worried about Kevin, but Kevin needs to be worried about this marriage."

"Wait, you haven't seen or talked to Kevin?" Andrew was really concerned now. He knew how Regina felt about the situation with DeShawn, but even she would surely be sorry to hear about his arrest.

"No, Drew, I haven't. And at this point, I have no interest in seeing or talking to him. He hasn't given a darn about anyone but himself, so he can carry on."

"Believe me, Gina, the *last* person Kevin has been focusing on is himself. He has been a wreck since DeShawn was arrested. It's really taken a toll—"

"*WHAT?*" Regina screamed into the phone. "Andrew, tell me exactly what happened. Please! Is Kevin okay? Where is DeShawn now? Oh no, what about Ms. Martin?"

"Hey, hey, hey. Calm down, sis. DeShawn will be okay, and Kevin is going to be fine. He has just been running himself ragged, and he hasn't been taking care of himself like he should. I don't want to lay a guilt trip on you, but the state of you guys' relationship has been an added burden to Kevin. The very last time we spoke, he said he wished he could talk to his best friend about all of this. That even if he could not get advice, he knew he could get a supportive shoulder and a loyal ear. And just so we're clear, he was not referring to me when he said *best friend*. He was referring to you. Because Kevin knew that you blamed DeShawn for his extra time away from home lately, he felt that he could not talk to you about the situation. Kevin feels helpless with DeShawn, rejected by you, and alone in his fight for and belief in that young man. Like I said, I'm worried about him. He is too proud to admit that he's down or having a hard time juggling everything, but I've known Kevin for more years than I care to count. And I know his defense mechanism when things get tough is to throw up walls. He builds an impenetrable emotional fortress around his head and heart, and nobody gets in until he's ready."

Regina was speechless. This was the first time in weeks that she'd even considered Kevin's position or feelings. In fact, she was so busy pouting that she had decided to meet her own need for attention. Aside from the fact that Kevin was her husband, he was also her best friend, and Regina realized she'd not been a supportive friend, but rather a selfish one.

"I don't know what to say, Drew. I'm going to sit right here in this house until Kevin comes home. As soon as I see him, I'll tell him to give you a...Hey, that's him coming in now. Call you back." With that, Regina hung up the phone.

As Kevin stepped into the foyer, he noticed Regina standing on the stairs. The last thing he needed was to get into an argument with his wife.

"Hey, Regina."

"Hey, Kevin."

"Look, I know we need to talk. Can it please wait until tomorrow? There is a lot going on right now that you don't know about, and I need to bring you up to speed." Kevin had plopped down on the bottom step and buried his face in his hands. He was startled when he felt Regina's hands on his shoulders, in massage-like motions.

"Andrew called. He was concerned about you and wanted to make sure you were taking care of yourself. Are you okay, Kevin?"

"Actually, no. I'm not okay, but I have to believe that things are going to work out. Nothing is going to get accomplished by me stressing. Hey, I broke the phone the other day. I'll replace it this weekend. Also, I want to apologize for being M.I.A. It's a long story, and we can talk tomorrow if that's cool."

"Kevin, you don't need to apologize. Well, maybe for smashing the phone, but the battery was weak in that thing anyway, so it's no big deal." Regina tried to make light of the situation. She really was angry with Kevin for making her feel neglected. At the same time, she had to admit that she felt more than a little guilty for not being more understanding. "I heard about what happened with DeShawn. I'm very sorry about that. Since you believe in that young man so much, he must be a good kid. I will make some food tomorrow for you to take to his mom. She must be out of her mind with worry, and cooking is probably the last thing on her mind. Whatever I can do to help, Kevin, you can count on me."

Kevin turned around and got on his knees on the step to face his wife. "Thank you, baby. That means more than you know. It's late, let's get ready to head upstairs."

"Okay, baby, I'll turn off the lights and lock up down here. Be up in a second." Regina pecked Kevin on his cheek and watched him tread up the stairs.

Kevin stopped midway up the stairs. "Cool, I'll meet you up. And check your phone; it's playing that annoying tune that chimes whenever you have a text message. Tell your sister or your girls don't get checked; they know good and well it's too late to be blowing up your phone."

Regina chuckled nervously as she grabbed her phone off of the end table. "Kevin, you so corny. What did Curtis Taylor, Jr. tell Effie's brother in *Dreamgirls*? 'You can't kill shit!'" Regina unlocked her phone and deleted the text from Mike without even reading it.

oh so now u can respond??? im teasin. r u ok? when i didnt hear from u the other day i got worried

sorry about that…just had a lot going on…hey can we meet sometime this week?

u know u just gotta say the word and its a deal. u wanna cum back n have me plant some more SEEDS n my garden tub?LOL

ha ha. very funny mike. i was thinking we can meet out somewhere. maybe grab a bite2 eat after work

ok cool. im not gonna b n this week but any day u wanna meet just let me know…just one request tho

whats that???

u gotta sit across from me, and u cant wear panties…i wanna put my foot up in it…isn't that what black people say when they eat something that tastes good…that somebody put their foot in it??? well thats some of the best pussy ive ever tasted so i really AM gonna put my foot in it… in public… at least dip a toe in that sweet pot o huny

bye mike...ill c u 2morrow

bye hot chocolate!

Regina wanted to burst into tears. After Kevin shared everything that was going on with DeShawn, she decided to be a better wife. She figured she could start being a better wife by being a better friend. That would mean ending this thing she had going on with Mike. Even as she reached out to Mike to start the process of doing the right thing, she had mixed feelings. A part of Regina still liked the excitement that she felt when Mike was freaky with her. She loved the feeling of being aroused and turned on. The other side of that coin, though, was the guilt and shame because she had allowed herself to have those feelings with someone other than Kevin. But still, Regina reasoned that Kevin had contributed to the situation by putting Regina and her needs on a back burner. If her dealings ever came out, which would only happen over her dead body, Regina had determined she would point out to Kevin that as long as he had handled business in the marriage, there was no opportunity for anyone else to move in. No matter, everything was about to be rectified tomorrow. Regina would meet with Mike at the little hole-in-the-wall burger joint near his house because it didn't start getting crowded until late evening, and she would tell him that they would have to stop seeing each other. Things wouldn't have to be awkward at work, either. Regina and Mike worked on opposite sides of that massive building. Unless they were in the cafeteria or one of the break rooms at the same time, they would rarely see each other at work. Thankfully, Regina had never heard any rumors about her and Mike, and sitting next to Cassie, she would surely have questioned Regina if she'd heard any gossip. That woman wouldnha be able to keep her mouth closed if she used super glue instead of toothpaste! Regina rolled her eyes, mentally kicking herself for thinking Cassie into existence.

"Well good morning, Regina. I didn't see you come in. You must have slipped right by me." Cassie was returning to her desk with her morning cup of coffee.

"Good morning, Cassie. I looked for you when I came in, but I guess you were downstairs or across the hall getting your coffee. Hope you had a good weekend." Regina turned back toward her computer, hoping that Cassie would get the hint that she was focused on getting to her work, not on having idle conversation.

"No, as a matter of fact, I didn't. Regina, you remember my brother, don't you? Well he and his snooty wife had some fancy shindig out of town, and guess who got stuck watching their little brat? Talk about busy—"

"Yes, Cassie, you hit the nail on the head when you said *busy*," interrupted Regina, before Cassie could get into her diatribe against her brother and sister-in-law. And she certainly did not want to hear another story about their child, whom Cassie only referred to as the *little brat* or the *little demon*. No child deserved to be referred to that way. "You know how Mondays are. I guess we better get to it, huh?" Regina turned around to her computer and tried to tune out Cassie's voice.

After Regina had logged into her computer, checked her voice messages, and read several emails, she could still hear Cassie's voice droning in the background. Despite her best effort to not listen to Cassie, Regina could still hear words and phrases every now and then. Regina actually felt a little bad for tuning Cassie out, given that she really seemed to need to vent. Regina offered a random "uh-huh" here and there just so Cassie would not feel ignored. Trying to be a gracious coworker, Regina offered a "wow, that's crazy" when she heard Cassie say something about the *little brat* being angry with Cassie for refusing to allow a boy to spend the night. As Cassie continued talking about being fed up with the lies, manipulation, and malevolent schemes, Regina issued an apathetic "that's terrible." It was only when Cassie mentioned that the *little demon* threatened to make Cassie pay by hurting herself and blaming her aunt, did Regina began to listen more seriously.

Regina almost fell out of her chair when Cassie said, "I'm telling you, Regina, one day my niece is gonna pull her tricks on the wrong person, and she is gonna be in hot water. She has a pattern of telling lies on people she thinks need to be taught a lesson for telling her no. I only hope my brother and his snotty wife wake up to her malicious lies and evil ways instead of pretending to be blind to her antics like they usually are. It's not just my brother, either. All of those parents whose kids go to St. Augustine are the same way. They think they can solve all of their kids' problems by throwing money at them."

Regina's ears perked up. For the first time since Cassie opened her mouth, she had Regina's attention. Kevin had not discussed much of DeShawn's case with Regina, but it was not for a lack of trying. Initially, he'd try to share information with her in an effort to get her opinion or just for her to be his sounding board. But after making it painfully clear that she'd rather discuss quantum physics than DeShawn's case, Kevin had stopped trying. But one thing that Regina did remember was that the girl who had accused DeShawn of raping her was a student at St. Augustine. She would have to ask Kevin that girl's name because Regina thought it began with an H, but she couldn't think of the name. Maybe it was Heather, or Hailey. No, Hilary or maybe Hannah. Regina wondered if this was just a major coincidence or if Cassie's niece was the same girl who accused DeShawn – falsely, it appeared – of violating her.

*****

"So this is where you spend your time when you are not at work, huh?" Kim had made a late night run to the drugstore and ran into Mike when she got inside. Actually, she saw his car in the parking lot, so she searched every aisle once inside the store until she spotted him.

"Hey there, Kim. What are you doing here at this hour?" Mike usually tried to get away from Kim as quickly as possible whenever she approached him. Tonight, though, she looked especially good, and he did not want to appear rude. "I don't know how wise it is for such a beautiful woman to be out and about this late."

"I know, right. I really need to be in bed. For some reason, I couldn't sleep so I had to throw on some clothes…you know, I sleep naked…and come and get some Doritos and ice cream. That always does the trick. This place is not too far from my house. What about you? Why are you out so late? And why haven't you been at work the last few days?"

Mike noticed how Kim threw in that comment about sleeping nude. She was always up to her tricks. Little did Kim know, tonight her bait just may hook a great white on her reel. "What's up with the twenty questions?" Mike teased. "Seriously though, I'm on vacation this week. I'm not going anywhere, just need some time off to relax. And I'm at the store now, if you must know, because I just came from meeting someone, and I stopped in here to pick up a prescription since this is the only twenty-four-hour drugstore near my house. The reason I'm in this aisle is to get a card for one of my pals. He is biting the bullet and getting married. Poor schmuck."

"Well who was your meeting with, the grim reaper? You look grumpy or agitated or something. I can't quite put my finger on it...*yet*." Kim was intentionally being suggestive. "It's been a while since I've seen you. You look great, like you're really slimming down. Are you losing weight?"

"No, not intentionally. I think I've just been too busy and am tired, is all. As far as my meeting, Ms. Twenty Questions, in a way, it was with the grim reaper because there are a few things that apparently needed to be buried. But no worries. What about you, why can't you sleep? You have to be at work in a few hours, so that's not good."

"I guess my mind was racing too much." Kim was setting her bait.

"Oh really, now? Why was your mind racing, Ms. Stoner?"

"I guess I've just been frustrated lately. It's these crazy sex dreams I've been having. They are just really vivid. I'm always really wild and uninhibited in the dreams, and I'm having sex for hours at a time with my partner. Every time I wake up, I'm left feeling frustrated because I can't get a clear picture of my partner's face. On top of that, I'm sexually unsatisfied. No matter how much I try to soothe myself, it just...never mind. I'm so embarrassed. You must think I'm so weird, huh?" Kim had hooked her bait. One quick glance showed the growing evidence of Mike's excitement.

Mike tried to hide his exuberance by placing the greeting card in front of his private area. Dammit, he knew he should have selected a bigger card. "Well, I can see how that could keep you up at night. What about your boyfriend? He can't fulfill those dreams? And why isn't it his face that you see in your dreams? Maybe life doesn't really imitate art, huh?"

"First of all, although I have plenty of friends, I don't waste time with boys. Secondly, I have not yet met the man who can fulfill my sexual dreams. Oh well, sucks for me, I guess. Like you said, I have to be at work in a few hours, and I've bored you enough, so I'd better let you go." Kim was reeling him in. And she hoped that Mike was a shark, not a darn guppy or minnow.

"Wait a minute. Did you get what you came in here for? Let me re-phrase, did you select the items you came to purchase? Because something tells me you are getting exactly what you came in here for. I am going to check out, and I can walk you to the parking lot. I wouldn't be a gentleman if I didn't see you safely to your car."

"I'll meet you up front. I just gotta grab an extra item." With that, Kim headed toward the prophylactics.

A few minutes later, Kim and Mike were walking to the parking lot. They were so engrossed in their conversation that they neither saw Cassie pull into the parking lot, nor heard her yelling hello to them. Mike knew that Kim could be trouble and dealing with her could be regretta-ble, but right now he did not care. Not even thirty minutes ago, Mike was wrapping up his meeting with Regina. They had met at a restaurant for what he thought would be an intimate date. Instead, she'd thanked him for being a great distraction during a difficult time in her life.

Mike normally did not get emotionally attached to the women with whom he was sexually involved. Regina was something special, though; she was different. Regina was the type of person whom others, men and women alike, just wanted to know better. She brought fresh air into ev-ery room she entered. She was a good conversationalist, because she was a great listener. She was beautiful because she did not try to be. She was natural and comfortable in her own skin. Mike would not describe himself as being in love with Regina, not by a long shot. However, she was one of the women he actually looked forward to hooking up with. Mike was disappointed that Regina wanted to end things with him, but he respected her and accepted her position. Mike didn't have hard feelings toward Regina. In fact, he was grateful for the pleasant change of pace from the people he usually dealt with. Still, Mike loved being with women, too much in fact. He was actually glad that he had run into Kim. Mike knew that Kim had been interested in him for a while now. Maybe it was time to give her what she wanted. Experience had shown Mike that the best way for him to get over one woman was to have another one under him.

Mike closed Kim's car door and leaned in through the window. Kim buckled her seatbelt and made sure her short skirt was pulled up high enough to reveal her pantiless vaginal area.

Kim saw Mike staring. She cleared her throat and said, "Up here, Mike. This cat can get your tongue later. It was really good running into you. Thanks for walking me to my car. I'll let you know when I make it home. Oh shit, never mind…I don't have any way of getting in touch with you."

"Here, put my number in your cell. Shoot me a text when you make it home." Mike told Kim his phone number and was in the process of saying goodbye when he felt a tap on his shoulder.

"Hey, Mike! I thought that was you. I said hello when I saw you and Kim coming out of the drugstore. What are you guys up to? I got a case of the runs and had to come get some Kaopectate. Hi there, Kim!" Kim rolled her eyes without speaking to Cassie. Without missing a beat, Cassie continued. "Well it's late, and I for one need to get some rest so I'm going to take off. See you later, Mike. Guess I'll see you tomorrow, Kim. Hopefully you won't be in such a rush tomorrow so you will remember to put on some underpants." And as fast as she appeared, Cassie was making her way to her car, leaving Kim, for the first time in a long time, speechless.

★ ★ ★ ★ ★

Although Kim did not particularly like people in her home, she was all too happy to host the girls for their weekly get-together. She wanted

179

to be in full control of the environment. That way, she could kick every-one out if she felt like it and still be in the comfort of her own home.

Regan and Regina shared a ride to Kim's, and Melissa arrived just as they were pulling into the driveway. When Kim opened the door, the ladies were already engaged in conversation. Melissa was telling Regan that she was surprised that Regan stereotyped people the way that she did. Regan looked to Kim for support once the door opened.

"Kim," Regan began. "Say you're in the bathroom or kitchen and your television is on. You hear the newscaster say someone got busted for operating a meth lab. What race is the suspect?"

"White." Kim crinkled her face as if to indicate that was a painfully obvious answer.

"Say that same newscaster then reports that there was a drive-by shooting. What race is that suspect?"

"Black. Why are you asking these silly questions, Regan?"

"Because Regina and I were talking about how shocked we remem-bered being when we found out the DC snipers were black, because that is usually the type of crime that white people commit. Well Melissa said that there is no way a person could determine the race of an individual just by the type of crime committed. So I was telling her I beg to differ." Regan looked at Melissa with an I-told-you-so expression.

Regina spoke up. "Melissa, everyone does it. Even though it is wrong, we all make assumptions about people based on very surface informa-tion. To be aware that we do it is to be in a position to correct it, but to deny that we do it is to live in a fantasy world, and things will never improve. If I hear of a person stealing someone's wallet, I think black suspect. If I hear of a person stealing someone's retirement savings, I think white suspect. Not that there isn't crossover every now and again. Melissa, you have never in your life made a judgment about someone based on an initial encounter or something?"

Melissa did not have to think long. She had to laugh as she answered Regina. "Actually, I was guilty of doing just that today at work. I had to take a complaint call about an account that one of our associates messed up. When the operator transferred the call to me, she announced that La-

Keesha Simmons was on the phone. I don't know why, but an image of an African American female popped into my head. My assumption was wrong. She was Caucasian."

"See?" Regan pointed out. "That's what I'm saying. That is just the way society is. You just never know, so you shouldn't really judge people, but we all do it all the time. If you see a male all tatted up and wearing some jeans and a t-shirt, you would make certain assumptions about him, especially if he was wearing an earring. But that man could be a surgeon or a pastor or any number of things we may not consider."

"Ok, now I feel bad," Melissa confessed.

"Why?" the other three ladies asked in unison.

"Well, I saw a guy in the mall, and I assumed he was gay because he had on Ugg boots and was getting his eyebrows threaded. At first I felt bad for even thinking those things made him gay, then he put on some lip gloss…with a brush. So I thought it again. It's hard not to make assumptions, I guess." Melissa felt convicted.

"Shit, he probably was, but so what?" Kim quipped, as she poured wine into everyone's goblets. "That's like saying a female who sleeps around is a hoe."

"She *is*," Regan responded. "I mean, here we go with the societal views again. It's perceived as wrong or immoral for a female to have multiple partners, but for a man, he is a stud or a mack or whatever. That is so corny."

Kim lifted her wine goblet toward Regan. "Now I'll drink to that."

"Heffa, you will drink to anything," Regan teased.

"No, I'm serious. As women, we should be free to do what we need to do to bring us happiness, relief, a break from the monotony, whatever it is that we need. Shoot, if I had a friend who was stepping out on her man, I'd totally support her." Kim was looking at Regina, and Regina refused to make eye contact.

Regan spoke up. "Kim, that is terrible. Why would you encourage something like that?"

"Because, for one thing, if she is stepping out, then her dude must have done something that he should not have done…or not done something that he should have done. Either way, he fell off his game. Plus, nine times out of ten, her dude is doing his own thing anyway, so whatever she does is just evening the playing field. It's scientifically proven that messing around is natural, normal, and even expected."

Now, Regina did make eye contact with Kim. She looked at her like she was crazy. Kim winked at Regina. The tension was so thick it was palpable.

Regan was the first to break the awkward silence. "Kim, you are crazy. What scientific proof are you talking about?"

"Easy. Messing around isn't new. It's been around since the beginning of time. That's why when it comes to relationships and stuff, I don't judge people…well except for that one hoe at my gym. That's 'cause she was a phony-ass heffa. But as long as you are keeping it real, then I say go for what you know. It must not be that wrong, or there wouldn't be all kinds of songs speaking to that exact situation. What's the verse to that one John Legend song? 'Stealing moments just to be with you, though it's wrong it's hard to tell the truth, but she don't have to know.' Ain't that some shit? Then that nigga goes on to sing, 'Oh it's getting crazy, I don't want to hurt my baby, and I know it's supposed to be the last time for you and I, but let's not end this way, just wait another day.' It sounds harsh, but that shit is real. He's not the cause of the cheating just because he sings about it. The cheating is going to exist whether he sings about it or not.

"But just to show that cheating is a normal part of life, look at the countless songs about it. "Part Time Lover" by Stevie Wonder, "If Loving You Is Wrong I Don't Want To Be Right" by Luther Ingram, "You Make Me Wanna" by Usher, "Oops I Did It Again" by Britney Spears, "Careless Whisper" by George Michael. The list is infinite. So you see? To be in a relationship is to be involved with cheating, as either the cheater or the cheatee. It's just a natural thing."

Although everyone was looking at Kim like she was crazy, Melissa was the one to speak up. "Wow. That is so skewed. But let me just address the songs. If the songs you listed prove your point, what about songs like "Dirty Diana" by Michael Jackson, "Cry Me a River" by Justin Timberlake, "Karma" by Alicia Keys, and one of my favorites, "If You Think You're Lonely Now" by Bobby Womack?"

"What about those songs?" an irritated Kim questioned.

"Those songs have the message that cheating has consequences, that what you do will come back. You reap what you sow, Kim, and *that* is the proven fact here. Nobody has ever planted a watermelon seed and harvested an orange. You can't throw something up and expect that it won't come back down. Those are facts."

"Whelp, whatever. I'm just trying to make the point here that people don't need to be ashamed of their dirt. They don't have to act all goody and perfect. We all have some...what did Stevie Wonder say..."Skeletons in the Closet." Huh, Regina?"

Regina was beside herself. She was ready to explode inside. She had no idea what Kim knew or thought she knew, but this was not about to happen. "I don't know about all of that. I just believe that every person is responsible for their own choices and behaviors. And it is that person's business. I have my hands full with—"

"So I heard," Kim cut Regina off. "Or at least you used to anyway."

Regina felt her face catch aflame as blood rushed to her cheeks. "Kim, thanks for having us over, but I think it's time for me to be on my way. You never seem to disappoint."

Kim creased her face into a scowl. "What's that supposed to mean?"

"It means that you have certainly met the level of expectation that people...let me speak for myself...that I have of you." Regina grabbed her purse.

Again, the room filled with tension. Regan and Melissa stood with Regina to leave. As they filed out of Kim's house, everyone was somber and their faces reflected their moods. Everyone except Kim. Her face reflected the pleasure she had derived from ruffling Regina's feathers.

*****

"Oh, no you don't! Get back down there. I didn't tell you to stop." Regina pushed Kevin back toward the foot of their bed.

"Aw, baby, can't a brother come up for air? Please? I'm starting to catch a cramp."

"No sir, a deal's a deal. I won at Spades, so you have to massage *each* foot for fifteen minutes. You are going to learn to quit betting against me."

Regina and Kevin were both making concerted efforts to jump-start their relationship. Just this week, Kevin noticed that Regina had been more emotionally present than she had been in months. As a result, he was more attracted to her than ever.

Kevin leaned forward on his elbows and faced his wife. "I love you, Regina Golden."

"I love you, too, Kevin Golden. But you still are finishing my foot massage, so *GET TA RUBBIN'!*" Regina mocked in her best Martin imitation.

"Okay, fine. Let me runget some gloves, though. Your feet are slicing my hands to pieces."

"Very funny. Too bad your smart mouth just talked you out of the surprise I had planned for you."

"What surprise?" Kevin sat up again.

"A surprise that you have been asking me for since we met. But never mind, I wouldn't want my sharp feet to get in the way or hurt you while I'm down there." Regina folded her arms across her chest in a defiant gesture.

Kevin dived on his wife and tickled her until she was practically stuttering. Regina could barely catch her breath as her husband smothered her with tender kisses. He started at her forehead and kissed every inch of his wife until he reached her toes. Two hours later, Regina and Kevin showered together. Kevin washed his wife's back, so he was unable to see her tear-streaked face. Regina silently wept over the way she had muddied her marriage. Kevin gently grabbed his wife's shoulders and turned her toward him. He pulled her to him, and they stood in the shower as one. Regina hoped that the stains of regret and pain she put on their relationship would wash away as easily as the soap with which they'd just cleansed their bodies, forever disappearing down the drain of life.

2 WEEKS AGO

"Cassie!" Regina caught Cassie off guard when she yelled her name so unexpectedly. "Remember last week when you were telling me about your niece?"

"You bet I do. Why? Don't tell me you have a youngster like that in your family, too."

"No, not that I know of. I don't remember what you said her name was." Regina now wished she had paid more attention when Cassie was running her mouth. Who knew that she might actually have something pertinent to say?

"Her name is Little Brat. Or when she is really acting out, her alias is Little Demon. Why do you ask, Regina?"

"I just couldn't get her off my mind. It's just a shame that she costs your brother and your family so much pain."

"Please, Hilary doesn't cost my brother anything but money," Cassie snorted as she dropped her purse onto her desk and headed out of the door to get her morning cup of coffee.

bay we gotta talk soon as we get home

who needs to waste time talking? we can just pick up where we left off the other night. and the timing of your text is perfect because i was just thinking about you

Kevin, i'm serious...we REALLY have to talk...found out some very important info...

ok baby. well is everything ok? do you need to leave work early, or maybe meet for lunch

*no bay its cool. it will keep until we get in.
love you.*

love you back baby girl

Later that evening, sitting in the middle of the floor eating takeout from their favorite gyro restaurant, Regina and Kevin discussed the situation with DeShawn. Kevin revealed that DeShawn had been found responsible for the rape of the young lady. He explained that Ms. Martin was taking the news very hard, but in an effort to not take time away from his home life, Kevin had been visiting with the family during the hours that Regina was at work. Regina felt terrible. She did not want Kevin to feel like he could not be available to people like he was in the habit of doing in order to keep Regina from being angry.

Regina explained that she didn't understand how DeShawn could be found responsible when the alleged victim's own friend could attest to the fact that the accuser had framed DeShawn. Kevin explained that the girl's friend had lied, that she actually said she did not know what happened. Regina knew that Kevin would not tell her the accuser's name. It was not released to the public, and the only reason Kevin knew was because DeShawn told him what happened and Kevin's own closeness to the case. She had information that might be helpful, though.

"Kevin, I know you can't tell me the accuser's name, but if I tell you a name, will you tell me if I'm right?"

Kevin did not respond. He did not move a muscle.

"Kevin, is her name Hiliary?"

Not realizing he'd been holding his breath for the last few seconds, Kevin expelled an audible sigh. "Wh ...why would you say that name, Gina? Where did you hear that?"

Regina ignored Kevin's questions. "Okay, so Hilary is DeShawn's accuser. Listen, baby, you have to get some information to DeShawn's attorney. It could make a difference."

Kevin ruefully shook his head. "No, baby, it's too late for that. You want to know the worst part, Gina? From what I understand, it was not just the DNA that sealed the deal for DeShawn. Reportedly, DeShawn presented a compelling argument to the judge, and his version of what happened was a convincing one. But in the end, DeShawn was his own worst enemy. Somehow, that boy got his hands on a cell phone, and the idiot…" Kevin's voice trailed off.

"What?" Regina scooted closer to Kevin. "What happened, Kevin? Did he call that girl?"

"No…worse! At least if DeShawn had called her there wouldn't be a transcript of what he said. That boy sent her text messages. He was calling that girl everything but her name. He texted her that she was going to pay for ruining his life. He just didn't do anything to help his case. All the work, time, and effort that I, his mom – everyone – put into this…I don't even know what to say. It's a done deal now, Regina."

Regina's heart melted over her husband's pain. He really loved DeShawn, just as he loved all of the kids at the center. Kevin believed in DeShawn, so this had to be a devastating blow. Regina had to restore his faith in DeShawn. "Baby, I'm so sorry. I know you wanted to believe DeShawn didn't rape that girl."

"Damn right I wanted to believe it. I still believe it. Things just don't look good. And to be honest, I feel like I let DeShawn and Ms. Martin down. He said he sent those texts because he was angry with the judge's finding. I get that, but it just makes everything worse. Now—"

Regina had to interrupt her husband so he could have some hopeful news. "Now you need to listen. I knew Hilary's name because I work with her aunt. In fact, I sit right next to her."

"Who?" Kevin asked, raising his eyebrows. "Nosey Cassie?"

"Yes…Cassie. She was telling me last week about her niece who was staying with her. I was half listening at first because you know how Cassie can be. But the more she talked, the more intrigued I became. She was saying how her niece has a habit of manipulating people and lying on people when she does not get her way. She even told lies about Cassie when she wouldn't let her have her way. This girl sounds like a real piece of work. Well, when I got to work today, I asked Cassie her niece's name. When she told me, I just knew it was the girl involved in DeShawn's case. I remembered you mentioned something about the school she attended. So you see, Kevin? There *is* a chance for DeShawn. Can't that information be used to help?"

"Damn, you are sexy."

"What? Kevin, where did that come from?"

Kevin simply stared at Regina for a moment. "It came from my heart. My baby over here playing detective. It is such a turn-on to have your support and to know that you care. I appreciate that, Gina. I'll call Mr. Thomas tomorrow. Tonight, though, I'm going to call Teddy and them."

"Who?"

"Teddy P. He said "Turn Out the Lights." Then, in the words of the other homies, I'm going to slap-it-up, flip it, rub it down."

"Oh nooooo!" Regina finished the Bell Biv Devoe song as she and Kevin crumpled into a heap together on their family room floor.

*****

"Oh well, that myth is out the window!" Kim plopped back against the pillows strewn across Mike's bed.

"I tried to tell you. I'm gonna run and get you a warm wash cloth. Do you need anything else…a cane, some crutches, a wheelchair maybe?"

Kim pushed Mike lightly in the back of his head. "Nigga, don't even trip. You good, but don't ever think you can hurt this."

"What the hell? What did you just call me?" Mike could not believe how crazy Kim was. He was always guessing with her. The same spontaneity and wildness that made Mike attracted to Kim also scared him. She was the type who might say or do anything…anywhere, to anyone. "In case you hadn't noticed, I'm not African American."

"I'm not either. I ain't got shit to do with Africa. And me calling you a nigga ain't got shit to do with race or ethnicity. That's just a term of familiarity, like homie…er, I mean like buddy or dude. You need to loosen up, Mike."

"No, dude, you need to tighten up…in *all* areas." With that, Mike jumped off of the bed and dashed into the bathroom. He knew that comment would piss Kim off a little, and he was glad. She needed to get a dose of her own medicine for a change. Little did Mike know that he had really touched a nerve.

Kim acted self-assured, actually arrogant, most of the time. She always projected a flawless image and a tough-as-nails attitude. Kim could not afford to risk anyone knowing how worthless she really felt. It was easier and oftentimes funnier to make other people feel inadequate rather than face her own inadequacies. Now she was wondering if she really did feel like a vacuum down there. She hadn't gotten any complaints in the past, and her vagina had retired more men than social security. Kim wondered what Mike thought about Regina's sexual prowess. *There is no way that lame-ass bitch is better in bed than me!* she thought. *And Mike has a lot of nerve to make a comment because he sure wasn't complaining when he was trying to get knee-deep in it.* Kim could not wait until he came back into the bedroom. She would show him that she was far more than enough. Meanwhile, she stretched across his bed and opened his nightstand drawers to snoop around. *Mike must really be a health nut because he has every kind of bottle a person can imagine in this bottom drawer,* Kim thought. *No wonder I didn't find much when I went through his bathroom closet the other night. All of his pills and vitamins are in the bedroom.*

"What the hell are you doing now?" Mike asked. Kim was so busy picking up and putting down bottles that she hadn't even heard Mike come back into the room.

"Nothing. I was just looking for a condom."

"I gotta reload for round two." Mike sat on the side of the bed and grabbed the remote control to turn on the television. "Do you wanna finish that movie we started?"

Kim came around the side of the bed where Mike was sitting. She dropped to her knees in front of him and put his entire flaccid penis into her mouth as she made a humming noise and massaged his testicles. With her free hand, Kim grabbed the remote from Mike and tossed it across the room. She emptied her mouth for a moment.

"No, we don't need to finish watching that movie," she answered. "But we can make our own if you'd like."

Kim resumed her position – slurping, licking, and sucking in such a way that Mike forgot all about being annoyed at her for going through his belongings. Before he knew it, Mike was indeed ready for round two, and a short time after that, round three as well. Mike made a mental note to tell Kim that she didn't need to tighten anything up, that she was probably one of the best partners he had ever been with. In fact, she was so good that he became too distracted to put on a condom the second and third time they had sex that evening. Mike usually made it a habit to never have sex without a condom. He knew he had to act safely and responsibly when being sexually intimate.

*****

Regina, Regan, and Melissa were on a three-way call, and Regina was giving Regan and Melissa an earful. She was letting them know how angry she was because she felt she'd been manipulated by them. Earlier in the week, Melissa had come to Regina's cubicle and asked where she wanted to go for their girls' night. Regina looked at her friend like she was an alien. Remembering their last girls' night, Regina thought to herself, *She must be from another planet...or galaxy... if she thinks I will ever break bread with Kim again. Break her neck or maybe her arm! But that's about it!* Seeing that she was not going to convince Regina to participate in their usual fellowship, Melissa left Regina's area, shaking her head but confident with the ace she had up her sleeve. A few short minutes after Melissa left, Regina's cell phone rang. It was Regan. She was telling Regina she'd heard the most bizarre rumor, and Regan wanted to call her sister to confirm that she'd surely been misinformed.

Regan told Regina that she heard that Regina was refusing to attend any more girls' nights. Regina told her sister that the rumor was accurate. Regan said that was fine, that she could understand how the rude and insensitive comments of an unpolished and surly wench could make

Regina change her behavior. Regan told Regina she did not know it was so easy for Kim to exercise power over her, but that was Regina's choice, so she had to respect that. Finally, Regina agreed to go. She made it clear that she was not going to take any of Kim's mess tonight, that Kim could get it as well as she gave it. And if she started any mess tonight, she would get more than she bargained for. Regina had also sent a text to her sister and her friend letting them know how she felt about them tag-teaming her.

Now, they were all en route to the winery where they agreed to meet. Regina insisted that they each drive separately, though, because she needed to be able to leave at a moment's notice. Regan and Melissa were thanking Regina for agreeing to come out and betting her that this would probably be one of the most fun and memorable times of all their get-togethers.

Regan was the first to arrive and then Melissa. Regina arrived shortly thereafter, and Kim was last.

Kim approached the bistro table in her normal audacious fashion. "Hi bitches! Did everyone drive tonight, or did anyone ride the sensitive train? It's good to see you, *all* of you."

"Too bad it's not mutual," Regina retorted. "To answer your question, though, I drove here. How did you arrive, the bitch bus or your broom?" Regina let it be known at the outset that she was not to be toyed with.

"Okay, Regina, I see you. Well, I'm going to be on my best behavior. We're all like sisters, and sisters sometimes have spats, right? I'm sorry if I was out of line last week. We good?"

As corny as Kim thought Regina was, she did like hanging with her and the other ladies. They were the closest semblance of friends that Kim had ever had. She did not think it was her fault that she was not the most polished when dealing with friends. She had not had much practice.

Wanting to lighten the mood, Melissa interjected, "I am ready to start sampling some of these wines. I heard they have a new ice wine. It's supposed to be really good, but ice wine is strong. I have to put something on my stomach. Should I get wings, or sliders?"

"Get them both," Kim suggested. "If you have a taste for both, just eat a little of both now, and then take the rest home and save them for lunch tomorrow."

"That's a great idea. I'll order both and eat the sliders now, because they taste like crap when they are reheated. I'll eat the wings tomorrow." Melissa knew she usually had the most trouble making a decision out of everyone in the group.

Even though Regina was initially steely – not just toward Kim, but toward everyone – she couldn't help but jump into the conversation. "Oh my goodness, Melissa is not the one to give options to. She can't ever say this or that, A or B, up or down. Our friend is truly indecisive."

"No I'm not," Melissa playfully pouted. I know how to make a choice and stick with it."

"Okay," Kim decided to test Melissa. "Coke or Pepsi?"

"Oh goodness, that is hard. If it's straight, I'd have to say Pepsi because Coke tastes too sweet to me. But if I'm mixing it with alcohol, I'd have to say Coke." As soon as the words left Melissa's lips, she knew she'd proven Regina's point. "Oh shoot, I didn't do well on that one. Gimme another one."

"Okay, Beyoncé or Rihanna?" Regan asked. She was really curious to hear this answer because she knew Melissa listened to both artists quite a bit.

"Oooh, you guys are asking hard stuff. I'm gonna say Jennifer Hudson as far as singing. But as far as being an entertainer, I'll say…let me see, I'd have to go with…shoot, I don't know." Melissa was starting to think she really was indecisive.

"Okay," Kim jumped in. "This is an easy one. Sprees or Sweet Tarts?"

"Thank you, Kim, that's more like it. Back in the day, it used to be Sweet Tarts, but now they are soft and crumbly like Smarties, so I'm gonna go with Sprees." Everyone at the table clapped, as Melissa stood up and executed a dramatic bow. "Now it's my turn because I bet I'm not the only one who sometimes has trouble committing to A or B, up or down." Melissa figured she'd turn the table on the ladies. "Prince or Michael Jackson?"

Nobody said anything. After a few moments, Kim spoke up. "She's asking you guys a question. Go ahead, Regan."

Regan raised her eyebrows and shook her head. "That's impossible. Both are geniuses. I'm going to have to pass on that one. How about you, Gina, Whitney or Mariah?"

"I just put food in my mouth, go to Kim." Regina was stalling. She loved Mariah during the *Vision of Love* and *Always Be My Baby* times, but not so much lately. Whitney was The Voice, so c'mon. Then again, Mariah has the octaves, but so did Minnie Riperton and Chante Moore. Geesh, she physically shook her shoulders. She was not touching that one.

"Pitiful!" Regan shook her head, feigning disappointment. "Okay, I'll make it easier. Kim, Brad Pitt or Matthew McConaughey?"

Kim was all too happy to answer that one. "That's easy, Brad McConaughey!" Everyone at the table erupted in laughter.

Since everyone was in a joking mood, Melissa thought of a way to really get them riled up with the ultimate prank. "Church's or Popeye's? Because I heard you people love fried chicken."

It was as if someone had hit the pause button on a remote control. There was no sound, no movement, nothing. Kim hit the play button. "You are a fool, Melissa! That was a good one. You almost caught a beat down, but that was good."

Regina and Regan exhaled, not even realizing they'd been holding their breath.

"I was totally joking because you guys always say I'm uptight. Did I offend you guys? I really didn't mean—"

"Girl, we know your corny butt didn't mean any harm." Regina was actually proud of Melissa for being a little risqué. "You made a great point though, Melissa. We can all get stuck when it comes to choosing between this or that. The choice is easy when it's a matter of preference, but when it's a close call between two great options, that is tough. Shoot, Justin Timberlake or Robin Thicke, football or basketball, Heath bar or Skor bar, Crest or Colgate, Target or Walmart, Boyz II Men or N'Sync, Jodeci or Dru Hill, Usher or Chris Brown, Cameo or The Gap Band? The choices are endless, which is what makes life so interesting."

Regan leaned over and gave her sister a one-handed hug. "Oh my goodness, that is hands down The Gap Band. I've loved them ever since they sang "Word Up". Remember that, sis?"

"Uhhh…no, and neither do you," Regina corrected her younger sister. "Why do you always get those groups confused, Regan? Cameo sang "Word Up", and that group had Larry Blackmon. The Gap Band had Charlie Wilson, and—"

Kim cut in, "And Charlie Wilson must have wine running through his veins because brotha man has sholl gotten better with time. I saw him last year, and he cut up! He was twice as energetic and entertaining as artists half his age. He sounds good, he looks good…shit, he could hit if he wanted to."

"He wouldn't," Melissa spoke up. "His wife looks more like me than you. But you're right, Charlie Wilson is definitely back. And guess who is largely responsible for that?"

"God?" Regina offered.

"Charlie Wilson?" Kim proposed.

"Both of you are partially right, but the answer I was looking for is R. Kelly." Melissa saw everyone giving her that here-we-go-again look. "No, I'm serious. R. Kelly wrote "Charlie, Last Name Wilson", and he produced several other hits for Charlie Wilson. If you listen closely, at the end of "Charlie, Last Name Wilson", he sings 'Kelly you bad.' Y'all keep sleeping on Rob if you want. Plus R. Kelly takes other artists' songs to another level when he collaborates with them. Y'all remember how he just took over Bow Wow's "I'm A Flirt" with his re-mix."

Regan put her drink down. "I didn't hear Bow Wow on that remix."

"Exactly!" Melissa declared. "Rob took it and improved it so much, he didn't need Bow. Kells gave it all the *wow* it needed. And that version sold better than the original."

"Well, Prince sang on "Yo Mister" with Patti LaBelle," Regina offered out of nowhere. The rest of the ladies looked at her as if asking where that little tidbit of information had come from.

"So what? Michael Jackson sang on Rockwell's "Somebody's Watching Me"," Regan responded, almost defensively.

"Well it looks like somebody shoulda been watching Michael's ass if you ask me. Namely that bootleg doctor," Kim interjected. "And Melissa, girl, I don't see why you are so enamored with R. Kelly's ass. Yes, he can sing, but I keep telling you he ain't all that." Kim reminded Melissa once again how she felt about Melissa's favorite artist. "And even if he is all of that musically, what about his little sick fetish for teenage girls? That's some sick mess, Melissa."

"Well I don't know about all of that. But I do know that Rob has never been accused or suspected of messing with little boys. I'm just saying. Plus, he never made a song about being a pedophile, like some artists have." Melissa was going to defend her favorite artist to the end.

"What are you talking about Melissa? Who are you talking about?" Regan was intrigued.

"It's one of your sister's favorite old school groups. Remember that song "Do Me Baby"? They tell you right in that song what's going on: *'Backstage, underage, adolescent, how you doing, fine she replied, I sighed, I'd like to do the wild thang...action took place, hey, kinda wet, don't forget the J the I the M the M the Y, y'all, I need a body bag.'* Now *that* is crazy, ladies. She is backstage, she is underage, and the action still took place. And now somebody needs a body bag. And they are promoting that mess by singing about it. How sick is that?"

Kim gulped her last bit of wine. "Dang, I have sung that song a million times and never paid attention to those lyrics. I make a motion that from now on, we leave Melissa alone about her precious R. Kelly."

"I second," Regina and Regan said in unison.

Again, everyone at the table erupted in laughter. By the time everyone was leaving, Regina admitted to herself that she actually had a good time and was glad that she came tonight. There were hugs all around, and when Kim hugged Regina, she held on a bit longer than usual. Why that was, Regina could not determine. Regret, affection, atonement?

*****

"You hold, I'll load," Regina told Kevin as they walked toward the car from the grocery store. An hour prior, when they went into the store, there was a light drizzle. Now, as they left, there was a steady downpour. Regina pushed the shopping cart filled with groceries, and Kevin held the humongous umbrella over their heads.

"Cool," Kevin responded. "Line those bags up nice and straight, and when we get home, make sure all the cans and boxes are perfectly aligned and facing the same direction. I already owe you a whooping for having a hand towel misaligned." Kevin loved the way he and Regina teased each other. He'd missed that over the last few months, and it was refreshing that they seemed to be getting back to their comfortable, fun way of communicating.

Regina began to unload the cart. "Hold the umbrella right, Kevin, dang. And keep it still."

"I'm holding it fine. I'm not getting wet," Kevin roared with laughter.

"Ha, ha; very funny. Why don't we switch jobs?"

"Okay, my bad, Gina, let me move this umbrella 'cause I see my baby is getting all wet." Kevin shifted the umbrella a little to the right.

"That's even worse, I'm getting soaked and it's cold. I thought you were concerned about me getting wet?"

"Uhh, yeah. No, baby, I wasn't talking about you. I was talking about the inside of my trunk." Kevin was almost beside himself laughing now. He must have gone too far because Regina snatched the umbrella out if his hand, leaving Kevin to unload the remaining groceries by himself… in the rain.

After they pulled into the garage, Kevin didn't get out of the car. He just sat there, staring out of the windshield.

"Hey, baby, what's going on?" a concerned Regina asked. "You seem distracted. Is everything okay?"

"I'm thinking about going to my parents' and getting one of my dad's guns." Kevin braced for a harsh reaction from Regina. He knew she did not like guns.

"Kevin, no! We talked about getting a gun when we first got married, and we agreed then that we would not have a gun in our home. Why do you suddenly feel the need for a gun? I wouldn't even feel comfortable with that at all, honey."

"I know, bay, I know. I'm not saying we should buy a gun, but I would feel more comfortable if we had one in the house, just for a little while." Kevin knew that was not going to cut it with Regina. She would insist on knowing what was going on.

"Kevin, why would we need a gun in this house, even for a little while? What aren't you telling me? No lies and no bull." Regina folded her arms across her chest to indicate that Kevin had better start talking.

Resigned, Kevin shared with his wife why he was concerned. "Baby, I didn't say anything, because I did not want to worry you. It's just that strange things have been happening for the past week or two, and I just feel like I need some added protection."

Although Regina was worried, she did not express it. She did not want Kevin to think she could not handle whatever it was that he needed to tell her. "What kinds of strange things, Kevin? What's been going on?"

"Well, at first there were just a lot of hang up phone calls. I would answer the phone, and sometimes someone would giggle into the phone, and sometimes they would just hang up. Then, a few mornings when I went to open the center there were sexually explicit pictures, like from a magazine or something, taped to the front doors. The last straw was the other day. When I got home from work, there were dolls on the front stoop."

"Dolls? What kind of dolls?" Regina was really starting to get freaked out.

"Like just regular dolls that a little kid would play with. They were taped together, a male and a female doll. The one set had a female doll's head taped to the crotch area of a male action figure. The other set had the female doll bent over, like on all fours, and the male doll was taped at the midsection to the rear end of the female doll. Bottom line, Gina, I think someone out there is angry that I supported DeShawn during that situation with that girl, and they are trying to send me a message. For the life of me, though, I can't figure how some psycho would know where I live. I don't have the greatest confidence in the justice system right now, and plus there hasn't been anything that law enforcement would consider serious enough to take action over. I would just have a better peace of mind if we had a little protection." Kevin pulled Regina across the console and into his arms. "I love you, baby, and I can't imagine the thought of anything happening to you or to our home. I don't regret my decision to support DeShawn and Ms. Martin, but I do regret the impact that it has had on you and on our marriage. I love you, Regina, and I'm not going to let anything happen to you."

Regina sat quietly for a moment. "Okay, Kevin, whatever you think is best. Just know that I don't like the thought of having a gun in the house. It scares me, but I trust you." With that, Regina reached over and mushed Kevin on the side of his head. "Now hurry up and unload these groceries. It shouldn't take you long since you are in a nice and dry garage."

She hurried into the house so that Kevin could not see her face as she lamented the fact that her husband was willing to do whatever he could to protect their home, while she'd been too selfish to do the same. Were those calls and antics really due to someone being angry with Kevin over DeShawn's situation, or were they due to something altogether different, something that Kevin had no idea about?

1 WEEK AGO

Kevin had left Regina in bed early in the morning to get some work done at the Golden Choices Center. He had been there on a limited basis since DeShawn's trial and sentencing. Even though Kevin felt that he left the center in good hands with two of the counselors there, he still knew it was time for him to get back to work. It was barely 7:00 a.m. when Kevin heard the front doors rattling, like someone was trying desperately to get in. Dammit! Kevin was ticked that he'd listened to Regina about that gun, instead of following his first mind. After he brought his father's gun to their house, Regina made Kevin promise that he would keep it locked in his closet and that he would not carry the gun on his person. Regina reminded Kevin that he went to law school, had a judge for a father, and an attorney for a best friend, so of all people, he should know that he could not legally carry a gun on his person without a permit to do so. Kevin warily gave in and promised that he would not carry the gun. At this very moment, as he crept around the corner and peered through the blinds on the doors, Kevin wished he'd broken his promise.

"C'mon, open it. I know you're in there, Mr. Kevin. Your car is outside. Unless you got a lil honey up in there or something."

Kevin unlocked the doors as fast as he could and flung the doors open. "DeShawn? Man, is that you? What are you…wait a minute, did you escape from that facility? You know DYS is going to be all over—"

"Chill, Mr. Kevin. No I ain't escaped from nowhere. Ask my moms. Moms, tell Mr. Kevin what happened." DeShawn was motioning for his mother to hurry over from the parking lot. She'd remained in the car while DeShawn went to the door, having told him that the building looked like it was locked and empty. But DeShawn insisted that Mr. Kevin was inside, and if not, he would wait at that front door for him until he arrived.

"Boy, I'm coming. Remember, I'm fifty-seven, not seventeen. And

I can't be running or even walking too fast with these heel spurs." Ms. Martin acted like she was yelling at DeShawn, but in actuality, she would have run a marathon right now for her son. She was delighted beyond description.

"I don't understand," Kevin said. He fist-pounded DeShawn and hugged Ms. Martin as they squeezed past him and into the lobby of the center. "Please, have a seat. What's going on?"

DeShawn spoke first. "All I know is they came and got me like in the middle of the night it seemed like. Me and my bunkmate were dead asleep. They told me to get my stuff 'cause I was leaving. At first I was scared, probably from watching too many movies. I was thinking about that part in *Tango and Cash*, and all I could picture was them taking my black ass, sorry Moms...taking my behind down to some dark, smelly basement and beating me until I confessed."

"Yeah, man," Kevin interrupted. "You do watch too many movies. But go on."

DeShawn chuckled a little. "So anyway, after I grabbed my stuff and we left my room, one of the guys said I was being released. They said that my moms was on the way, and when she got there and signed the papers, I was free to go. I cried...I mean, I let moms cry on me when she saw me, then we came straight here. That's it."

Kevin was as shocked as he was happy. He looked as Ms. Martin.

"Don't look at me; I'm as surprised as you. When I saw the phone number for the facility come up on my caller ID, I was worried. I was scared something had happened to DeShawn or that maybe he'd done something to get in trouble again, like he did with that cell phone."

"C'mon, Moms." DeShawn looked like an embarrassed six-year-old for a moment.

"Well I'm just saying, son, that's what came to my mind. When your phone rings late at night or early in the morning like that, and your only living child is locked up, you just..." Ms. Martin began to snivel at first; then she was outright bawling. She did not have the words to express how blessed she felt. She and DeShawn had gone through an emotional ordeal and to have him unexpectedly released to her was a lot to absorb and process. "I'm okay, y'all, I'm just happy. It's like when you were in that car accident that time, DeShawn. I was thankful and happy that you were alive and not more seriously injured. Then, when I saw how mangled that car was, I cried because the possibilities of what could have happened, of how bad things could have been, flooded my thoughts and emotions. It's hard to explain, but I'm fine. I'm better than fine, I'm blessed!"

Kevin was happy, too. He visited with the Martins for another thirty minutes or so, until Ms. Martin suggested that they go home so De-Shawn could get a decent meal and shower and both of them could get some much needed rest. Kevin had no idea how or why DeShawn had been released. Ms. Martin believed that it was a miracle and the work of God. Kevin did not know if it was God or not, but someone had been working behind the scenes. Once the Martins left, he immediately called Andrew to find out who the wizard was behind the curtain.

"Hey, bro, what's up?" Andrew answered the phone sounding as if he were half-asleep, which Kevin knew should not be the case, since Andrew woke up at 5:00 a.m. seven days a week, three hundred sixty-five days a year.

"It doesn't sound like you are. You okay, man?"

"I'll be okay, just a bit under the weather, I guess." Andrew was actually heartsick, but he was not in the mental space to admit that to anyone – not to his wife, not to his best friend, not even to himself.

"Hey, man, I'm sorry to hear that. You know if you need anything, just holler. I wanted to share some good news, or should I say something I just found out because I'm sure it isn't news to you. Did you know DeShawn got released?"

Andrew was silent for a moment. "Yes, I believe I did hear something about that. Congratulations, man. I know I wasn't the kid's biggest cheerleader, but I'm happy for him and his family. That includes you, because you have been like an uncle to him."

"Thanks, man, I appreciate that. So what happened? I know you and Mr. Steele have connections in every branch of law and government."

"Kevin, even if I knew, which I don't, you know I couldn't share that information with you. What, so you could go and tell Gina? Then who knows where it would go from there with her bigmouthed friends, especially that one. What's her name, with the fat ass?" Andrew knew exactly who Kim was. He had gotten oral sex from her once in Kevin and Regina's bathroom when they were all there for a Super Bowl party.

"Don't play like you don't know Kim's name. Didn't she have it written on the top of her head?" Kevin joked with his friend.

"Man, please, that was an alleged event. Nobody can prove what did or did not happen. And why are you bringing up the past? I thought we were talking about DeShawn. You need to be focused on talking to him about his future. Is he planning to go to school? I heard he was nice on the football field. Is he just as good in the class room?"

Kevin knew Andrew was trying to change the subject and avoid discussing what he really wanted to know. "Man, he's good. Now what happened? I'm not going to say anything. Who would I tell? Gina? Telling her is like telling myself. That girl is my rib."

"I like the sound of that. I'm glad you two are back on track."

"Yeah, me too. We're getting there. I just got caught up in this case and was neglecting what really mattered. Regina has supported me and this center from day one. I thought she would understand…no, let me be honest, I thought she would tolerate my crazy hours, and that was wrong. What I was doing was taking her for granted. She got her little attitudes from time to time, but Regina was a soldier. She held me down and waited for me to come to my senses. One thing is certain though, Drew. I will spend the rest of my life making sure that my wife feels like she is number one in my life, because she is. Now what happened?" Kevin wasn't letting Andrew off the hook. He could do this all day.

Andrew cracked a smile for the first time in two days. "Dude, I'm about to hang up on you. I told you I'm not feeling well. And I really don't know."

Kevin was getting irritated with his friend, but he knew not to push because Andrew would not be swayed, but rather frustrated and defensive. "Okay, whatever, man. If that's your story, then I'll have to respect that."

Hearing the disappointment in Kevin's voice, Andrew offered a bit of encouragement. "I'll tell you what. Let me do some digging, make a few inquiries, and I'll see what I can find out. Cool?"

"Cool!" Kevin's mood improved immediately. "Well, get some rest... after you do your digging, of course. And I'll holler at you later."

As much as he loved Kevin Golden, Andrew Steele knew he could never share with him the truth of why DeShawn was released. Andrew's father had been instrumental in DeShawn's release. Whether it was fear, respect, loyalty, or a combination, Andrew had agreed to take what his father had shared with him to the grave. Judge Steele had summoned Andrew to his home and shared the crazy story with him. One of Judge Steele's friends, a former judge himself, had a young wife and a teenage daughter. The family was quite wealthy, and the daughter was beyond overindulged, she was spoiled rotting. Judge Steele had made a point to say *rotting* instead of *rotten*, for he said this young girl was like milk or meat or a piece of fruit that was in a perpetual state of become more and more rotted. Despite the financial wealth and abundance she enjoyed, she was morally bankrupt and destitute. Her life seemed to consist of a collection of lies, misbehaviors, and bailouts from her father. This time, she had falsely accused a kid, some football star from another school, of raping her. Judge Steele went on to say that his friend had been truly pissed with his daughter and resolved to not reveal her latest lie. He was going to make her leave his home when she turned eighteen and graduated high school. He said that she was toxic, and he did not know how to help her. His daughter had accused a kid of raping her. Given his daughter's sexual promiscuity, the former judge had his doubts about her allegation, but he didn't share that with anyone. The accused kid was tried in juvenile court, found to be responsible for the crime of rape, and ordered to a detention facility with DYS until he turned twenty-one years old. The former judge initially had some sleepless nights over the incident, but his $1000 bottles of Cognac proved to quiet his mind and thoughts. A few days ago, Judge Steele explained, his friend was look-ing over some transcripts from the case and saw a name that caught his attention. The name was Debra Holyfield. Andrew had told his father that none of this made sense to him; he did not understand why Debra Holyfield was significant to DeShawn or to the former judge whose daughter had lied on DeShawn. Judge Steele hushed Andrew, and told him to just listen. Debra Holyfield had been married, with three children. Her oldest son, Deon, had been killed by a drunk driver. Several years after that, Debra Holyfield's daughter was diagnosed with a terminal disease. She and her husband divorced, and Debra took her maiden name, Martin. She also changed the last names of her dying daughter and her youngest son, DeShawn. Andrew had slapped his hand over his mouth, partially in disbelief and partially to keep from regurgitating. Andrew's mind had rewound like an old VHS tape. All the images inundating his mind made him woozy. He remembered, years ago, when his father was in this very study, yelling at another judge for killing a kid because he had been driving while intoxicated. Judge Steele promised to remain the man's friend and ally as long as he confessed to the police and entered rehabilitation. The judge was forced to retire and was never criminally charged. The former judge continued to earn a lucrative salary, and for a while, he even stopped drinking. The former judge had no idea that Ms. Martin, DeShawn Martin's mother, was actually the former Debra Holyfield. In fact, the former judge had never known DeShawn or Delisa's names, he just knew that Debra Holyfield had two children other than Deon, whom he had killed. Throughout the entire situation, he never connected DeShawn Martin to Debra Holyfield, now known as Debra Martin. As soon as he made the connection, the former judge called his old friend and mentor, Andrew's father, Judge Steele. Judge Steele made some calls, pulled some strings, and within a few days, DeShawn was released. Andrew left his father's house that day feeling like he didn't really know anyone anymore. Especially his own father. He was still sick about the entire situation.

*****

Even though Regina was in a good place with the ladies, she still felt hesitant about meeting for girls' night, instead of being with Kevin. She and Kevin had been reconnecting in a great way over the past few weeks.

And since DeShawn's release, things had been even better. It seemed as if a huge weight had been lifted off of Kevin, like he had been unburdened. Kevin was more free and relaxed, and Regina enjoyed spending every moment with him that she could. Still, she knew they had never been ones to smother each other, so she agreed to meet with the ladies. Kevin had actually encouraged her to go hang out, telling Regina that he was getting tired of babysitting her. That comment earned him a punch in the arm.

"Hey, divas!" Regina was all smiles as she walked to the table where Melissa, Regan, and Kim were already seated.

"Look at you! You have a glow. Kevin must be puttin' it down," Regan teased her big sister.

"Girl, whatever. Don't hate me just because I got me a good man."

"Why?" Melissa asked.

"Why what?" Regina was as confused as Kim and Regan were.

"Like, why is Kevin a good man? Well, specifically, why is he a good man for you? You guys know I date all kinds of men. Last night, I made of list of qualities and attributes that I would like in a man, but no one man seems to have them all. So it made me wonder, if I could only have two of the attributes that I listed, which ones would be required for me to have what I would consider a good man." Melissa was interested in hearing what everyone had to say.

"Wow, Mel, that is really deep," Regina observed. "So what were the attributes that you listed?"

Melissa whipped an envelope out of her purse. "I couldn't find paper, so I had to use this. I listed: sense of humor, physically fit, handsome, honest, a master at sex, a great communicator, hardworking, and financially stable. The two that I picked were sense of humor and great communicator."

Not surprising to anyone, Kim was the next to speak. "Well I say financially stable has to be first because if he is broke, ain't nothing to talk about and ain't shit funny. After that, I'd say handsome. Don't nobody want a frog, give me Prince Charming. If he has money and looks good, I can make the rest work."

Regan shook her head. Kim was a nut, but she did make her laugh.

"Well for me, he would have to be honest, which I don't know if that exists in males. Honesty translates to loyalty, and I don't know a single man who has never cheated. Along with honesty, he'd have to possess a strong work ethic. A hardworking man is very attractive to me. What about you, sis? Since you married Kevin, we know looks were not important."

"Good one, Regan. We'll see how good Kevin looks next time your scary butt needs him to come and get a bird out of your house."

"What? Girl you thought I meant your Kevin? No, I meant Kevin Costner. Now gone and tell us why you married my handsome brother-in-law."

"For me, it was his sense of humor. Kevin and I are always playing and laughing and being stupid. That is key in our relationship. Also, I'd say his work ethic. His work is his passion, and you just don't see that very often these days. Since you guys always want to make choices and lists and all of that, I have a good one. And we can only pick *ONE*, Melissa Sullivan! So if you could have any celebrity who is deceased, really be alive, who would it be? Mine would be Maya Angelou."

"No," Kim protested. "She was not a celebrity. She was just popular because of Oprah."

"What? Kim, do you know how ignorant you sound?" Regan had flipped into teacher mode.

"How much did you hear about her until she became Oprah's mentor, or whatever she was. Shoot, we didn't even read her books during Black History Month back in school. If I could have someone still be alive, it would be Tupac," Kim announced. "His music, movies, all of that would be legendary. What about you, Little Miss Regan?"

"Y'all already know, Michael Jackson forever, baby! Who would you choose, Melissa?"

When Melissa inhaled deeply and cocked her head to the side, everyone knew there was more than one name coming. "Boy, that is tough. I mean, all of the Jims and Jimmys: Hendrix, Croce, Morriso.. Then you would have to say Elvis. I mean, c'mon, he was like, the King. Then Tammi Terrell, just because she was so young and beautiful and sadly died of cancer. She and Marvin Gaye made the most beautiful music together. But wait, if Tammi was here, then Marvin would have to be here. Oh, what about Bruce Lee? John Lennon. Oh my goodness…oh my goodness…wait, how could I not say MLK and JFK? But then part of me wants to say Princess Di because she could raise her sons." When Melissa finally finished naming people, everyone had cleaned their plates and nearly emptied their glasses.

Regina spoke next. "Let's finish with a toast to life. We can't bring any of those wonderful people back. And when we go, nobody will be able to bring us back. So I want us to toast to committing to lives well lived." Everyone touched glasses to Regina's water bottle.

✶✶✶✶✶

"I'm sorry I'm not being a great host tonight, I think I'm just tired." Mike and Kim were sitting in his living room listening to music. They had dinner earlier but not much conversation, and not any sex.

"That's okay, Mike. I'm cool. It's just fun to hang out. You are a great host. Do you wanna go in your room? I can remind you of what I'm great at." Kim didn't know what the problem was. For the last few weeks, she and Mike had been banging like firecrackers. Now he was being all corny and moody.

"No, I'm gonna take a rain check, if you don't mind. I'm actually about to call it a night. Walk you to your car?" Mike wanted to be alone. He had a lot on his mind, and he didn't need Kim's distractions right now.

"Sure, Mike, walk me to my car. Let me grab my purse, if that's okay." Kim acted like her foot got caught on the rug, and she fell to her knees, right in front of where Mike was sitting on the couch. "Clumsy me! Can you please help me up?"

When Mike stood to offer Kim a hand, she pulled his gym shorts down to his ankles and pushed him back against the couch. She was going to make him reconsider not wanting to have sex with her. At first, Mike resisted Kim's touch. But the warmth of her mouth and the tingling sensation created by her tongue on his penis were more than he could handle. Before she arrived at his house, he had determined that they were

209

not going to have sex. However, this was altogether different. He did not want to be too rude of a host. So Mike leaned back and watched Kim work her magic. As the rabbit was about to escape the hat, Mike leaned back, closed his eyes, and erupted down Kim's throat. Mike looked down and saw that his toes were curled into the carpet. He'd heard about that, but he wasn't aware that someone's toes could really curl. He cleared his throat as Kim coughed and wiped her mouth.

"Help yourself to the guest bathroom down the hall," Mike offered. "I'll be right back. I need to go into my bathroom for a moment. When I come back, we need to talk before you go. I want to discuss something with you."

Kim did not want to hear anything from Mike about cutting things off and not seeing her again. She put on her shoes and went to grab her purse off of the table. Instead, she grabbed Mike's cell phone. She could not believe how stupid he was for not having a lock code on his phone. Kim scrolled through Mike's directory. Bingo!

"Kim, I have to tell you something really important, so..." Mike was talking as he was walking up the hall toward the living room where he expected Kim to be waiting. She was nowhere to be found.

Meanwhile, on the other side of town, Kevin and Regina just had one of the best nights of their married lives. Although they had both been busy running errands and had not seen each other all day, that evening they enjoyed dinner and a movie and some of the most passionate, intimate, and varied lovemaking ever. After they showered and rubbed lotion on each other, Kevin and Regina got into bed, knowing they had to go to work in the morning.

"Thank you for a wonderful date night, Kevin," Regina softly whispered as she lay with her head on her husband's chest.

"You're welcome, baby. Thank you for being a wonderful date. You wanna gimme that special favor before we go to sleep? Your head is already halfway there?"

Regina jerked her head up and looked at Kevin. "Don't get punched, boy. It's not your birthday, so I'm good. But you can eat at the Y if you want. And I might have something to tell you tomorrow."

"Okay, Gina, whatever, baby." With that, Kevin dove under the sheet and pleasured his wife until she screamed her way to her climactic end.

PRESENT DAY

The sound was deafening. Oddly, there was no pain. Regina lay there, unable to hear anything but the ringing in her ears. She noticed that Kevin was sobbing bitterly, his body jerking with each painful tear that fell from his eyelids. After a few moments, Kevin composed himself, angry that he had gotten so overwhelmed with emotion. "Why, Regina? How long have you been cheating on me?" Kevin's voice was almost a whisper.

"Kevin, I am so sorry. Baby, where this is coming from?" Regina had no idea what had changed in the last eight hours and why she was awakened so violently out of a sleep that had begun so gratifyingly.

"Hmph, that's funny, 'cause on my way from the bathroom, I hear your phone buzzing at four-something this morning. I have never checked your phone in all the years that we have been together. I picked up the phone to silence it and to see who I would be cussing out later on for being so rude – either your sister, Kim, or Melissa. Imagine my surprise when I see the name Mike on the text."

Regina gulped hard, a bitter mix of air, blood, saliva, and shame jammed in her throat. She panicked, trying to imagine what Mike could have texted to her, then she got angry that he would dare text her at 4:00 in the morning. In fact, he should not have been texting her at all, no matter what time of day or night it was. Regina could not wait until she saw Mike at work and could tell him off! What was that fool thinking?

Kevin spoke through clenched teeth, "Go 'head…start talking."

This had to be a dream. Regina could not grasp that her life had taken a 180-degree turn in a matter of a few short hours, while she was asleep no less. "I just…I don't know Kevin. I am going to call off so we can talk about all of this. The most important thing is that I love you, and I'm sorry. My feelings were hurt, Kevin, and I just needed to feel loved… special…attractive. I needed to feel anything other than neglected. We used to be best friends, but that stopped. We used to have sex on the regular, and that stopped, too. Hell, we hadn't even laughed or held hands in the last few months."

"Hold up, wait a minute. Are you sittin' up here saying this is my fault, Gina? You can miss me with that bullshit!"

"No, Kevin, it's my fault. I take full responsibility for my actions. But baby, we can't ignore the fact that something was missing, though."

"Sure the fuck was missing. That would be you, Regina! You went missing from this marriage when you decided to step out on me. Bottom line, at the end of the day, do you love this nigga?"

"*WHAT?!?* No! Kevin, no I absolutely do not love him."

Regina wondered what the text had said. Reading her contorted face and seeming to read her mind as well, Kevin began to read aloud:

```
"u crzy girl. I luv when u have ur pretty brown
lips wrapped around this gr8 white shark. u swal-
lowed that load like a champ. cant w8 2 return the
favor. still gottta t/t u tho
```

"So this nigga is *white*, Regina? You getting all freaky and shit with some corny-ass white dude, and a muthafucka in here can't get some head to save his life? Wait, it must've been his birthday though, right, 'cause you sure as hell reminded me that I can't get shit unless it's my birthday. Damn, looks like it's a lot I don't know about you, 'cause the only loads you do in this house is loads of laundry…oh my bad, and loads of lies." Kevin was now pacing the room and his conversation was as scattered as were his thoughts. "All the shit I been going through, and this is what you do? Wait a minute, you been settin' me up the last few weeks, huh? Playing me for Boo-Boo the god-damn fool." Kevin was beyond enraged. He was prowling around their bedroom like a crazed lion, and Regina feared she would be devoured in short order. She knew that Kevin's ego had been bruised, crushed in fact, and she had to figure out how to calm him down. His booming voice snapped her back from her thoughts. "Who all knows about this shit?"

"Nobody, Kevin, I swear."

Kevin stopped and glared at Regina. "Now is not the time to be lying to me. Now who knows about this?"

"Well, I just -- Mel – she found out by accident, and of course my sister. But that's it. But listen, it's not like—"

Kevin cut Regina off. He did not want to hear any lies from her. "So I'm the joke, huh? Stupid-ass Kevin is the dummy? I bust my tail, Regina. This house, keeping you dressed and looking fly, buying you expensive purses and shit just to put a smile on your face. I felt guilty for working so hard, doing something right, something positive, and you sitting up…"

Kevin's voice trailed off. He stared at the hole in the mattress, a part of him wishing he'd have fired that shot into Regina's throat, which had swallowed another man's…his heart would not allow his head to complete that thought. Another part of him was glad that he had not let himself do anything to risk his freedom. At that moment, Kevin realized that Regina had to go. He knew he could never be intimate with his wife without thinking about the fact that someone named Mike had been inside of her, in both holes as far as Kevin could tell. On top of that, he would always wonder if Regina was thinking about another man while she and Kevin were being intimate. The trust was gone. The precious vessel that was their marriage had been shattered beyond repair. Even if glued and pieced back together, it would never be strong enough to hold the love, trust, and respect that used to be contained therein. The strength and integrity of their vessel had been compromised. What was once priceless was now worth nothing. In fact, it was worth less than nothing because instead of having zero value, their marriage held a negative value for Kevin. Kevin's mind was awash with emotions and questions. *Why did she do this to us? Why would she put me in a position of having to do what I have no choice but to carry out? Did I ever really know this woman? Did I miss signals to indicate that this was going on? And what was up with all the lovey-dovey stuff the last week or so?* He was about to lose it. He had to put some space between him and that woman on the bed who resembled his wife.

"Regina, I'm going into this bathroom, and when I come out, you need to be gone." Kevin looked toward Regina with an expression of disgust, not able to meet her eyes. In his mind, her eyes were not worthy to hold his gaze.

Regina knew she deserved that and more. She thought about how she had violated her covenant with God and her husband, disappointing both of them in the process. As humiliated as she felt, it was all her doing. If she had been so unhappy with Kevin, she knew she should have poured the same energy, excitement and imagination into her marriage as she had poured into her dealings with Mike. That ship had sailed, the milk had been spilled, and the bell had rung. There was no way to unsail, un-spill or unring. Hindsight was always 20/20, but now Regina determined that she needed to focus on looking ahead. The first thing she wanted to figure out was why this was happening. It was weird that Mike had sent that text, when they had not had any dealings in the last few weeks. Regina had not known Mike to be petty or creepy, and he in fact seemed to be comfortable with the fact that she no longer wanted to deal with him. He was almost relieved, now that she thought about it. Regina was anxious to confront Mike. That would have to wait, though. At this moment, someone far more important than Mike required Regina's attention. The only man, the only person in this world who she wanted to focus on was Kevin Golden. Who knew how long it would take for Kevin to forgive her? How would she even begin to get Kevin to trust her or believe a word she said? Honesty would be a good place to start. Regina could never tell Kevin all the details about her dealings with Mike. Those descriptions of dinners and bathtubs would only serve as lighter fluid to an already intensely burning fire. She did want to share with Kevin the one truth that time would not let her hide, and that would hopefully make Kevin want to fight for their relationship.

"K-Kevin," Regina shakily called out to her husband.

No response.

"Kevin, you alright in there?" Regina would not allow Kevin to be embarrassed anymore by her lies and her secrets. She would be honest with him, as honest as she could be without causing more damage, and they would then be able to move forward unified and stronger than ever. Frightened but determined, Regina went to the bathroom door and tapped lightly. "Kevin, will you please answer? I need to tell you something that will change everything. Kevin, I'm pregnant."

Not a sound.

Regina stood at the bathroom door for the longest minute in eternity, waiting for Kevin to respond. That minute seemed like hours. Regina stepped away from the bathroom door, wanting to crawl back into bed and somehow sink into the hole that Kevin had shot through the mattress. Pausing to look at all the pictures of her and Kevin throughout the room, Regina smiled sadly. Why had she allowed herself to get so caught up? Why had she not counted the consequences of her actions? Had being made to feel wanted and attractive been that important? What about her partner? Kevin had never, not once tried to change Regina or hold her back in any way. He was always encouraging and supportive, no matter what she wanted to do: her jewelry making business, baking ventures, interior decorating partnership with her sister. The things she and Kevin shared were based in real life. Both the struggles and the strides were made hand-in-hand. They used to say they were back-to-back, them against the world. No temporary fantasy should have outweighed the proven, real life relationship with her husband. Seeking her own pleasure and gratification, Regina knew that she lost sight of what was important. Kevin hated her right now, but Regina vowed to spend the rest of their lives doing two things: being a good mother to this child and trying to win back Kevin's love and trust.

While Regina was in the bedroom wallowing in regret, Kevin was in the bathroom drowning in grief. He tried to convince himself that his love for Regina outweighed his anger toward her. *Her one mistake should not overshadow all of the years she's been a loving and loyal wife, outstanding friend, and amazing partner.* Kevin was indeed angry; he knew that he and Regina had a lot talk about. *If she wants this thing to work, her ass is coming to counseling with me. I'll find a way to forgive Regina because I love her.* Kevin determined he would be like his father. Mrs. Golden had cheated on Kevin's father while Kevin was away at college. He remembered losing respect for his father and thinking he was weak when he made the decision to forgive his wife and not leave. Several years later, after Kevin graduated and was working as a teacher, he asked his father why he took the soft way out and had not handled the situation with a stronger hand. Why not man up? Mr. Golden shared that it took greater strength to act contrary to his feelings. He explained that all feelings – good ones, bad ones, painful ones – are temporary. He said he had to dig deep to find the strength to act in such a way that his temporary feelings would not dictate behavior that would have far more permanent consequences. Kevin's respect for his father was restored and multiplied after that conversation. Kevin remembered having resentment toward his mother for quite a while after he learned of her affair. However, with the help of his father and a counselor, he was able to forgive his mother. The counselor assisted Kevin through that situation by advising him to process that breach of trust like a death, something that needed to be grieved in a healthy process. He would insist that Regina set up counseling for them immediately. If she was willing to work through this mess, he would do the same. Kevin was about to come out of the bathroom when Regina tapped on the door and made an announcement that simultaneously knocked both the air and all sensibility out of him.

About to crawl back into bed, Regina stopped and turned around when she heard the bathroom door open. "Did you hear what I said, Kevin?"

"Yes, Regina Golden, I heard you," Kevin said, his voice barely audible. "I was calling 9-1-1."

A single tear began to roll down Kevin's cheek. Regina was dumbfounded as she looked at the broken man before her. He was more than broken, he was obliterated. Lost in thought, Regina failed to notice that Kevin had cocked the gun in his hand. As the reality of the situation set in, words eluded Regina. She mouthed "I love you" as Kevin pulled the trigger. The single tear on Kevin's face was the last image Regina had of her beloved and betrayed husband.

BOOM!

3 DAYS LATER

The church was packed. Almost everyone from Bright Star had come to show support and pay respects to Regina. Most came out of genuine concern. Some came out of curiosity. Both Melissa and Kim were to sit in the front row with the family. Before the service, Melissa happened to look up and see Mike quickly duck out of the church doors. She started after him, when someone grabbed her arm from behind.

Melissa narrowed her eyes, "Yes, Cassie?"

Cassie failed to notice how irritated Melissa was. "Yeah, Melissa, I heard you helped with the arrangements. You are a good friend for that. By the way, is it true that this was all because of an affair that Regina had? Some people in the parking lot were saying the affair was with another Bright Star employee. I sat next to her for all those years, and she just never seemed like the type. You just never know people, do you?"

Melissa was flabbergasted. *I cannot believe this cow has the nerve to bring her typical rude and nosey mess to this funeral*, Melissa thought. She was about to light into Cassie when Alicia approached.

"Just so you know, Melissa. There has been an in-depth review into Mike's actions to see if any company policies or conduct codes were violated. He was on the verge of being terminated, but as of yesterday he has resigned."

Cassie drew in a deep, audible breath. Slapping her hand over her big mouth, she quickly walked away from Melissa and Alicia and headed toward the bathroom.

"Thank you, Alicia, your timing is perfect as always," Melissa scowled at her.

"Any time. If there I anything I can do, please—"

"You can stay as far away from me as possible," Melissa cut her off. Melissa had to remind herself that she was there for her friend. *This day is about Regina, so I'll do everything in my power to not lose my temper with some of these ignorant, insensitive people. And speaking of insensitive, where in the world is Kim?* Today was supposed to be all about Gina, and Melissa had very little tolerance for anyone's mess, including Kim's. They needed to be there, front and center, for their girl.

"Can everyone please be seated," the minister began.

Melissa kept glancing toward the rear of the church, looking for Kim. Members of Kevin's and Regina's families occupied the first few pews on each side the aisle. Melissa, not wanting to walk up front since the service had already started, decided she would just sit in the back and wait for Kim. Regina was at the front of the church, Melissa was at the back of the church, and Kim was nowhere to be found. After the funeral service, Melissa went to the parking lot. She needed to get some fresh air before coming back to join in fellowship with the families and other guests. After today, nothing would ever be the same. Sure, life would go on, but there would be a new normal for everyone involved. The old normal was killed when Kevin pulled that trigger. Poor Regina. Melissa absentmindedly strolled the parking lot, trying to clear her head. She chuckled to herself because she knew that if she circled the parking lot a million times, her head would never be clear of all the madness from the last three days. Melissa turned to go a different direction when she saw Cassie talking with a couple other women just ahead. Melissa was too late; Cassie had seen her and began to walk toward her. Cassie threw her arms around Melissa and began to sob. Not knowing what to do, Melissa patted Cassie's back and assured her that Regina was going to be alright. Cassie shook her head no. After taking a moment to gather herself, Cassie reached into her purse and handed Melissa a folded piece of notebook paper.

"Kim asked that I give this to you, Melissa. She said that it was for Regina."

Melissa took the paper and folded it again so that it fit into the palm of her hand. "When did you see Kim? Was she inside? Did she leave already? What did she say?"

Cassie started crying softly. "No, she was not inside. Shortly after the service, some of us came outside to get some air. As we were standing here, Kim drove up. She said something about there being two more funerals soon. She handed me that paper I just gave to you, and she drove away. She looked as if she had been crying."

"Thank you, Cassie." Melissa went back inside the church. After looking for a few minutes through the throngs of people, Melissa finally saw Regan at the front of the church with her beloved older sister. Regan sat down on the first pew and patted a spot next to her, inviting Melissa to join her. For a while, neither Regan nor Melissa said anything.

Then Regan spoke, "I talked to Mike. He came here before the service started, and said I needed to know something very important, that he did not know what, if anything, Regina had told me."

"Go on, I'm listening." Melissa forced herself to exhale, as she realized she'd been holding her breath.

"He said that he and Regina had never had sex. He said that they had met for dinner a few times, and she had been to his home several times. Mike said they had exchanged sexually explicit text messages, and even some pictures, but having sex was a line that Regina refused to cross." Regan paused, as if considering how to proceed. "Melissa, Mike said that he respected Regina and was glad that they never had sex for two reasons. He said that when she told him that she could not see him anymore, she shared that she might be pregnant. It was important to her that she not disrespect the life that might be growing inside of her by contaminating its home. He said something else too, Melissa." Regan began to sob.

"It's okay, honey. Take your time. I'm not going anywhere." Melissa hugged Regan and let her have her moment.

"I'm sorry. Mike said that he has full-blown AIDS. He said that was the reason that none of the women at Bright Star ever talked about their dealings with him. He told them all up front about his situation, and if they still wanted to be intimate with him, it was their choice. He said they may have been scared or embarrassed about disclosing to anyone else that they'd been intimate with him, so although there was constant speculation about with whom he was having sex, nothing was ever confirmed. Mike said he almost always wore condoms when he had sex because it would have been irresponsible to do otherwise."

"*Almost* always?" Melissa interrupted.

"That's right. Mike said that Kim had always been bad news as far as he was concerned. He said that, unlike my sister, Kim was rude, mean-spirited and disliked by most people at Bright Star. Mike went on to say that he did not want to be too graphic, but he made deposits into all of Kim's receptacles. He said that one time, he and Kim had gotten caught up in the moment and had unprotected sex. Then, on another occasion, Kim had caught Mike completely off guard and performed fellatio on him."

Now Melissa began to cry. This was a lot of information to process, and her mind was shut down right now, so her heart was working over-time. "So he and Regina...so Regina never... So Regina could not have been infected, correct?"

"That's right. He also said something that I'm still trying to wrap my head around. Mike told me that Kim was the reason that we were having a funeral today. Mike said that he sent an explicit text about oral sex to what he thought was Kim's phone. As it turned out, Regina's telephone number had been typed into the contact for Kim's name."

Regan and Melissa both looked at Regina's smiling face. The gigantic pictures on each end of her gold coffin made her presence loom large in the room.

"So when Kevin said he shot her when she said..." Melissa's voice trailed off as she started crying again.

"Yeah, I know. I was thinking the same thing. Kevin thought Regina was carrying Mike's child, when that was impossible. Kevin killed his wife and his own child. It's weird, but I don't hate Kevin. I'm not mad at him at all. I feel so sorry for him. Andrew said they've had him on suicide watch since his arrest. Kevin is in bad shape, Mel. Andrew said Kevin has wanted to die since he found out that Regina and Mike did not have sex. I don't know how we are ever going to get through this."

Melissa cradled Regan in her arms as they rocked from side to side. "Together, that's how we will get through it. We don't have any other choice."

Regan, her mother, and Melissa had all vowed to do whatever they could to help Andrew in his defense of Kevin. He was just as much a beloved family member as Regina was. Andrew had assured everyone that he would do the best that he could for Kevin, as would his father and Kevin's own father. Knowing everything that she now knew, Regan was relieved that they decided not to reopen Regina's casket for a final viewing. She motioned for the funeral home staff to come and wheel the coffin out of the room. Regan and Melissa each grabbed flowers and walked behind the casket.

Melissa stuffed the paper down to the bottom of the huge plant she was carrying. Before sitting down with Regan, she had read what was on the folded pieces of paper; one small piece of paper was wrapped inside of a piece of notebook paper. Melissa had made the decision that they were better being buried with Regina. The one small piece of paper was a note in Mike's handwriting. It mentioned something about liking chocolate. The other piece of paper was in Kim's handwriting. It looked like a poem or composition of some kind. Melissa decided that she would try to focus on the fact that Regina was indeed in a much better place. That did not alleviate the pain of her loss, only time could do that. But Melissa would live the rest of her life in honor of Regina. She would try her best to make decisions and choices with the end in mind. Kevin and Regina Golden were good people who, like most others, made bad choices. Their lives would not be in vain as far as Melissa was concerned, but rather painful reminders that our choices always impact us as well as others. Good or bad, right or wrong – our choices determine our conclusion.

ENOUGH

by Kimberly Denise Stoner

When I was in the womb, there was another with me.
I entered this world, while the womb became the other one's tomb.
At first there were two, but one had to do.

As a child, school was a bore.
The teachers were mean and the work was a chore.
Still, I did okay, earning mostly B's, but since they were not A's,
it was not enough to please my parents-
Were so smart, many accomplishments they achieved.
Buying me the best of everything would make me like them,
or so they believed.

My teen years were fun, I traveled the world.
I mostly hung with adults, or either with boys my age,
but never with girls.
I tried to have girlfriends, but they all called me phony,
Which never made sense, 'cause I would always buy them stuff,
I was tired of being lonely.

Finally I grew up and fell in love. This man was an angel:
good, kind, sweet, and fine.
He had my loyalty, my heart and my love.
He cheated…I found out. He lied…I forgave.
He did it again, and a third time too, finally I left.
My heart shattered in two…million shards.
Never again would I get played, that pain was too hard.
I was hurt and depressed, it was rough, but it turned out for the best,
'cause it made me tough.

One baby short, life can be cruel.

Not an A student, no friends at all, and getting played like a fool.
You look at me and judge me, thinking I'm rough.
The truth you don't know, I've never felt I was enough.
I wear expensive clothes, weaves, and shoes. My make-up is flawless.
My home is filled with material possessions, all kinds of stuff.
The real reason is that I'm trying to feel worthy, to at least look like
I'm worthy. But it's still not enough.
I use material, money and attitude to look the part, but too bad none of
that can dress up my heart.

Part of me knows I need to stop this madness,
get in touch with my pain and internal sadness.
My head and heart just have so much hurt,
disappointment and madness.

One died, my mother cried. I tried, girls shied. He lied, I lost my pride.
I was wrong, not strong. I was weak, had a mean streak.
Regina is dead and it's my fault,
I tried to harm her, and harmed myself by default.
I did people wrong, I know it's true, that's a jacked up way to be, but
how can I be good to others, when I can't be good to me?